The Trick to Time

The Trick to Time

KIT DE WAAL

VIKING
an imprint of
PENGUIN BOOKS

VIKING

UK | USA | Canada | Ireland | Australia
India | New Zealand | South Africa

Viking is part of the Penguin Random House group of companies
whose addresses can be found at global.penguinrandomhouse.com.

First published by Viking 2018
001

Copyright © Kit de Waal, 2018

The moral right of the author has been asserted

Set in 11/13 pt Bembo Book MT Std
Typeset by Jouve (UK), Milton Keynes
Printed in Great Britain by Clays Ltd, St Ives plc

A CIP catalogue record for this book is available from the British Library

HARDBACK ISBN: 978–0–241–20710–9
TRADE PAPERBACK ISBN: 978–0–241–20711–6

To Bethany and Luke, as always.

Five o'clock, Monday morning, there's a purple light far out at sea. When they pulled down the old wreck of a factory between Mona's building and the next, they gave her the gift of a view, and because she's three floors up, if she leans against the window at an angle, now she can just see over the chalets and beach huts to the dawn-bruised clouds and the rosy hue of early-morning sun. She makes toast and a cup of tea and waits for light. The third night of not sleeping.

Mona notices then, in an identical flat in an identical building across the new narrow road, someone else can't sleep and has the lights on at an ungodly hour. He's a floor below her, standing at his window looking out at the blurred horizon. He's her age, perhaps a bit older, grey hair swept back, in a dressing gown maybe with a thick shawl collar, and although Mona can't see the belt, she imagines it's made of gold rope with tassels on the end. Before she can look away, he turns and catches her staring.

They face each other like two characters in an opera, lit from above, waiting for the music to start. Then, with great elegance, he makes a gesture with his head, something between a bow and a nod that reminds Mona of the films she watched as a girl, sumptuous, Technicolor movies, ladies in crinolines and generals with brass buttons, splendid and handsome and chivalrous. She smiles and raises her mug in salute. Hopes he gets the joke. She hears her toast pop up in the kitchen. When she turns back, the man has gone.

She brushes her teeth, dabs cream on her face and rubs it in, notices again the blue of her eyes paling with time, the give of the skin on her cheeks. 'You're as pretty as Christmas,' he said and she believed him but that was a long, long time ago.

She chooses a gingham dress in oyster pink but it's the end of the summer and no weather for sandals. She belts up her mac and slings a satchel over her chest. Downhill all the way.

Mona's is first on the lane to open up, not yet eight. She unlocks the shop door and turns the sign from 'Closed' to 'Open'. She walks straight to the kitchenette at the back and puts the kettle on. It's a little chilly for the end of September. She kicks the fan heater into life and it purrs warm air on to her feet.

'That's my girl,' she says.

Under the sink she finds a duster and some polish and walks back to the front of the shop. In the window there she has seven of the standard dolls, sixteen inches each one, five seated and two standing courtesy of an ingenious little contraption the carpenter made, a plain wooden stand with two arms that grip the doll round the waist and the neck. The display has an autumn theme with miniature squashes Mona bought at the supermarket, twigs and leaves from the communal gardens, and all the dolls dressed in green velvet, tan leather, burgundy wool and tweed the colour of Highland heather.

Mona dusts all over and puts a quick polish on the window. She rearranges a leg and an arm. Then she dusts the centre display where some of the dolls have fallen over. All this movement must happen at night, because before she locks up she spends half an hour tidying and settling but somehow every morning she finds the dolls have shifted and moved.

So she props them up properly, lets their legs dangle over the side, sits them facing the front, saying hello to the customers. But it will be an extra quiet Monday because of the biting wind and because it's much too early for people to think of Christmas. There's all of October yet. Come November, the end of November, things will be different but she doesn't want to think about November before she has to.

At last, the cafe is open and Mona nips out.

'Morning, Mona,' says Danny and slips an almond croissant in a brown paper bag. He adds a flapjack and winks. 'Bit of extra for my favourite blonde,' he says and when Mona smiles he leans over the counter and whispers, 'There's more where that came from. Sugar and spice on tap. Imagine it,' and winks again.

Mona puts some change on the counter. 'I've got five years on you, Danny,' she says. 'Dog years.' She makes for the door.

'I can work with that,' he shouts. 'Anyway, who's counting?'

She makes coffee to wash down the croissant and licks the sugar from her fingers. She'll need to flick a duster over the toys, the building blocks and trains on the lower shelves, over the miniature vans, the wooden alphabets and children's names, mobiles that hang from the ceiling, pull-along dogs and cars, aeroplanes and elephants, all carved from beautiful bits of wood, natural or under matt varnish with the grain showing. But they can wait.

Instead, she carefully polishes the glass cases of the specials, the tall dolls that each have a wardrobe of clothes and a printed sheet about the making of them and the wood that was used. Every doll comes with a name, and a sort of birth certificate. Mona suspects that she might have doubled up over the years. By rights she should have kept some sort of register, but she never imagined she'd still be at the dollmaking after more than twenty-three years. Too late to start an efficient census now. The damage is done.

Each of the special dolls reclines on a silk bed wearing a costume that Mona has handmade over weeks or months, their smooth, elegant bodies painted in two coats of flat, alabaster white. Their cases have compartments at the back with two extra little outfits hanging on a wooden peg. Mona's made costumes from every era, Elizabethan, Georgian, Edwardian, Renaissance. She's dressed dolls for great country houses and air-raid shelters, for weaver's cottages, jazz clubs and field hospitals. She spends hours with books and magazines ensuring her designs are true yet unique creations, made to fit.

Ah, now the shop is warm. Mona sits at the counter, rubs her hands together to get them going and then takes the lid off the plastic drum she keeps at her feet. Most of her customers, especially the ones in Japan and America, like to think of every garment being sewn in a thatched cottage by an old lady with a thimble and half-moon glasses. The truth is that there's very little now that can't be done on a good Singer sewing machine and the bulk of the work is done at home. Nevertheless there are bits of embroidery and finishing that take nothing short of a needle and thread and a couple of hours under a good light so Mona reserves hand-stitching for quiet shop days.

She has a man to finish today. He has an orange suede jerkin and faded serge pantaloons. He has a green jumper, a rope belt, leather boots and a navy felt fedora. His red paisley neckerchief she will edge by hand with bright-green silk cotton. She holds the thread to the light and sees it waver in her breath. She kisses it, dampens it, pulls it through and draws out a length.

She makes a double stitch and sews carefully, tugging the thread after each delicate stitch, each movement of her hand and balletic stretch of her arm repeated over and over until the doll, who she will call Francis, has a new neckerchief. Then she will make his second outfit, one for the evening. Francis is a watchmaker by day but at night he plays the piano at the dancehall in town. He plays honky-tonk and Mona smiles because she has no idea what honky-tonk is. But she likes the word and Francis likes it too. She picks up his arms and makes him dance a jig. His heavy head wobbles on his neck.

'*Di-didilly-didilly-dee.* So, Francis, you will need a black evening suit.'

She has just the thing at home, an old tuxedo. She's used the sleeve already for an urchin's waistcoat but this time she will cut right into the back for Francis and give him satin lapels to boot and a velvet dicky-bow. She might even fashion a cummerbund because Francis has a twinkle in his eye and a taste for the ladies. But he's not a young man, Francis. He's in his prime. Forty-five maybe, fifty would be pushing it. Mona holds him up close and whispers.

'Who's counting?' Mona asks him. 'I'll tell you who. Old Father Time and his dreadful abacus, that's who. Sixty on Saturday. Can you believe it, Francis? Me? Sixty?'

It's nearly noon before a customer opens the door. Mona knows who she is straight away just by the cut of her but she waits while the woman has a look round, picks up a doll and comes at a creeping angle to where Mona sits behind the counter, hand-stitching a white ruffle shirt.

'Gayle sent me,' the woman says. She has huge pools of eyes, sore and glassy, with a beautiful tumble of hair the colour of October leaves. She's as thin as a reed, white as milk; she might be thirty-five or ten years younger. That's howling grief for you. Mona gets up and comes round to the other side of the counter, takes her hand.

'Yes, I was expecting you. Hello, love.'

The woman's coat is belted tight like the scarf round her neck and the grip she has on Mona's fingers.

Mona smiles. 'Now then, have you got something for me?'

The woman nods and opens her handbag. She brings out a little parcel, wrapped in white tissue paper tied with a white velvet ribbon.

'Grand,' says Mona. 'Someone bought this for you, did they? We'll take a look at this when you visit. Now, have you got a number for me?'

The woman purses her lips and swallows. Mona waits because some things are hard to say.

'I'll tell you what, let me give you this.' Mona takes a business card from the counter and writes her address on the back. 'That's me. Shall we say next Wednesday at 4.00 p.m.? Would that suit you?'

The woman nods and Mona smiles. 'I just need the weight.'

The woman's voice is a whisper when she speaks. 'Five pounds seven ounces,' she says and she looks around as though she's told a secret.

'Lovely. Five pounds seven ounces. Good. All right now, I'm Mona and you are?'

'Christine Burrows.'

'Now then, Christine, four o'clock on the eighth of October. It takes a little while, at least an hour, sometimes more. Have you got other children? Do you need to pick them up from school or is that time all right?'

'No others,' she says, 'four o'clock is fine,' but she looks at the white parcel with the white ribbon on the counter. She touches it with the tips of her fingers and the paper crinkles.

'Don't worry,' says Mona. 'You'll see it again. I'll take very good care of it. Special care. You've done the hard bit now, haven't you? You've come all the way here and spoken to me. Wednesday week at 4.00 p.m. The address on the card. Come alone.'

Mona pats her on her shoulder because anything more would make the woman collapse. Anyone can see that.

2

Joley comes in after lunch. She smells of hairspray and roll-ups. She dances around the centre display with her arms out, fingers splayed.

'Guess what?'

'You got it!'

'Yeah!' Joley pirouettes, flies round the counter and into the little office opposite the kitchen. Mona follows.

'Oh, that's grand, Joley. I'm so pleased for you, love. When do you start?'

Joley takes off her denim jacket and puts it on the back of the office chair. She sits down and turns the computer on.

'Six weeks.'

'Six?'

'You should have let me show you before. I've been telling you for ages.'

'I know but . . . I'll have to get someone in when you've gone,' says Mona. 'I can't do it myself.'

'You can! I keep telling you, Mona. You can!' Joley puts a bar of chocolate on the desk and takes white headphones out of her pocket.

'What did you wear?' asks Mona, looking her up and down. Her vest covers nothing, not the navy ink on her tattooed arm, not the generous inch of cleavage, not the creamy skin of her abdomen.

Joley laughs. 'Wish you'd seen me. I wore, like, this black dress that my mum bought in, like, the nineties. And these?' She raises her feet and shows Mona her heavy black boots. 'And then I did my hair like yours, all tidy and straight in a sort of bun thing. Mum said she didn't recognize me.'

'Chignon, Joley.'

'Yeah, I used a sort of plastic doughnut that gives you this kind of bouffant.'

'Well, it did the trick anyway. Joley Carter, Teaching Assistant. They'll call you "Miss" and everything,' says Mona, straightening the denim jacket and giving Joley a little hug. 'I'm very pleased for you, love.'

Joley turns her face up and smiles. Mona can see the child in her, see the toddler, the baby in the crib, but when Joley turns back to the computer she's as fast as a cat, her fingers flying over the keyboard, her eyes darting over the screen, her black hair sprayed into impossible peaks and knots, like a doll herself or an alien. God, the place will be dead without her.

Mona goes to the toilet and looks in the mirror. Tidy and straight, is she? Maybe she'll take her hair down or pin it up at the sides. Too old for a hairband, too old for a fringe. It's still modern though, isn't it, a chignon? Mona's lipstick has disappeared, eaten along with her sandwich. And she could do with a manicure. That's what she'll have done at the Spa on Saturday. And a facial. And a back massage. She'll have a healthy lunch and ruin it with wine. She'll have bubbles in her glass and bubbles in the Jacuzzi. She'll have afternoon tea with clotted cream. Proper tea in a proper pot, the way her mother used to make it. An old enamel pot it was – everyone had one in those days in that corner of Ireland – that was filled and refilled throughout the day, fresh leaves, fresh water added and kept hot by a thick felt cosy with red embroidery that her mother made. She made everything herself, clothes and curtains, coats, Mona's dresses and a strange all-over apron of coarse brown material that she called 'sackcloth' because it only appeared for the annual spring cleaning.

Mona's mother always pretended that the day was an almighty chore. She would enlist the help of Big Maureen O'Shea who also took in washing and ironing. She'd arrive at the front door with a pail, a couple of scrubbing brushes and a clutch of dusters, but mostly the two women would sit and drink tea. Very little cleaning was even attempted but a desperate bout of dusting was crammed into the last couple of hours of an April afternoon after which Big Maureen would waddle home with ten shillings, a cake, a pie and some of Mona's old clothes for the little O'Shea twins.

Mona must only be four or five years old, swinging her little legs on a kitchen chair while she's colouring in at the table. The two women chatter near the sink.

'You weren't at the wedding, Kathleen,' says Maureen O'Shea.

Mona's mother wrings the mop in the bucket and catches her breath. 'No, I wasn't well. I've had a terrible chest. Was it good? What did she wear?'

'Molly Kavanagh?'

'As was.'

'As was, is right. As will be again if what I hear is correct.'

Mona's mother looks up suddenly. 'Go on!'

'Listen while I tell you, but look . . .'

As long as the two women are emptying cupboards and scrubbing and splashing the flags with water, Mona takes no notice. But the conversation about Molly Kavanagh makes Mona look up from her colouring book and the two women stare at her. Without saying a word, they both turn and look at the rain drumming against the kitchen window.

'She can't go outside,' Mona's mother says.

'No,' adds Maureen.

Mona's mother wipes her hands and goes to the dresser. 'We'll have to be careful.' She pulls a drawer open and Mona hears the rustle of paper. 'Now then, lovely,' says Mona's mother, putting three wrapped sweets on the table in front of her. 'You carry on with your colouring and you can have those sweets one after another, sucking them slowly. Good. And draw me something. You concentrate on that while we do our work. All right?'

Mona pops one of the sweets into her mouth. It's sharp and lemony and makes the water start from the back of her throat. She will draw a flower for her mother and a fisherman for her father

9

for when he comes home from work. She wants to ask her mother what her favourite colour is but when she looks up the women have walked to the stove and are making more tea.

'So?' says Mona's mother, nudging Maureen. 'Wasn't she only married Saturday week?'

'It didn't last twenty-four hours.'

'What didn't? Do not tell me that Stephen Hooley has disgraced that poor girl. Was he drunk? What did he do? He's always been a fast one, that boy.'

Maureen O'Shea turns her head slowly and Mona has time to look down and carefully colour in the petals on her little flower.

'Well, they went on up to the house after the wedding. As would be expected, after the celebrations had finished. The flowers were lovely, Kathleen. Molly did them herself. She's as plain as an old coat, God bless her, but the blooms were grand and there's not much to choose from this early in the year.'

'Go on.'

'Well, it's night-time and they've retired for the nuptials, if you know what I mean –' Maureen O'Shea nods in the direction of Mona – 'and Stephen Hooley has a friend.'

'A friend?'

'Yes, a friend he's kept well hidden all during his courtship with Molly Kavanagh. And the friend is eager to see her. Very eager.'

Mona's mother sniffs. 'I see.'

'But when the friend is introduced into the room, so to speak, Molly is horrified. "What's that?" she screams. Says she doesn't like the friend and he must be put away.'

Mona's mother has her mouth wide open. 'But the girl has lived on a farm all her life. What did she think was going to happen? She has two brothers, for pity's sake. Did no one tell her?'

'Well, from what I hear, she knew all about the existence of friendship but had no idea that – that the – er – friend would be – had intentions of, well, you know, would be inserted into . . .'

'Her friend?'

'Precisely. But Stephen Hooley, after months of denial, is banking on his powers of persuasion. "Don't worry, Molly," he says, edging his friend closer and closer, "he doesn't bite." '

Mona's mother begins to laugh, one hand splayed on her chest, great gulping gasps that rock her backwards and forwards. She has to grab the handle of the kettle. Maureen O'Shea's face is creased and red.

'She hit him! Molly Kavanagh leaps out of the bed, picks up a shoe and lamps him one!'

'Him or the friend?' says Mona's mother through her laughter.

'The friend was out of it like a shot! He shrank away,' blusters Maureen O'Shea and the women howl and scream and it's ten minutes before they recover. Mona watches them with a smile on her face, with her crayon poised over her drawing, drinking in the sound and the sight and the love in the warm kitchen in the grey April light. She would remember it for ever.

When Mona's father comes home that night and they're eating dinner together, she hears the same sound of fun in her mother's voice as she tells him about her day.

'Tell Dadda, Mammy,' says Mona.

'Tell him what, pet?'

'You know, about Stephen Hooley's friend?'

'What friend?'

'The shrinking one.'

The laughter seems to last for ever, her mother weeping again and wiping her eyes with a corner of the tablecloth, her father shaking his head and begging for an explanation, and Mona between them knowing she has made a wonderful joke.

Joley puts the New Orders file on the counter. 'You don't need to get anyone else, Mona. I can show you. The printing's easy. Then all you'd have to do is concentrate on Orders. You fill in the invoice, put it in with the doll, write an email from the pro forma file, press send. When the –'

Mona pushes it aside. 'I don't even want to think about it, Joley.

I've enough to do without trying to get my head round spread-sheets or whatever they are.'

'The spreadsheets are even easier.'

'Next week, I'll have a go next week.'

Joley taps the file with her finger. 'Time's ticking,' she says.

3

There's a pile of new orders. All for specials. One from Korea, one from America, one from New Zealand, and a pair of dolls, male and female, wanted in South Africa. That's a lot of orders for one month along with all the Christmas extras. Mona makes herself another cup of tea and stands at the window watching the lane. It's filled up now. There are young women in denim jackets and others in T-shirts despite the chill, mothers with toddlers, toddlers with ice creams, their little hands and faces covered in chocolate stickiness, everyone trying to eke out the last of the Indian summer.

Saturday will bring the day trippers with windbreaks and towels on the beach, sauntering along George Street, sniffing scented candles and handmade soaps, trying on plaited leather bracelets and hand-sewn purses. Across the road they'll wonder who on earth can afford the cashmere blankets in Grey's. They'll weave in and out of the antique shops and vintage emporiums, up and down, up and down the street, until finally settling at the White Horse for a late lunch. On their way to the car park, they'll spend a fiver in the pound shop and when they get to Mona's they'll stare and point and hold their babies up to see the wooden skittles and Noah's Ark.

But Mona's routine is no less predictable. Monday to Saturday, it's the shop, and then dollmaking on Sundays and most evenings. On Wednesdays the shop shuts for half a day and Mona takes the international orders to the post office or sometimes she'll see the women that Gayle sends to her. She hardly alters her schedule except for Christmas and New Year and her annual trip to Val or Val coming down for a bit of sea air.

One year, one February, the snow was atrocious. Mona didn't open up for five days. She put her snow boots on and visited the carpenter a couple of times, collected a few dolls and scurried back home, holding tight to handrails and hedges all the way up the hill. And another year Geor e Street flooded and no one could get in. So all in all, it's only the rare act of God that interferes with her plans.

Mona closes up at four and walks to Clearwater Lane, which has all the best charity shops. She's out sourcing stock whenever she can, imagining and dreaming and planning outfits for her dolls, the thing that sets her apart, that keeps her business thriving. She knows what looks good with what. She can look at a silk blouse with a satin cuff and see what it might turn into, which doll might wear it and how she might take it apart. Mona's always on the lookout for scraps of leather and wool, or an evening bag covered in tiny beads and buttons that she will painstakingly tease apart. She always needs lace for edging dresses and underskirts, also for the ruffs of shirts. She uses string or heavy thread for laces in boots, sequins and little bits of fashioned metal for jewellery, pendants and necklaces. And real hair of all colours – curls are a bonus. She sorts through the rails and carousels at Save the Children, Oxfam, the Blue Cross and Toby's Hospice but there's only a meagre yield: a navy suede jerkin, a rusty brooch with loose stones that she can pick out to decorate a dress, a Fair Isle cardigan that will be felted for a miniature carpet bag and two stained tablecloths with gros-point edging.

Then there's just time to pop in on the carpenter before she heads home. She takes the long way down to the seafront, turns left away from the pier and the arcades, the ice-cream parlours and young men slouched over the railings, throwing their cigarettes on to the stones. She walks slowly in step with the long breaths of the sea. An early mist creeps over the water. She heads east towards the cliffs. This isn't the tourist end of the beach; the buildings, all but one, are anonymous workshops and industrial units huddled under pewter cliffs that leach grey water from some leakage inland. Great lumps of rock scatter the beach. But even this end of town is being tarted up with oyster shacks and the Ropemaker's Grill, local ice creams and the promise of the Old Town Heritage Centre.

The carpenter's workshop is on the first floor. She can see it in the distance – it juts out, cantilevered almost over the old warehouse beneath. The wooden shutters are open as always, like great flat arms that beckon the great flat sea that sweeps all the way out, right to the edge of the world. Once, on a winter's evening, Mona saw a crimson sun half dipped in the water and another time she hung out of that window and saw the clouds shuffle and sweep across the sky, the sunlight suddenly slicing through them and dancing over the waves.

It's a beautiful space. You couldn't help but make something beautiful in it. It smells of trees and forests, of resin and oil and sawdust and metal and all the minerals that make up the sea. It smells of food if he's been cooking on his two-ringed stove in the corner, bacon sometimes or a fried egg, fish and chips if he can't be bothered. Certain places, certain corners of the open space, smell of coffee or whiskey, and although he keeps it scrupulously clean, his toilet smells faintly of stale urine, like the back alley of a pub – but that's men for you. Just as you walk in, there's an alcove behind a faded velvet curtain, sapphire blue with a maroon fringe, something belonging to an old theatre or cinema, the sort of place that might pair those colours together and think it looked all right.

Once, by accident, many years ago, Mona had pulled the curtain back. There was a single bed against the wall, all made up neat and trim with a stripy flannelette sheet and a grey blanket, as old as the Crimea, tucked in tight apart from one corner he'd overlooked. It was all she could do not to nip in and make it perfect. She stopped herself. It wasn't her business.

She opens the thick wooden door at the bottom of the metal steps. It's never locked. There's always been a carpenter here, a carpenter and an apprentice, one taking over from the other, their names carved on the heavy oak lintel, six in total but no youngster these days. The stairs are metal, open tread, slippery when they're damp, and she's suggested a couple of times that he fixes a rubber tread on each step for the sake of safety and peace of mind. He says he will but nothing changes.

She knocks at the door that leads to the big open room and walks in. 'Only Mona,' she shouts.

She can't see him. She dips her head under the bulk of a wooden beam, walks round the workbench and the black pot-bellied stove in the middle of the room. The windows are open and the sea breeze makes the sawdust dance in the light. On a shelf near the window, he arranges the dolls by finish, from those ready for fine sanding to the rough ones, works in progress or in pieces. He lays the ones she can take on a table underneath with the finished toys. She comes so regularly there's only ever three or four at most.

Mona loves the feel of a new doll, all loose-limbed and naked. The way they clack and tangle together reminds her of the crabs brought in at Kilmore Quay. Each wooden carcass has an egg-shaped body and smooth tapered limbs with articulated joints. The head has a small pointed chin, a peak of a nose and a medieval look. The carpenter sands them well enough but every now and again there's a little rough patch he's overlooked so she keeps a stock of fine-grade sandpaper for finishing. She uses light, quick, gentle strokes, blows the dust off, wipes it with a damp cloth, especially in the crevices, and then leaves it a while. It's nothing she would ever tell the carpenter but all the same she's become just a little finickety about texture over the years.

The carpenter always works with his back to the door, bent over, sawing or sanding, whittling or chiselling, both hands to the job, his long hair falling in jagged shanks. From behind you'd take him for a hippy maybe but you'd be wrong and if you ever got a close look at his eyes or saw past the beard, you would know it. He's not a man to care about hairstyles or fashion and more than once Mona has found him with his head shorn and the ponytail making ash in the wood burner. But under it all, he's broad and strong, his face worn and manly, with a smile, if ever you see it, that would make you blush.

And there he is, at the back by the lathe, planing something, slow and deliberate, his head inclined to the side in the dim light.

'Afternoon,' she says. 'Though it's barely that.'

He hardly raises his head but moves his hand. His greeting. She's learnt to wait, to winkle out a conversation. She runs her finger along the top of a small wooden armoire, antique.

'Who's this for? It has a lovely deep sheen. Yew, is it?'

'Yew, yes.'

'I need a five-pound-seven-ounce baby,' she says. 'And I'll put the kettle on if you've a few minutes.'

He stands up and stretches his back. His jeans hang at the back and the front and if it wasn't for his belt, Mona would see everything. 'Five pound seven,' he says, 'that'll be a little one.'

'Balsa?'

'Too light.'

He walks over to the holding bays that line the workshop where he stacks his stock of wood and planks and off-cuts. Mona follows. He scratches his beard and crouches down on his haunches. He shifts blocks, weighing them against each other, muttering. His ribs furrow his shirt. Mona wonders if he's hungry, whether she should offer to get them both fish and chips. She dare not go as far as a meal in a restaurant. He springs up suddenly with a dull piece of pine.

'This is right,' he says.

'Good.'

Mona goes and fills the kettle at the little sink in the corner. It's all bleached clean and shining; a little shelf to the side has a new bar of soap, a rough cloth, a folded towel.

'Freezing wind today,' she calls behind her. There are only two mugs, draining upside down on a wooden breadboard. There's a beautiful little walnut cupboard wedged into the corner, with a bowed door and a marble top. It holds his life. Money, teabags, birth certificate, tablets, plasters, pencils, an old photograph. Mona could tell you every scrap in there. She takes out the teabags and wipes over the marble top.

'You wouldn't think it was September.'

Suddenly he's next to her.

'No?'

'My hands are like slabs of ice,' she says and holds them out. 'Feel them.'

'There's always the promise of winter,' he answers and leans past her to fill the mugs. She smells him, herby and sharp, like leaves in a forest. She puts her hands in her pockets and shuffles out of the way to the window. Down below, squatting on the pebbles, are a young man and his girlfriend.

The two of them are piling one big stone on top of another into a sort of totem pole and even from this distance Mona can hear the girl laughing and the young man's baritone jokery. Their clothes are so insubstantial, her blouse buffeted by the wind, his T-shirt rising up at the back. They know nothing of the promise of winter, those two.

Mona turns back to the room and takes her tea. 'I brought biscuits,' she says, dipping into her bag. 'Chocolate.' She fights with the wrapper, takes one and puts the rest in the walnut cabinet. She takes eighty pounds from her purse and tucks it under the jar of coffee where he'll see it.

'Did she get it?' he asks.

'Who?'

'You told me that girl that works for you was after a job.'

Mona takes a step towards him. 'Yes, she'll be gone in six weeks. I have her until then.'

'Well, then,' he says.

'She wants to train me up. She thinks I can do it myself but I've never been good with figures.'

'You?'

'Yes, me, on the computer.'

He says nothing. She picks up the dolls and toys he has made and puts them in a canvas bag. When she looks again, he has gone back to his work.

'Oh and I'll have to bring back the yellow birch dolls from last week. They're stained on the leg, two of them.'

'Stained?' He moves towards her and stands at the window.

'Or something like that,' she says. 'There's a sort of brown mark on the legs. I don't want to paint over it.'

'Bring them back. I'll take a look.'

'I thought you'd want to see them.'

'Spalting. Discoloration.'

'Yes?'

'Fungal infection on the wood probably. People pay good money for spalted wood. You wouldn't want it on a doll. Can't think why I didn't notice it though. Don't paint over it. It might show. It would look like a mistake. And it's not a mistake. Might make you look sloppy.'

She hears him swallow his tea, hears the grinding bob of his Adam's apple. They are close together looking out at the two young lovers, giggling still, their stone construction uneven and listing. If she moved an inch she could touch him, elbow to elbow. He moves away.

'Bring the dolls back,' he says. 'The pair of them.'

4

Soon, Mona's mother seems to be crying all the time and not from laughter. Mona's walking up the wooden stairs in her dusty sandals, straight in from the garden, and just as she gets near the bedroom door she hears the sniffing and mewling and she tiptoes down again, out the back door, through the hard stone lane, over the yielding dunes and down to the fringe of the Kilmore shore. Sand as soft as powder all around the wide curve of the bay. She splashes and plays and gets her sandals wet and stays away for hours. Away from her, away from her. Mona's ashamed of herself now but at seven or eight children can be heartless.

One day, Mona's father comes striding after her with his shirt untucked, his house slippers sinking as he walks. When he reaches where she's playing, he stands still and, for a moment, says nothing. He looks like he's been sleeping or crying himself.

'Mona,' he says, 'what do you think you're doing?'

'Playing, Dadda,' she replies.

'Where do you think you should be? Where did I ask you to be, now?'

'With my mother.'

'Doing what?'

'But, Dadda . . .'

He crouches down until his big head is level with hers and takes both of her hands in his. He tugs on them.

'Is it boring with your mother, Mona? Because she can't get up and run into the waves with you like she used to? Because she can't sit you on her lap and brush your hair, because she doesn't get out of bed? Is that it, Mona?'

As he speaks he picks strands of Mona's white-blonde hair from where it blows across her eyes.

'Yes, Dadda.'

'One day,' he says, and his voice is kind so Mona knows she isn't getting a telling-off, 'one day, you will want these hours back, my girl. You will wonder how you lost them and you will want to get them back. There's a trick to time.'

He stands up, brushes the sand from his trousers, and Mona jumps up on to his back for the ride home. He lollops over the dunes with her hands round his neck and her chest against his ribs.

'What's the trick, Dadda?'

He likes to explain things so Mona expects a good long answer that might delay them getting back home.

'You can make it expand or you can make it contract. Make it shorter or make it longer,' he says.

'How?'

Mona clings to him. She looks out to sea for one last glimpse before it sinks over the brow of the hill and her father turns his head also.

'By the sea all life's worries wash away,' he says.

This is typical of him, quoting something from a poem or a book and not answering a straight question with a straight answer. And anyway, the sea must be losing its special powers because Mona's father is worried all the time these days and he's right here by the sea in the wrong trousers and the wrong shoes without even a comb through his hair. And it has nothing to do with making time grow.

'All life's worries wash away?' she asks. He nods and says no more.

When they get home, Mona goes straight upstairs to her mother, sitting up in bed wearing the horrible knitted hat, the one with bits of hair stuck to the sides, the same black hair that once used to cascade over her shoulders or rest like a plaited rope on her back. But Mona can see straight through the wispy veil that now barely covers her mother's scalp; whole skeins of her loveliness are tangled in the knitted bonnet or lie loose and dark on the pillow-case like dry seaweed on the rocks. And then there are the sores at the corners of her mother's mouth. Sores that make Mona turn away from a kiss. God forgive her.

Mona's mother takes a piece of linen out of her sewing basket and holds it up to the window.

'Come, look at the light through the weave,' she says. 'See? It's the colour of your summer skin, Mona.'

'Yes, Mammy.'

'When you grow up, when you're a big girl, you'll go to other countries, Mona. To Italy and France and Spain. Far, far away, where it's hot every single day and you'll go browner than this.'

Mona can feel her mother's eyes all over.

'You'll be tall, I think. Yes, tall you'll be and very, very pretty, *a stóirín*.' She strokes Mona's arm. 'I can see you now. Walking down a street that has a French name, the Rue something, and it's not summer, it's winter, yes, let's say it's a crisp December evening and maybe you'll be hand in hand with a husband or a sweetheart. You'll have a coat with a fur collar and a pair of leather boots with buttons up the side.'

'What else will I have?'

'You'll live on a wide boulevard or maybe up by the strand in Rosslare in a big house with two cats and a rabbit. Two children – no, four children and a maid. Yes, shall we give you a maid, my little treasure? Shall we give you a maid and a cook and someone to open the front door to visitors and curtsy?' Mona's mother puts her nose in the air and speaks in an English accent. 'I beg your pardon, madam. Miss Desdemona is not to be disturbed.'

But as Mona laughs, her mother loses the smile on her face.

'You know, I might not be there, Mona. I might not be with you.'

'Why?'

'Because you have your life to live and you won't want your mother with you all the time, will you?' She begins to tack the linen with long, even stitches. 'And because I might not be well enough to see you grow up.'

'I'm growing quickly. Dadda said.'

'Yes, you are. But I'm getting sicker quickly too. And if it was a race, Mona, I think you would win.'

'Mammy,' says Mona, 'you can live with me when I have my big house.'

Mona sees how her mother's nightdress gapes at the neck, how her face is sunken, the colour of the grey rocks on the beach. 'And the cook will make you a nice dinner with lots of bread and butter. And jam,' Mona adds.

Her mother's reply is a squeeze from her cold hand and a little cough.

It goes on for hours, their sewing and imagining and making each other laugh. Mona stays upstairs until it's nearly dark, until her mother leans back against the iron bedstead, until her blinks get slower and slower and her sewing drops on to the covers. Mona creeps off the bed and tiptoes down to her father, who is still in the wrong clothes sitting in front of a dead fire.

'Good girl,' he says.

5

Mona tries to sleep. Knows she won't. She walked the long way home from the beach hoping the exercise would wear her out and she fell into half-consciousness as her eyes closed. But she's still awake, pressing her eyelids together and thinking back to her mother. How old was she when she died? Thirty-eight? No age at all. A young woman still.

Mona makes a cup of tea and walks to the window. Middle of the night and he's there again, the General, looking out to sea. She watches him until he turns round and waves. She salutes him again with her mug in the air and there is a moment between them, more than a few seconds. He gives a little bow and withdraws back into his room.

Mona watches the morning come with nails of rain that drive against the glass. If this isn't a day for a break in her routine, nothing is. Stay home, that's what she'll do. Stay home for once, for the whole morning. Why not? Let Joley look after the shop on her own for a few hours. She'll not get dressed, she'll sew for the whole day and just enjoy herself.

Mona has plans for a doll, a new one with a just-painted, quiet and thoughtful face, long, delicate limbs. She might make a serge pinafore from a canvas jacket sleeve and a calico blouse from a pillowcase in the white and cream section of her stock. Or what about a kilt from a bit of tartan blanket and an Aran cardigan from an Aran cardigan? Half a yard of ruby jacquard lies waiting on her desk – well, it's a table really and her workroom is just the biggest bedroom with the best light, with space for the dolls and supplies, space for a sewing machine and a workbench that could sit eight for dinner. She sorts methodically through shelves layered with cloth for a bit of contrasting corduroy. She has fabric of every variety, in pleats and bolts of strict colour gradation, and a tea chest of frilly peels of lace. Second-hand curtains trail off hooks on the back of the door. There's often great folds of them in the charity shops and at jumble sales – not that there are jumble sales any more. The Methodists and Christadelphians used to run them grand, with heaps of good-quality stuff sold for pennies, books and bric-a-bac, a tombola, home-made chutney, a cake stall and a tea urn. All gone now. Mona usually pays close on ten pounds for a good suede coat or a crewel-work runner. But it's worth it. She finds a bit of furry suede that matches the ruby jacquard and as she's about to cut, the phone rings.

It will be Valerie and it will be about the weekend. Mona knocks her elbow on the door jamb as she rushes through the door and rubs it like she's trying to bring a shine.

'Hello?'

Yes, it's Val. Mona listens, drops her shoulders and her voice.

'Oh no. Sorry to hear that, Val. Not again. She's worse then. What happened?'

It's not about Saturday. Well, it is, sort of. She listens to Val's tale and asks questions where she should. 'Your poor mother. Where did it happen? Corporation Street? What was she doing in town? Lost? Was she alone? Oh no, Val.'

Mona hears the strain in Valerie's voice, knows its source, the mother's fall and the fact that Val never likes letting anyone down. So Mona makes it easy.

'No, you can't leave her. Stay where you are. Don't worry,' says Mona.

Her elbow has stopped hurting.

'I'll be up in November as usual. We can do it in November. We can go out for a meal. Yes, of course. No. Don't be daft. No.'

As she listens, Mona lowers herself on to the arm of her favourite chair, the one she has angled to the television and the tall windows that overlook the gardens.

'I'll be fine. You've got to be there, Val, love. I won't hear of it. No.'

But Mona has stopped listening to her friend 177 miles and three hours away. She's nodding as though Val can see and keeps a light touch in her voice.

'We knew this was coming, didn't we, Val? When she came home in those leopard-skin leggings, remember? We said she wasn't right then. Not at eighty.'

She giggles along with Val, who says she will ring the next day. 'Don't worry about me. You get going. Where is she? The QE's a good hospital. Take her that bed jacket in, the one that makes her look like Liberace. That'll cheer her up. And take her the leggings to match. There's a lovely outfit for you. Oh, we shouldn't laugh, Val. No, go on. Get off. Yes. Bye, love. Bye.'

She clicks the phone in its cradle and walks back to the swivel chair in her workroom. She picks up Belinda and turns her round. All she wears is a coat of primer and undercoat and two of chalk white paint; her eyes are green with a full-stop pupil. The doll's face is as smooth and fine as porcelain although a trained eye could just see the grain in the wood under the alabaster paint. Mona wipes her eyes with the pad of her thumb.

'What would you like, Belinda?' she asks. 'I mean, if you could have anything? Wouldn't be work clothes, would it? A party dress, is that it?' Then Mona lays the doll down again and walks out of the room. 'Talking to yourself, Mona. Talking to yourself.'

She puts the kettle on and while it boils she tidies the kitchen, folds the dishcloth and places it like a poultice over the tap. She takes a mug from the cupboard and spoons in coffee from a jar.

'Or if not talking to yourself,' she continues, 'then talking to a piece of wood. Not sure which is worse.' She pours the boiling water and adds milk. 'Wood, Mona. Definitely the wood.'

She walks slowly back to the lounge and sits in her chair. The midday sun falls like yellow paint on the frame of the French windows. It will taint the white gloss and fade the drapes. It will leach the red from the carpet and bleach the rug and Mona doesn't care. She sits with the mug on her lap and thinks about Saturday and how she will feel when she actually turns from fifty-nine into sixty. She imagines getting into bed on Friday night and falling asleep or trying to. She was not always scared of old age, would have welcomed it once upon a time when there was someone to grow old with. They made so many plans and she thought she had time for all of them but she was so bloody young then, they thought that life went on for ever.

She blinks and looks around her living room. It's not too late. She could invite a few people over. Make canapés. Buy canapés. Couple of bottles of white wine. Beer. Or even a sit-down meal. She turns to look at the drop-leaf table with both its leaves dropped.

'Huh,' she says. 'And when were you last needed?'

Maybe she should have an impromptu party at the shop, an open house, come one, come all, fancy dress, Venetian masks. They could spill out on to the cobbles and conga down George Street, drunk and careless. She jumps out of the chair and shimmies towards the kitchen but stops at the sight of herself in the mirror. She's not dressed, the collar of her dressing gown is up at the back and her hair is untidy. The General will have seen her like this. She straightens and smooths and adjusts her clothes but it's too late, the horse has bolted.

She pours her coffee down the sink and sighs. 'Tricia might be up for a night out,' she says aloud. 'I'll pop down right now.'

Downhill, left round the park, turn right. All over town there's building and renovating going on, all the old shops becoming artisan bakeries or organic groceries, and Tricia's road will be next to turn. It's still a bit scruffy at this end but someone's bought up the old hardware shop at the corner. Its ancient wooden counter lies sideways in the street, its innards all exposed, warped by the rain, the varnish peeling like diseased skin. The big yellow skip outside the shop is full to the brim and the red-painted sign that says 'Robinson's Ironmongers' rests on top, rusted and buckled.

Mona steps over the rubble on the pavement and walks a few yards on to Tricia's. The windows are steamed and dripping.

Trish is in one of the chairs near the front of the salon facing a

27

mirror, a brown towel on her shoulders. Deep purple dye has crept from her hair on to her forehead and neck.

'So you're going for dark and sultry now, Trish?' says Mona, sitting in an empty chair.

Tricia raises her eyebrows. ' "Midnight Raven", supposedly.' She squints into the mirror and scratches her scalp with the end of a comb. 'Or "Crows After Closing" as I call it.'

Mona laughs. 'Are you busy on Saturday night, Trish?'

Tricia's eyes dart left and right. 'Saturday night? Why does that ring a bell?'

'Oh, don't worry if you're busy, I just –'

'No, no.' Tricia taps her forehead with a finger. 'Let me think. Oh, hang on, I've got something for you.' Trish examines herself from all angles. Touches the dye with the tips of her fingers and then peers at the colour.

'Adele! Adele, get here.'

Tricia raises her eyes to the ceiling.

'Honestly, Mona, I've got another one straight from college. New. Thick. Deaf.'

A blonde whippet of a girl hurries in.

'Adele, remember that ponytail from last Saturday? Go and get it. Second drawer to the right of the fridge. Then get this gunk off my head. Quick. Hurry up. Hurry. Ponytail first then rinse me.'

Mona slips a plastic bag from her pocket and flicks it open.

'A ponytail? That's grand, Trish.'

Trish swivels round in her chair.

'You'll like this, Mona, love. Listen, little girl, about eleven I'd say, comes in here with her dad. Sat right there. Wants the sides shaved and a great big quiff like some pop star. Can't remember the name now. So I'm thinking this. Contact visit. Mother and father separated. He's got the golden child for the weekend and the golden child's got him by the balls. So I say, "How about a bob? Or some choppy layers?" but he's like, "Whatever she wants, lady," and I'm like, "You'll regret this, buster." She was a right little madam, wasn't she, Adele? Adele?'

Trish eases herself out of the chair and storms to the back of the salon.

'Adele? Come on! I'm itching like a leper. The ponytail, Adele. Have you got it? Give it here.'

Trish holds a long white-blonde skein of hair up in the air.

'Look at the length of this. Honestly, I said to the dad, I said, "Listen, love. I get the picture. It's your precious weekend. You want to spoil her a bit. And she's a pretty girl. I know what they're like at that age. Only don't take her back home looking like a dyke. Her mum won't like it." Anyway, you know me, I've talked him down off the ledge and I've just about convinced him that she's better off with a good trim and the little madam starts performing, pouting like a toddler, folds her arms over her flat chest, dredges up two fat little tears, and he's all "All right, darling. All right. Don't cry."'

Trish swings the ponytail like a lasso.

'Ours is not to reason why, Mona, love. So here it is. One ponytail. One long regrowth for the girl and one dad in the doghouse.'

Mona takes the hair, silky, heavy in her hand. She wonders what it felt like when it was alive, when it was swinging on the girl's back, lying on her pillow. She tucks it in her carrier bag. Trish's new girl rinses the purple dye away and as soon as Trish is upright, she goes straight back to the mirror and frowns.

'It'll look all right with a blow-dry.' She catches Mona's eye. 'Honey, Mona. If I've said it once. Honestly, go honey-blonde, it would really suit you with your face and skin tone. A few golden highlights and a few inches off the back. Take years off you. Centuries even.'

'Centuries? There's a monumental promise.'

'Go on. Treat yourself.'

Mona shrugs. 'I'm all right like this, Trish.'

'Says who?'

'Me and the mirror.'

'Yeah, well you've been coming here fifteen years, pet, and times change as do fashions. Modern is my motto. Move with the

29

times. Take my word for it, Mona, three inches off the back, highlights, lowlights and a blow-dry. You wouldn't know yourself. One inch for each decade it will take off you. That's a good deal by anyone's standards.'

Trish is talking over the hairdryer, tugging her black curls with a big brush. 'On the house, Mona, and I don't say that very often, do I?'

Mona shakes her head and pats Trish on the back.

'Thanks, love. I might. I'll come in here one of these days wearing a basque and fishnets and I'll get some bright-red extensions. How's that?'

'Peroxide ringlets go better with a basque. I won't tell you how I know.'

Mona laughs. 'Ringlets it is. Now, will I put something in the charity pot? What's it this time?'

'Puppies, I think. Or blind donkeys. Can't remember now.'

'Ah, well,' says Mona and as she finds her purse and drops a two-pound coin in a blue plastic bucket by the till, she calls over, 'What's going on next door?'

'Kebabs and burgers apparently. Imagine the smell! Fried meat and melting lard. They'll stink us out. Can't say I'm happy about it but at least they're tarting the place up.'

'Thanks, love,' Mona shouts on the way out. She's past the kebab shop and on her way home before she starts laughing. 'Crows After Closing,' she says. She forgot to ask about Saturday.

6

Mona's mother sleeps most of the day now and her father has taken a chair upstairs and stationed it next to the window in the sick-room. That whole summer Mona's down at the beach. Her father's almost stopped hearing Mona's questions, stopped telling her off about things and reading her stories at bedtime. He's even stopped going to work at the post office and reading the newspaper. If he isn't upstairs, he's sitting hunched by the cold fire like he's willing it back to life. Women from the village come and leave stews and cakes. Mona can come and go as she pleases.

Sometimes she presses shells into the wet sand until she has the shape of a doll, one big shell for the body and lots of little shells for the arms and legs. Seaweed makes a good head of hair, wild and dark. Then she runs off again and scours the coves and inlets for something special, something beautiful for the head and face, a smooth flat stone maybe, the opalescent shell of a crab, a piece of amber ocean glass, but more often than not, by the time she comes back with her treasures, the sea has been and taken the body back to itself and eventually that's what happens to Mona's mother.

One day, Mona comes home from school to find the house is full of people. Her father is nowhere to be seen. One woman keeps saying, 'The poor baby, the poor little creature,' and it takes Mona weeks and weeks to realize that the poor child is herself. Mona runs through the house, brushing against neighbours that litter the hall and kitchen, looking for her father. Hands reach out for her, all of them sighing, saying, 'Come on here till he comes back,' or, 'God bless her, keep her inside,' but Mona slips out of their grasp, she shoves them away and runs out of the back door and down to the sea.

She finds her father there holding his head, howling like a

banshee, his mouth wide open and his throat swollen with the effort of making a noise loud and deep enough to argue with the waves and the injustice of life. Mona stands by him and takes his hand. They scream together until they are fetched back by someone, until they are sitting down in the best room, like visitors in their own home, served tea from the special china and fruit cake smothered with butter. Mona and her father sit hand in hand until everyone leaves, then he puts his arm round her, nestles her into his chest.

'We had her for a long time,' he says, 'longer than they said. And we loved her to the end.'

'Yes, Dadda, we did.'

'It was a precious time, Mona.'

'Is that the trick, Dadda?'

He says nothing for a long, long time then wipes his sleeve across his face.

'Yes, Mona, it is.'

In the days that follow after the mother and wife is taken away, they often walk down to the beach and round to Forlorn Point to cry with the sea, and afterwards she shows him how to play, how to make dolls from shells and stones, seven or eight at a time, until her father says, 'Come on, lovely girl. Time to go home.'

And he does make it a home. By the time Mona is twelve, she's nearly forgotten what it is to have a mother. Her father keeps the house almost by himself, tidies and cooks, sweeps the flags from front to back, moves ornaments to dust beneath them, and Mona doesn't have to help if she doesn't want to. But she always does and they change sheets either side of the bed, bash the dust from the rugs, clean the windows and boil the ham as a team, her father six feet four inches and Mona small and quick.

Never a month goes by without a visit to Bridie O'Connor in the village. There was some connection on her mother's side of the family and every so often her father tells her to put on a nice dress and a ribbon, polish her shoes and look presentable. No matter what Mona says, the visit is never postponed or abandoned and eventually she stops complaining.

She holds her father's arm as they walk past the tall hedges, through the main road and off down a little lane to Mrs O'Connor's big whitewashed house.

'Why doesn't she visit us instead?' asks Mona. She is fourteen.

'Good question,' her father replies as though he'd never thought of it before.

'At least then I could do the mending or shell the peas while she has the clock stopped.'

Her father laughs and squeezes her arm in close.

'Ah, she's a conjuror all right is Bridie O'Connor. I've never known a longer hour. But.'

And his 'but' says everything. Mona knows the words that come after. But she's family, sort of, and she loves you. But she's lonely. But she lives alone. But it's the right thing to do. But we have to think of more people than ourselves alone. But have a heart, Mona.

So they both smile when the front door is opened and they each give the woman a kiss on her powdered cheek. Mona walks through to the kitchen and helps to bring the tray into the front parlour. She pours the tea and cuts the cake that she has baked and brought in a covered basket. She's watched closely by Bridie and her father while she lifts three slices on to delicate china plates and passes them round, but when all these little tasks have been performed, she has no choice but to sit down and wait.

Her father does most of the talking and Bridie O'Connor sits and chirps and chimes in every so often, asking questions she surely knows the answer to or at any rate questions that bore Mona to tears.

'Your father says you're doing well at your studies, now, Mona. Is that so?'

'And are you using a lotion on those hands, Mona? A girl needs pretty hands.'

'Who are your friends at school?'

Bridie O'Connor is a slight woman with thick auburn hair that she must set every night in big plastic rollers so it fluffs up in extravagant waves. She's immaculate. She has whole sets of Crimplene suits and tailored dresses, stockings of opaque beige, shoes of patent black with a pointed toe and frosted pink lips. Sometimes she wears a mother-of-pearl brooch or a string of pearls and, at Christmas, a sprig of enamel holly on a silver pin. She always has a silk scarf, either on her shoulders or on her lap or the back of her chair, and she sits to one side with her knees together, her ankles neatly crossed, and while Mona's father talks she looks over at Mona and smiles to bring Mona into their dragging conversation.

The choices for entertainment in Kilmore are utterly dire. There's Bridie's parlour or the same four walls that Mona looks at every night, her father with a book or the newspaper and the same old programmes on the same old television that closes down early and never seems to show anything worth watching anyway. Everyone under twenty feels the same. They leave one by one until there are barely three teenagers in the village. Mona watches them pack up and leave at the first opportunity. Fiona and Maeve go to London, Paulie Byrne flies off to Detroit where he has a cousin with a restaurant and Bernadette Hooley marries a Scottish bricklayer she met on holiday and moves with him to Glasgow. The farthest Mona gets is Bridie O'Connor's stuffy sitting room and the visits that come around too quickly.

One summer's night on the walk home, Mona's father stops in the street.

'You were rude,' he says.

Mona marches ahead. 'She's sweet on you,' she throws over her shoulder. 'And she's about a hundred.'

When he catches up, Mona's father lays his arm round her shoulder. 'I have all I need here,' he says. 'You'll be married before me.'

'Who to? We never go anywhere. I hate this place. I hate Wexford and I hate Ireland. Everyone goes off and lives a great life abroad and I don't blame them. It's all right if you're old.'

'Like me, then?'

34

'Yes!' Mona shrugs him off and strides home. If she ever has to sit again and watch Bridie cross and uncross her legs, fiddle with the tiny gold cross round her neck and roll the stem of her sherry glass between her fingers she will go absolutely mad. She is barely spoken to some Sundays with her father and Bridie trading items from the newspapers and tragedies from the television and folk wisdom that makes Mona wince. When a fishing boat saved a drowning man, it was 'Heroes see opportunities where others see danger'; when the elderly thatcher fell from his ladders and someone else took over his job, Bridie shook her head and said, 'There's no shame in the workman who passes on his tools,' and what made Mona finally stand up and announce that it was time they were off home was Bridie's pithy response to the article on the front page of the *Echo* that said a famous film star was house-hunting in the area. 'Ah well,' she said, 'you can't always believe those journalists. After all, paper never refused ink.'

It was that sort of attitude that would keep any self-respecting millionaire with an ounce of taste or common sense out of the area for good. It was that sort of little-mindedness that had Mona sitting at home night after night with an occasional visit to Enniscorthy for the pictures or, saints be praised, to the pathetic metropolis of Wexford itself once in a blue moon.

Mona veers right past their little cottage, leaving her father at the front door, and stamps her way down to the beach. She throws stones at the waves until her arms ache and then, in tears, sits down on the wet sand as the wide sky turns from turquoise to pink and the silver clouds stretch and settle on the horizon.

She hears him coming and wipes her face. He settles a blanket on her shoulders and sits down next to her.

'I'm not getting the sand out of your suit. You can do it yourself.'

'I will.'

'And I'm not going to Bridie O'Connor's ever again. You can go on your own.'

'I see.' He hands her a piece of chocolate. 'You're giving up then.'

She chews quickly and swallows. 'Giving up on what?'

Her father breaks off half the bar and passes it to her. 'Wipe your lips. Here,' he says and uses his handkerchief on her face.

'Giving up on what?' she says again.

'On your obligations.'

She blows all the air from her lungs and rolls her eyes. 'Jesus Christ, she's not my bloody mother.'

The silence is painful and she knows she shouldn't have said it so she tries to cover it up with a thousand words.

'I mean, for God's sake, Dad. She's what, my second auntie twenty times removed or something and we go all the time and when I'm there it's just you and her and I may as well be on the moon. She only asks me out of politeness and she doesn't even do that very well. I mean, you said I was rude but she's so busy making doe eyes at you she doesn't even notice me. It's Robbie this and Robbie that, and then I have to make the tea and you and her talk about the newspapers all the time. Did you know that you say the same things every week? Did you know that? Honestly, I could set my watch by it. The fishing, the weather, the government, the new marina, wars and wars and wars and then a little bit of comedy courtesy of that terrible programme she's always watching that isn't even funny.' And on Mona goes. And she knows she should stop so eventually she does.

All the chocolate is gone and she's in tears again. He pulls her up on to her feet and hugs her all the way home. That night, he calls her down from her bedroom. He has a box of photographs on his lap and he pats the seat next to him.

'Look,' he says. 'Here's your mother. She was seventeen. Not much older than yourself.'

Mona has seen this photograph before. Her mother in a tailored suit with a pillbox hat and white gloves at a wedding.

'See the bride,' he says.

Mona brings the photograph up close. It's black and white and blurred but she can see the pretty girl with the dark-brown hair, both hands on her posy, in a tight lace dress and high heels.

'Bridie,' he says.

'Bridie?'

'Bridie.'

'Bridie is the bride?'

'Bridie Templeton is the bride. She's about, oh, something like twenty-five there I should think. That makes her eight years older than me. Not quite a hundred.'

'Jesus.'

'Bridie is your mother's mother's sister's child. Got that? Your mother's mother, that's Granny Flaherty, her sister married a man who already had a child. That child is Bridie. They are related by marriage. They were.'

Mona stares at the picture and squints to try and make out one single feature that she could match with the ageing woman in the tapestry chair.

'She has only us. You and me, Mona.'

'And Mr Michaels and —'

'Yes, she has a number of friends and some relatives but she only has us that she loves. And only us that love her.'

Mona says nothing.

'You don't have to make promises to keep them, Mona.'

She passes the photograph back to her father and goes to the kitchen. She puts the kettle on the stove and opens a packet of biscuits. She arranges them like she would at Bridie's and lays cups and saucers on a tray although it's something they never do at home. She finds a bit of lace and drapes it over the teapot.

She puts the tray on the coffee table and pours a cup for her father, who sits sorting through the photographs on his lap. When he looks up and sees what she has done, he smiles and the light catches his watery eyes.

'Ah, Mona.'

7

The first day of October and the turn of the season. Mona's up on Wednesday morning just before dawn. She opens the curtains and there he is doing the same thing, the General again, not sleeping. He won't see her pillow creases from that distance. This time he gives a proper wave, a royal hand held twisting at the wrist, and he looks at her so long that Mona blushes when she waves back. She thinks she sees a smile and she is first to turn away.

A quiet day and early closing. At one o'clock, as Mona's putting on her coat with the keys in her hand, the door opens. The woman that walks in is forty years old maybe, wearing a waxed jacket over jeans and a polo-neck jumper, chunky and well-worn. She has a ruddy face and no make-up, with the look of a life spent out of doors. It was weeks ago but Mona remembers being told to expect a horsewoman and here she is. The woman scans the display and picks up a doll.

'Can I help you?' Mona asks.

The woman turns the doll upside down so the little lace skirt flops over the doll's face. Mona gestures to the window.

'I have the male of that doll, just there behind you,' she says but the horsewoman lays the doll down and shakes her head. 'Not sure why I'm here,' she says. 'Gayle told me to come. It's not my idea.'

'Well, it's nice to meet you anyway,' says Mona and holds her hand out. The woman's touch is so slight and so quick that Mona is left with her hand out in the air for a few seconds. She turns it palm up.

'Did Gayle ask you to bring something for me?'

'Yes but I haven't got anything left. I threw all that sort of stuff away.' The woman has her shoulders back, her face defiant.

'That's fine,' says Mona. 'And not unusual. What about a weight?'

'Weight?'

Mona puts her keys down and walks round the counter so she is standing close up to the woman. She picks up the doll with the lace skirt.

'These, for example, are only about three pounds, less if you don't count the clothes. It all depends on the wood the carpenter has used. He makes them from off-cuts from his other jobs or rarely a bit of driftwood or something reclaimed. This particular one, I think, by the feel of her would be two pounds and ten ounces. You get a feel for them after a while. Course, it's all kilograms now but that doesn't mean much to me at my age. Do you get all that millilitre stuff or are you a gallons and pint kind of person?'

'Gallons, I suppose. Never really think about it.'

Mona straightens the doll and sits her carefully back where she was. 'My generation struggle with grams, we really do. I still think of a two-pound bag of sugar or half a pound of butter and I always will.'

The woman turns away while Mona is speaking and looks up at the shelves where the big dolls sit in their glass cases. 'I've never been into dolls. Didn't even have one when I was a child. Never saw the point.'

Mona follows her gaze. 'Oh, it's a myth that girls love dolls, isn't it? We just want something to love. It might not be a doll at all. Might be a cat. Or a teddy. Or a horse.'

The woman's hands are hidden in her coat. Mona can see through the pockets, see the bunched-up fists, hear the woman grinding her teeth at night, feel the sinews strain down her jaw. 'I had a pony,' she says.

'Ah. And I had my father,' says Mona.

They look at each other and Mona smiles and nods. The woman hardly moves her lips when she speaks. 'Eight pounds two ounces,' she says. 'Three point seven kilograms.'

Mona reaches out. She touches the woman gently on her arm and nods. 'What's your name, love?'

'Sarah,' she says.

Mona moves to the counter and writes her address on a business card. 'So, Sarah, you can come and see me in a couple of weeks' time. Shall we say, Wednesday the fifteenth of October at four o'clock? It takes a little while so if you have other children at home . . .'

The woman frowns. 'What is this? I mean, what do you do? No one's actually told me what you do. Gayle told me to come and see you but actually that's not enough information. What happens at these sessions? How much is it? I'm expected to just go to a stranger's house and do what? I don't want to turn up and find it's all been a waste of time.'

Her hands jerk in her pockets but her body is stiff. Her voice and her eyes are wild. Mona could weep for her.

'It's free. There's no charge. It's a gift. And we just talk, Sarah. Honestly, we just talk.'

The woman doesn't move. Mona touches her arm again.

'You leave it to me. You've done the hard bit, haven't you? Coming here? It's a difficult thing. So come to this address on Wednesday the fifteenth at four o'clock. Bring a shawl or a blanket or anything else you like or nothing at all, it's up to you, but some people have something special and they like to bring it with them. You just come and leave the rest to me. Come alone.'

The woman stares at Mona and opens her mouth, but nothing comes out. She walks away and leaves the door open.

Mona walks the long way to St Barnabas to catch the end of the group. She doesn't like to get there too early and disrupt the room but sometimes she eases the door open to listen.

If it wasn't for the big cross on the front, you'd mistake St Barnabas Church for a shopping centre with its new red brick and wired glass. They try, God bless them, and there's something for everyone: Afternoon Art, Write Yourself Well, Restorative Yoga, Meditation for Motherhood. Mona's given most of the classes a go at one time or another, she even volunteered at the Dementia Club when they were desperate, but she started off at the support group and she's never really left.

The session is just coming to a close when Mona arrives. She looks in and listens. Gayle sits in the middle of the circle, her hands resting in her lap, wearing her little half-smile and a dress with a handkerchief hem. She takes a deep breath.

'So, is there anything anyone would like to say before we wrap up?'

It's rare for anyone to jump in at this point as all the women want to get away and the few men hardly ever speak.

'Okay, then,' says Gayle, 'let's be quiet for these last few moments. You can close your eyes if you want to. Remember to breathe. You're going back to your day now. Think about leaving here and being back in the present. This is not about forgetting but about living with memories. Being mindful. Being here and now. Remember to breathe.'

Some of them have tissues. They wipe their eyes. They don't want to go back to the present. Gayle's very good though, she talks them into it.

'Some of you will be going shopping. Maybe you're visiting a friend after here. Catching the bus. Home to do some housework. Think about what you're going to do with the rest of your day, with the rest of your evening, with the rest of your week. We've talked about some distressing things this afternoon and we've been able to explore our feelings. Let's try and leave those thoughts where they are. Let them go. Remember to breathe. We're coming back now. Letting go so we can safely and quietly re-enter the day.'

Nothing then, just a cough and a sniff, a shuffling of feet.

'All right?' says Gayle. 'Okay. Anyone want to make any closing comments about anything? About what we can talk about next time maybe? Or what they've got on for the rest of the day?'

The girl that speaks is pregnant. 'I'd just like to say thank you because I was really in two minds about coming, you know, with this.' She strums her fingers on the round drum of her belly. 'I'm, like, still scared and everything but I think if I can just keep telling myself that it never happens twice . . .'

A sound of agreement from a woman with her back to the door.

'Thanks, Laura,' says Gayle. 'Anyone else? No? All right, thank you. Next meeting is on the twenty-ninth of October. Details in the newsletter.'

The chairs make a scraping sound on the plastic floor, they pull on their coats, the women picking up their handbags, the men stacking chairs. Mona stands aside as they push the door open in twos and threes and walk past. When the room is empty, she goes in.

'Hello, Gayle, love.'

Gayle's heavy arms squeeze a little breath out of Mona, a little sound. 'Got time for a coffee, Mona?' she says. 'Spring to Life are doing Drink 'n' a Bake for one pound sixty-five.' She makes her fingers into quotation marks and bites her bottom lip. 'Can you bear it?'

Before Mona can find an excuse, Gayle shakes her head. 'No, nor me. Come on, let's try that new place by the park. Have you been in yet? I've got half an hour before my train. Come on.'

She takes Mona's arm and they huddle together round the edge of the estate and back towards Old Town.

After a few minutes, Gayle gives a little nudge. 'You all right, Mona?'

'I'm sixty on Saturday,' she says.

'Well,' says Gayle, pulling her a little closer, 'if I look like you at sixty, I'll be more than happy. What are you doing for it?'

'Not sure.'

Gayle stops dead. 'Well, we can't have that. Come on, it's a big one. Something to celebrate.'

'I had something planned but it fell through and . . .'

'Settled,' says Gayle. 'We'll go to the Fat Pug. Nice quiet meal.'

Mona takes a deep breath. 'Thanks, Gayle, love. I didn't fancy sitting in with a bag of crisps. I'm never good at this time of year.'

Gayle lowers her voice as they round the corner into Old Town. 'You should come back to the group, Mona.'

Mona shrugs and says, 'I might,' but all she wants from the group is that last five minutes when everyone is quiet, when Gayle tells them to come back into the world, like coming up for air, when Mona thinks of letting it all go.

Then she sees him. The General. Even though it's only the back of him, she's certain. And while Gayle talks about the benefits of talking and the strength of the shared experience and the lovely mothers and the few poor men, Mona walks on, nodding and agreeing, and finds she is following the General through the back lanes, his beige mackintosh turning corners all the way to the edge of the park, all the way to the new Viennese patisserie, and he goes inside. Mona hesitates.

'Don't you want to go in? Come on,' says Gayle as she pushes the door open. It's warm inside and bright but hot air on cold cheeks means Mona's face will redden and she'll look like she's blushing or embarrassed. Her hair will be limp or wild, she has no idea which. No lipstick.

The General is right in front of them in the queue, broad and tall, taller than Mona's father, and his hair is swept back almost on his collar. He shuffles forward and they follow.

They've gone to such an effort with this place. Little marble-topped tables are all set for two with miniature china vases and flickering votive candles in smoked-glass holders. Chocolatey bent-wood chairs, a black-and-white tiled floor. A sweeping mahogany counter displays huge cakes under glass cloches, creamy gateaux in pink and brown, light sponges studded with fruit. Underneath on wooden shelves are pastel buns and biscuits, fat eclairs with a slick of sticky icing, and at the far end of the cafe, a bright, steaming coffee machine that pistons away and an old-fashioned till that pings and sings like a piano. It's all very lovely.

'Ooh,' says Gayle, bending over a tray of pastry swirls. 'What do you fancy, Mona?'

As soon as Gayle speaks the General turns his head so quickly that Mona is caught again, looking at him. He smiles and turns round to face her.

'Ah, I did not recognize you with your clothes on.'

Gayle looks at Mona from the corner of her eye and then back to the cakes. She begins to study the display as though her life depends on it, bending down and peering close.

The General holds out his hand and Mona takes it. 'May I introduce myself, now that we meet in the flesh as it were. Karl,' he says. His hand is enormous and warm. Mona's seems to disappear inside it. He doesn't let go but shakes once and then again. 'I am waiting,' he says. 'This is, I think, where you respond.'

'Mona, Mona.'

He inclines his head. 'Mona Mona?' Because he smiles and raises his eyebrows and because Gayle is contorting herself trying to keep out of the way, Mona laughs.

'Desdemona. Just the one. I'm Mona.'

'Ah,' he says, '*enchanté*, Desdemona.' He makes a little movement with his feet and again the incline of the head. 'And this is?'

'Gayle,' says Mona. 'Gayle, this is Karl. He's my neighbour.'

Gayle straightens up, already smiling. She holds her hand out and Karl's shake is quick.

'So,' he says, 'we've all come to make someone's dream come true, no?'

'Sorry?' says Mona.

Karl bends to whisper. He smells of a tonic or cologne, something you would smell in a big department store, manly and expensive.

'It is someone's dream this cafe, no? Look. How beautiful that people still dare to dream. You agree?'

'Yes, yes,' says Gayle, but Karl speaks to Mona.

'Maybe they have taken out a loan from the bank and bought these charming tables and chairs. And maybe they have sold their grandmother's ring to buy the coffee machine. It's a gamble, isn't it? But they are thinking it will be a success. No, they are certain. What do you think, Mona? Is it a happy ending?'

He leans in close and Mona looks away at the rainbow glass lanterns in the ceiling and the stiff lace curtains, at the empty tables and the single woman in the corner.

'Yes, I think it will work. I hope it will anyway. People always need to eat and drink, don't they?'

44

Karl claps his hands and turns to Gayle.

'I agree,' she says.

'Good! Now if you will forgive me, I must quickly buy myself a coffee and disappear. I'm a little late.' But he doesn't move away. 'Perhaps,' he says, 'I will see you tonight at the window. Or should I say, in the morning. We do not sleep, you and I.'

'Well, I try but . . .'

Gayle has turned back to the cakes in a gesture of disinterest.

'Let's see what happens,' he says quickly. 'Or perhaps I will see you here next week. Wednesday at the same time, two o'clock, shall we say? Let us see. If so, I look forward to it.'

'Yes,' says Mona. Then he turns and speaks to the girl behind the counter. He buys a very small cup of coffee and downs it in one without even taking a seat. He smiles at Mona and then he is gone.

Gayle chooses a table near the window and they sit with their coffees in little porcelain cups, their cakes on delicate gold-rimmed plates, a little fork each.

'This is Topfenknödel apparently,' says Gayle, comparing her cake with the picture on the menu.

'What does that mean in English?' says Mona. 'Dumplings swimming in jam? Or sweet fried baby cakes languishing on a bed of cherry compote? I should have had those.'

'Yes, you should. You can afford to put weight on and I can't. What's yours called?'

Mona peers at the little pictures. 'Mont Blanc,' she says and forks a square of tart into her mouth. 'I thought that was a mountain. Not a good advert for a two-thousand-calorie dessert if you ask me.'

There's so much condensation on the window that Mona won't be able to see Karl walking away down the street but she looks anyway.

'Nice man,' says Gayle.

'Yes, he is,' says Mona. 'I don't really know him but we wave to each other.'

'He likes you.'

'I don't know about that but he seems nice.'

'So,' continues Gayle, 'did either of them turn up?'

'Both,' replies Mona. 'Christine and Sarah. Christine I'm sure about but Sarah will take her time if she comes at all.'

'It's a pity,' says Gayle, mashing her fork against a few remaining crumbs. 'Her husband's worried about her. Thinks she might be having some sort of delayed reaction. Twelve years delayed.'

Mona closes her eyes. Twelve years is not so long. 'I'll make things ready just in case.'

Mona sleeps that night. She sleeps and has the lovely dream. So rare, the lovely dream, when her memories don't turn into nightmares. Bright sunshine. Blinding almost. She's sitting up in her hospital bed in a white nightgown, with a blue mohair bed jacket, a satin bow at her throat. She has a catalogue. She has a nurse. The nurse is Val. After a short deliberation, Mona chooses a beautiful, honey wood casket with brushed gold handles and an ivory cross that lies protectively along the top, just as long and pale as the child inside. And always in the lovely dream she knows she is dreaming. She can speed it up, she can slow it down. So this time, Mona wafts across soft green hills, like the hills in Wexford, to a private chapel of weathered stone where a kind priest kneels down and prays with her over the wooden box. He says long prayers that make her cry. It's always the crying that wakes her in the end, the itch of tears sliding off her neck or pooling in her ears. And then sleep again, a long, long sleep.

8

'Happy Birthday, my lovely girl. Happy Birthday, Mona.'

When she wakes, she remembers Desmond's on the Market Square in Wexford where her father took her for her sixteenth birthday. She had a knickerbocker glory, which every single child in town had been wanting for weeks. There was biscuit crumbled at the bottom then three different colours of ice cream and chocolate and raspberry sauce and a shining maraschino cherry on top. White cream oozed over the side of the glass as Mona dug her spoon in. Nothing else remains of that day, just the colours of pink and brown and white and red and sticky drips on sticky glass. Sticky fingers that Mona licked one by one. So long ago now.

It's a sunny Saturday on George Street and Mona's little shop is busy. If she'd been at the spa with Val, Joley would have been all on her own today so it's worked out well after all. There's a steady stream of customers and even Mr Morgan the local tinker, wrapped in layers of filth, his long teeth sparse and brown, shuffles in. Mona gives him five pounds and he tries to give her a hug. 'Bless you, lady,' he says, which unexpectedly brings tears to her eyes.

Then at lunchtime when she nips into Danny's cafe, he comes round the counter and plants a chaste kiss on her cheek, like she's his maiden aunt.

'Big one, is it?' he asks. 'Forty?' He gives her a fat slice of millionaire's shortbread with her sandwich and she picks at it for the rest of the afternoon. There are a few cards on the mat when Mona gets home. One from Val, of course; Mike, who never forgets; Sarah next door; Joley's mum. Six would have made one for every decade. Mona feels a pang for the ones that don't come.

She won't eat because Gayle's booked them a table, and anyway, Danny's shortbread has done some damage to her appetite. By seven she's ready in black trousers with a good pair of heels and a white silk blouse with diamanté at the neck. Hair up, earrings and a gold chain. Her tailored black jacket that still buttons at the waist and a suede clutch bag. At the mirror in the hall, Mona takes a deep breath and smiles at herself.

'Come on now, girl! You're not a bad-looking old stick at all!'

The Fat Pug squats on Moreton Street in Old Town. It bulges out on the ground floor, leans on its neighbours above, lurches and twists inside, not a straight or true line in the whole building. Mona has to dip to go through the door and tiptoe on the pitted, uneven flags. Gayle is already waiting.

'You're here! Happy Birthday. I thought we'd have one in the back and then go upstairs for our table.'

'Lovely,' says Mona. There's a flame in the wood burner and candles on the pub tables; Gayle is all sparkly and bright in one of her wafty dresses with a linen stole over her shoulders. 'I like your outfit, Gayle. You look great.'

Gayle orders two glasses of white wine and carries them both to the snug. 'I can't get the door with these,' she says. 'You go in first.'

But as soon as the door opens there's streamers and clapping and noise and cheers and the whole room is full. So many people, everyone has come, lots of friends and neighbours, Joley and Turk and Trish and Sarah and even Danny who said nothing earlier on and then Mike and Angie with the twins. And Joley's brought her mum and Trish has brought her husband and the Whippet of all people, bless her.

They sing 'Happy Birthday' at the top of their voices and then cheer at the end, shouting, 'Speech! Speech!'

So unexpected. So beautiful. Mona can hardly speak. Gayle twirls her wine glass. 'Go on, Mona,' she says.

'Twenty-three years I've been here,' Mona says and clears her throat. 'I only came for a couple of weeks. Didn't think I'd stay. Then I met Gayle at the community centre and, well, I've made my life here and I think of it as home because, as they say, home is where the heart is. Cheers to you all, my lovely friends, and thank you for coming.'

And then there are cards and presents and bottles of wine tied with ribbon and a lovely buffet with platters and platters of food, and too much to drink and laughter at Trish's very off-colour jokes and then someone puts some loud music on and the Whippet and Joley dance on the carpet and Danny gets drunk and tries to give her a proper kiss on the lips and plays his air guitar when she says no and some young people come in from the bar and they all seem to know each other and Mike has a jive with Gayle and the night goes so quickly that Mona is opening her front door at half past eleven before she knows it. She struggles in with a bouquet and a big bin liner full of gifts and eases her shoes off in the hall.

'Well!' she says as she puts the kettle on. 'That was grand.'

She unwraps a necklace and a make-up compact, a beautiful silver pen and a scarf from Trish, extravagant chocolates from Joley's mum who owns a sweet shop, a leather notebook from Mike who makes leather notebooks and a tiny little birthday cake from Danny with a kiss on top. The cards are lovely and hilarious.

I'M NOT 60! I'M 50 PLUS VAT. With lots of love from Trish xx
STAND BACK! I THINK WE'RE GOING TO NEED A LOT OF CANDLES FOR THIS ONE! Love from Angie and Mike xx
CHEER UP! SIXTY IS ONLY FIFTEEN IN SCRABBLE. Love Barbara x

She gets undressed and hangs up her blouse. She can wear it another day – you don't want to wash silk unless you have to and she spilt nothing on it. Her feet ache from the high heels. She lies down but she's too full to sleep and she's had a bit to drink. She gets a glass of water but it's no good. She turns over and over and then starts out along a path she shouldn't. It always leads her back to him.

1972. A fresh Irish girl seven months in a foreign country, in the enormous city of Birmingham with a new job and a little room of her own in a four-storey boarding house. Money in her pocket. Outfit? A little bunny jacket in pink fur, flared denim loons with red embroidery up the side, platform clogs and a pink handbag with a gold chain. Every stitch brand new. And what is more, in a moment of ferocious madness, Mona's had her hair cut, cropped short like Twiggy. All her blonde curls have gone and her eyes are as huge as plates.

Outside the Locarno on Hurst Street you have to make a sort of calculation about where to stand. All the girls have to queue up and look pretty. To cluster or not to cluster, that is the question. On the one hand, clusters are good for the nerves, but on the other hand, too many girls in one group puts the boys off. It takes guts to approach a herd and, even worse, you can get lost in the crowd. You can't look like you're on your own under any circumstances but two of you is grand.

So Mona is with Nuala, another girl who rents the biggest room in the boarding house on Bradford Street near the Irish Centre. Nuala is married with a baby and she's twenty but looks fifteen. Her husband gives her the night off every couple of weeks but all the rest of the time he's away working on a building site in Daventry. Sometimes during the long evenings, Mona sits with Nuala and bounces the baby on her lap.

Nuala can talk. Nuala can talk, chatter, gossip, gabble, moan and lament. When she's not missing her mother in Mayo, it's her two older sisters, both married to farmers, three children apiece and chickens at their feet. Nuala sobs and talks about going home all the while though she's only six months in the country and sometimes she says how much she hates her life and the dirty city and the squalor and black people everywhere who smell funny and how saving up is so hard and wouldn't even Daventry be better than Birmingham and she can't stand being all alone so far away from green fields. So Nuala's husband takes Mona aside and persuades her into inviting Nuala out for the night and making sure she has a good time. He slips her the money for drinks and breathes a sigh of relief no doubt when the front door is shut.

All the boys lounge on the low wall outside the Locarno, smoking and showing off and looking over at the clutches of girls giggling in the queue. But, actually, most of the boys are men almost, hard about the face in too much cheap aftershave. Mona can spot the ones that mean trouble. There's him there with the shirt open to his waistline, hips as narrow as a pole, his little rump all muscly and firm. He stands apart from the others in his clumpy shoes and flares, smoking a cigarette like he's a film star. The sort that would get a girl pregnant as soon as look at her. Mona is fascinated against herself and wonders what he would be like to kiss.

Then there's one with a black eye and a yellow shirt that's seen better days. Blood on the cuffs probably. Say no more. And then four or five huddling in a shabby group, wrong clothes, more than a whiff of whiskey about them before the night has even started.

The truth is, the Locarno isn't Mona's sort of place. If it wasn't for Nuala and her love of dancing they'd be somewhere quieter. According to the husband, dancing is what Nuala misses. She's known for her dancing, he says, and Mona has to bite her tongue. The dancing that Nuala has done in the dark of a little pub in a Mayo backwater will not, under any circumstances whatsoever, be like the dancing that goes on at the Locarno. Nuala might have some competition.

No, Mona's favourite place is a little pub in Moseley called the Prince of Wales where all the kids from the art school go, where they talk in their chewy accents about paintings and music and politics and big ideas and why the government is wrong and what about women's rights and what about homosexuals, aren't they all right too, and where a black man and a white woman hold hands and kiss right in front of you and where she's seen at least two men with ponytails and one woman with a green streak in her hair. Green. And where there is no jukebox but someone has an acoustic guitar and someone else has a flute, and there's no shoving at the bar, just the low buzz and hum of conversation and laughter.

And yet it's the Locarno where she meets William. She's standing arm in arm with Nuala, who's talking, of course, about will they get a drink right away or the terrible cost of the cloakroom and what if she's late home and the baby is still crying. Mona is paying as little attention as possible, watching the boys and thinking of the long night ahead, when one of them comes right over, breaks out of a big group of lads and starts walking across no man's land with everyone watching. He looks like a man on a mission, striding like he's about to start a fight or he's seen someone he recognizes. Tall he is, like a new tree, a boy with his hair too long and a face that could be on a magazine, taking his jacket off in the freezing wind. He isn't smiling either. Everyone's watching. Then, as bold as you like, he walks up to Mona and simply arranges his jacket over her shoulders. She doesn't speak or move, the surprise strikes her dumb. He pats her arm and walks away.

'Who's that?' asks Nuala. Mona shakes her head and the queue starts moving. She looks around but he's disappeared into the throng. She puts her hands on her cheeks to cool the blush but as soon as she's through the door he appears again and this time he's smiling. He slides the jacket off Mona's shoulders and winks.

'Did you know you were shivering? I could see it across the way,' he says.

'I beg your pardon?'

'Shivering,' he says, and he shudders to show her what he means. 'I'm William. I'm from Ireland. It's the accent.'

He moves his fringe and tucks it behind his ears. He shoves his hands in his pockets and looks like he's about to say something else but then Nuala jumps in.

'We're from Ireland! We are too! Mayo,' she says, pointing at her chest, 'and Wexford,' she says, pointing at Mona.

William nods but doesn't shift his eyes from Mona. 'Galway,' he says, 'Clarinbridge. Do you know it?'

'Why would we?' says Nuala.

'No reason,' says William, 'just talking.'

He waits while they pay and get tickets for their coats, he walks behind them into the dance hall and stands in front of them at the bar.

'I'd like to buy you a drink,' he says, 'and I would have paid the two of you in but I've no money.'

Mona and Nuala look at one another. He's so plain and countrified that he hasn't even made up an excuse. And he's not embarrassed. He carries on, loud over the music. 'I start my new job on Monday and until then I only have enough for one pint and the night bus home. I could walk, I suppose.'

The girls say nothing. They shuffle forward, pressing towards the counter. William has his hands in his pockets, looking at Mona like he's waiting for an answer.

'I could walk, couldn't I?'

'I don't know,' she says. 'Where do you live?'

'Gravelly Hill.'

'I don't know where that is.'

It's a few moments before he speaks. Mona stares at him and he stares back. His smile starts in his eyes.

'Shanks's pony for me then. What'll you have?'

He's with them all night. He dances with Nuala. He dances with Mona and she has to admit, country boy or not, the lad can move. He throws his head back and closes his eyes – anyone would think he was in his bedroom. People give him room. Nuala has her eyes out on stalks and Mona steps back and watches his hips and the shirt that sticks to his chest. He has absolutely no idea that he's become the main attraction and in the end Mona bursts out laughing. When the music stops and he opens his eyes, he laughs with the innocence of a child.

Not only does he walk home himself but first of all he walks the girls home through the backstreets of the city to the long hill of Bradford Street. He makes them take an arm each and they laugh and chatter all the way to the door. Nuala skips inside as soon as they reach the gate and Mona is left alone.

'Will I come tomorrow to see you?'

'I don't know.'

'It's Sunday and I'm not working. We could go for a walk.'

'I'm not sure.'

'I'd like you to say if you can. It would mean a lot to me.'

Mona looks at his face, handsome, not pretty, and as clear as the sun. She nods. He leans in and kisses her on the cheek and then offers her his hand.

'Two o'clock,' he says, shaking on the agreement. He walks backwards, away from her, his hands in his pockets, his smile the last thing she sees before she goes inside.

It's midday on Sunday when she wakes up. She meant to get up early and ring her father but she slept in. William was the first person she thought of when she woke up and what to wear when he called and where they might go and what they might do. And did she actually, really and seriously, have the chance of a boyfriend?

It's the landlady at the door. 'Phone for you, love.'

Mona runs downstairs in her slippers. Her father's rung again. She missed his call on Friday and yesterday. She won't tell him about William because he'll ask questions and worry, and anyway, there might be nothing to tell. She'll remind him about Christmas, that she's definitely coming home for the three days she has away from the factory, and that yes, she already has the fare, and yes, she'll get a ticket soon. She's out of breath by the time she picks up the phone.

But it's not her father. It's Bridie O'Connor.

9

Sometimes the rain is beautiful. The stones on the beach turn copper and bronze, violet and silver, curves of broken shells glisten pearly white with green-veined opalescence, and all from a drop of water. Mona never covers her hair. Cold. She pulls her scarf round her neck, too tight, and has to ease it off a little. Wet. Sea-sodden air and giant curls of water pushing in, over and over, black-and-white slaps of sea as loud as a train, as a thousand trains. She loves the sting of wet sand on her skin and the sharp lick of salt on her tongue.

The carpenter is standing at the mirror above the sink stripped to the waist and when he turns she can see the sheen of sweat on his broad chest. He has cut his hair; it sticks up tufty and uneven like a convict's.

'Only me,' she says, the words struggling out. He says nothing but splashes his body and face with water until it drips from his chin and runs down the dip in his breastbone. Mona watches as he puts on a clean shirt, denim, soft and faded to the palest blue.

'I've got another order for next week,' she says and finds her voice.

'Yes?'

'Eight pounds two ounces.'

'Heavy.' He picks up a small bottle of something. He's not a drinker but just occasionally she's smelt something on his breath and once or twice he's been out when she's called and she's found him at the pub on the corner, on his own, with a small whiskey and a pint of beer.

He takes a swig and points the bottle at her. 'Did I see you on the beach just now?' he says.

'Just walking.'

'The five-pounder is done. Didn't take much. It's been ready since yesterday,' he says, draining the bottle and going over to his bench. He picks up the lump of wood and places it in her arms. She weighs it, puts it in a carrier bag from her pocket.

'Eight pounds two ounces?' he says. 'When do you need it for? It will have to be pine.'

'The fifteenth, week tomorrow, Wednesday.'

He nods. 'It'll be done by then.'

A few times, in an emergency, Mona has waited while he makes the babies. She sits by the pot-bellied stove, or makes a cup of tea, or if it's fine she stands at the window while he works. She loves to watch.

It's not the shape, it's the weight that matters, so if the wood is more or less the right size he starts with the planer. What she gets depends on the grain and the bit of wood he starts with and also what he thinks is best. He's a law unto himself because he's an artist so Mona has to take what he gives her. She's had all sorts. If she's given him a good long time to make it, the baby is in two hinged parts. Other times, it's egg-shaped or a lozenge or an oval, but always smooth and always beautiful. Something you could keep for ever.

The shaping takes a good while. She could probably do it herself by now if she had the strength and the time, but then again, maybe it's harder than it looks. He sands by hand with standard oxide paper, smoothing and caressing in sweeps along the grain. Then finer sanding and sometimes, if there's no rush, he will chisel detail around the eyes. But that's unusual. Mona never asks for definition. As he works, he weighs the baby on a set of scales, digital ones these days. He measures and weighs and works and weighs and measures and works, and it goes like that until it's exactly what she wants.

It's not just the babies and dolls he makes. Other times she's watched him working on a cabinet or a table or a grandfather clock. The light is poor and the room is draughty and gawping but he doesn't notice. He bends his back to his work and moves as deliberate and dainty as a dancer. He's sinewy and strong for a man well past his middle years. Mona has been there when he's carried – with his bare hands, mind you – a dresser or sideboard over to the furniture lift. He's heaved it on to the platform and hauled at the pulley that takes it to the storeroom on the ground floor.

He has his world to himself with no radio or television to intrude, no woman or child, and she has certainly never seen friends if he has them.

'Will I make us a cup of tea?'

'Go on.'

He doesn't stop his work. Puts a lump of wood on the bench and begins turning it right and left, up and over. There's a few things he's done for her over the years, the rope-edged mirror in the hallway and the long rosewood table she uses in her workroom, a little corner cupboard from her father's house in Kilmore. Lovely, lovely things, a lifetime of memories waxed into the grain.

Mona goes home for her father's funeral. She gets off the bus that has brought her all the way from Dublin. Hours it took, stopping all the time to let people on, then she had to change in Wexford, and by the time she gets off she's bitten her nails to the quick.

She walks with her little case through the village she hasn't seen for nearly eight months. The shopkeepers wave and people raise their hats to her. Mothers of her old school friends cross the road to say sorry. They hug her close but she catches them eyeing the length of her skirt, the cling of her blouse and the cut of her coat. What should she wear to come home if not her best clothes? Even while they're consoling her, she can hear their disapproval. Nothing changes in this little backwater but there are things she has missed: the green-grey of the early-evening sky, the smell of ploughed fields and the herby smell of peat that settles like fog in the village lanes, the sand that sweeps in from the beach and heaps at street corners, the shape of the fat trees rising out of low plains, a slow walk along the shore with her father, his last words.

She opens the door to her father's house. Bridie O'Connor is there to meet her, one arm in plaster in a sling, her face scratched and white as a candle. She embraces Mona awkwardly.

'Go in to him,' she says.

The front room has been cleared of furniture except for a long table and on that table is her father in his coffin. There is flickering light from the candle and sweet perfume from the white flowers. The curtains dance in front of the open window. The room is as quiet and still as an empty church. In the corner sits Old Banjo Flaherty who has sat up with the dead since before time. He keeps a steady nip on a bottle of whiskey but never falls asleep nor takes fright. He raises his eyes and nods at Mona.

'A good man,' he says. 'God bless him.'

Bridie is at Mona's side, guiding her, edging her forward. 'He's at peace, now, lovey.'

Mona leans over the coffin. Her father's hands are wrapped in his rosary, his hair is combed and parted, he looks well, like he could get up and say it was all a mistake. He still has his wedding ring. Will he be married still in heaven? Is her mother waiting there? Mona hears the guttural noise that leaves her throat and tries to keep it inside.

'I'm sorry, Dadda,' she says.

Bridie and Old Banjo will sit together until the morning. Mona's father will have company for his final night. They tell Mona to get some rest, that she will need her strength for the morning, that this is a job for the old and not the young. Mona does as she is told, a stranger in her own house, and shuffles upstairs, undressing in a trance and lying still on her back between cold cotton sheets. She's hardly closed her eyes since she got the news and sleep comes no easier now. The single bed she dreamed in for seventeen years feels hard and foreign, the morning light too bright behind the thin curtains, and the silence is as loud as a brass band. She gets up too early and wanders the rooms in her bare feet, collecting memories and bits of things: her father's watch, a sprig of cloisonné flowers that her mother wore as a brooch, the enamel bedside clock that woke her father every morning, two rosaries and a framed picture of her parents on their wedding day.

She opens the wardrobe in her father's bedroom and touches his tweed overcoat. His good suit and best shoes are on his body downstairs, but there is the suit he wore every day to the post office where he weighed parcels and stamped savings books, day after day. And for what? To die alone before he was sixty.

He has a spare pair of trousers, three shirts and a waistcoat. Up by the front door will be his work shoes, his waterproof and hat but that's the sum of him. Mona feels suddenly poor and insubstantial, as though there's not much left of her in the world, as though a good breeze could blow her away and leave no trace, her mother and now her father gone and his few belongings hanging sparse and lonely. She is an orphan. She sits on the bed and, as her shoulders heave and shake, she prays that her tears are for her father and not for herself.

She sees then at the bottom of the wardrobe, by an old hatbox, the linen doll she made with her mother. It sits crooked, unfinished, dusty, with no face and no hair, and she realizes that her childhood self had made it to look like her mother – sickly, thin and bald. She grabs it, crushes it to her face.

The coffin is to leave from the house. The neighbours will line the hall, the front garden, the street outside. There'll be one car and Mona is to be in it. As soon as it's light, Mona hears Bridie O'Connor downstairs.

'There's tea for you, Desdemona,' she calls, and when Mona comes down, Bridie is putting the big brown pot on the table with two teacups. None of the mugs her father used.

'Thank you.' Mona sits down. She watches Bridie limping around the kitchen. 'I'm sorry,' she says, 'about the accident.'

Bridie makes a big plate of toast and puts it in front of Mona with a dish of butter. 'It was no one's fault, Mona, least of all your father's. He skidded on the ice and the car went over. I've said it before, that corner is treacherous, but there you are. I escaped and he didn't. That's my sorrow and yours. He didn't suffer, at least we can say that.' She pushes the toast an inch nearer to Mona.

'I can't,' says Mona, leaning back in her chair.

'No, not yet, lovey. But you will in a few minutes after a sip of tea. It'll be a long day so you'll need something, and your father wouldn't want you collapsing, would he?'

Mona groans and Bridie places her good hand on Mona's arm and gives a little squeeze.

'Think of everything you do today as being done for your father. Your dignity, your bearing, greeting your guests, Mona, your hospitality and kindness, it's all for your father, God bless his soul.'

Mona tries to control the tremor on her face and lips. Bridie too is fighting the tears.

'Now, now. He never felt abandoned by you, lovey. He understood you wanted to be living your own life.'

Mona stares at the old woman. 'I never abandoned him.'

'No, that's what I said. He knew that. He never said one word, even when he was lonely, you know. He was glad you were so happy. Pleased for you, he was.'

'I would never abandon him. Never.'

Bridie O'Connor opens Mona's fists one after the other and places her hands together, palm to palm, like when Mona was a little girl, saying her prayers.

'He loved you, Desdemona, and he was very, very proud.'

Then Bridie pours a cup of tea for Mona and for herself and butters the toast and Mona watches her struggle with her one good arm and won't help. Why couldn't it be Bridie in the coffin laid out on her polished mahogany table in her big white house that's already like a crypt? Why didn't she die and Mona's father escape with just a sling and limp? Who would miss Bridie O'Connor? While here was Mona, wretched and broken-hearted, having to listen to Bridie talking all the time about how the events of the day would unfold and how Mona's dress and behaviour would be as important as the hymns and prayers, that people's eyes would be upon her over everything else, her decorum would be a final gift to the father she hadn't rung for a week before his death and hadn't visited for the best part of a year.

He never said a word to Mona about going to England but she knew in her heart he was devastated. Mona had been full of it, how there were jobs for the asking in Birmingham, adverts in the Irish press and whole areas of the city given over to the Irish community, how there was nothing in Ireland and what a backward place she had lived in all her life and how there was certainly nothing in Kilmore to keep her there. She'd been on and on about it on their final visit together to Bridie O'Connor.

'Your father isn't nothing, is he, Desdemona?' Bridie had asked in her sweet voice. Before she could answer, Mona's father jumped in.

'Young people should take chances,' he'd said. 'Yes, take a chance, Mona. Your old Dadda will be here when you get back.'

But he wasn't himself, he went quiet for weeks, going about the house in a sort of daze. He became over-talkative, asking her again and again to take a bit more money and where exactly was she to stay and was she sure they had a telephone installed. He admitted, he told her, that he was going on too much and worrying about nothing but that was his role as her father. And then one evening, just before she went, he asked her up to his bedroom. He showed her a little wooden box on the dressing table.

'Anything you would like of your mother's is inside there. There's her wedding ring and watch, a crucifix and a brooch she inherited from somewhere or other.'

Mona could hardly keep the frustration out of her voice. 'Dad, I'm not getting married. I'll be back all the time.'

He shrugged. 'I only wondered if you wanted anything before you went. And I wanted you to know that these things belong to you.'

He put his hands in his pockets and took them out again. They stood in front of the mirror side by side with not a sound in the house.

'That's all I wanted to say, Mona, pet.' He put the wooden box back in the drawer. 'Maybe I chose the wrong time.'

Mona had never seen her father embarrassed before, had never felt a moment's awkwardness with him all through their life together.

'It's all right, Dadda,' she said.

And hadn't he taken her all the way to the ferry and shoved forty pounds in her pocket and kissed her goodbye in front of all the other waiting passengers and then asked her if she wanted sea-sickness tablets? And didn't he say that it wasn't too late to change her mind and there would be no shame in it? What could she have said? What could she have done differently?

And then it's over. Bridie O'Connor tells her not to sell the house. 'It's too soon for big decisions,' she says. Bridie can rent it out and Mona will have the money in the by-and-by, and anyway, there are memories stashed between the bricks and mortar and Mona might one day want to come home.

Everything is muffled, Bridie's advice and instructions, the thundering grief, the weather, the slanting rain and savage wind that blows right through the buttons of Mona's cardigan and into the marrow of her bones.

Before she knows it, she's on the ferry back to England, with her father's old suitcase instead of her own. She climbs up to the top deck and stands by the iron railing, watching the grey-green cliffs of Wexford harbour disappear. She never abandoned her father. He said he was fine with her going. Didn't she ask him over and over? Didn't he make light of it? Didn't she believe him? Didn't she offer to come back and didn't he say no? And didn't he tell her to go off and live her life? And when somebody has an accident and bangs their head and their heart gives out, can you ever see it coming? Ever? She was on the first plane and the first bus and she could never have known what life had saved up for her, never.

She begins to cry again from red eyes that haven't been dry for days. In the suitcase by her feet is the linen doll. She bends down, undoes the lock and takes it out. Why had her father kept it? Why hadn't she? It's so light and flimsy. She stands up and holds it in front of her. Her mother's linen and, stuffed inside, her father's socks. She cries until her throat aches.

And there he is at the top of Bradford Street. William is sitting in the evening light, his hands in his pockets, waiting on the wall outside Mona's boarding house. He sees her and runs. He takes her case and takes her hand and it's as if she's known him for ever, not just a single day, and it's as though he was with her all the time and would be with her for the rest of her life. He stands her case on the top step of the house.

'You can't come in,' she says.

'I know. It's the same where I am. You have to be married.'

'Yes,' she says. 'That's the Irish for you.'

'I got your message. The landlady gave it to me when I came. I'm sorry for you, I am. Are you all right, Mona?'

'Not really.'

'No.'

She takes her key from her pocket and rolls it around between her fingers. 'Thank you,' she says.

'I'll be here tomorrow, straight from work. You can count on that.' He leans forward and kisses her cheek. 'And the day after.'

By Christmas Nuala has talked her husband all the way back to Mayo and for Mona, William is everything.

It's the draught and the hardness of the stool that brings Mona back to the workshop, to the scratching of the carpenter's saw. He's saying something.

'Mona? Mona? I said I got some English oak today. From Wilson at Redhouse Farm. Not much but enough. Turning blanks, seven of them. Pick them up next week. Good colour.'

'Oh? What colour would you say?'

'Like a biscuit or the crust on a loaf of bread.'

'I was thinking you might make me a black doll, a couple of

63

black dolls. Dark, dark brown. Maybe I won't paint them, just varnish.'

'We've done that before, haven't we?'

'Yes, I know. But not for ages and I saw a beautiful African girl the other day, couldn't stop looking at her.'

'There's a few bits of dark wood over there. Have a look yourself.' He nods towards the bay and Mona walks carefully past him, lets her fingers linger on the planks, all of them dusty and dull.

'Oh, I'll leave it to you. Make four, I think. Four twenty-twos. Will you do the varnish as well?'

'I will.'

Then there's nothing for it but to leave. She holds on to the bench, a little giddy from her long journey back down the lanes of the past. She won't mention her birthday nor Val not coming. He didn't come to her party. Who would have invited him? He'll tot up anything she owes him, scribble something on a bit of paper and pass it to her, or she'll just stow some cash where he'll see it.

Time to go home.

10

Love is like being on the swings at the park, pushed too high, and right at the top the metal ropes buckle and she floats, still and weightless before the links catch and she hurtles back down and then up, up, up again, floats for a moment and, swoosh, back down. That's what William is like, the little time at the top when she is still and weightless, floating, her heart in her mouth.

There's bits of her father in him too. He's not as tall and he's not as broad but he has his easy smile and open face as though he thinks the best of her and the rest of the world.

He calls for Mona every Sunday night. They take the bus down Stratford Road, getting off early and walking the long way to the College Arms, along Showell Green Lane, down Woodlands Road with the big houses, past Springfield Road and back on to Stratford Road. Then they walk the same way back later on. The College Arms is all right but what they really want is to be together, quiet and uninterrupted.

A single Victorian mansion takes up the whole corner of Woodlands Road. A stone path lined with lavender and box leads from a black wrought-iron gate to a red front door with a brass knocker. Big bay windows, stained glass and heavy curtains with no nets. One evening those curtains are open.

'William, look,' says Mona as they pass. They slow their steps. There is no one in the huge front room, lit by a tall standard lamp with a fringed shade.

'There's luxury for you,' he says.

'I know.'

They stop, arm in arm, and take it all in, the oil paintings and sofas with white lace antimacassars, embroidered cushions, rugs, little side tables with barley-twist legs, porcelain figurines.

'Imagine it's ours,' William whispers, 'and I'm late home. You're in the kitchen waiting for me.'

'What's the kitchen like?'

'Ah now, that's your department.'

Mona doesn't hesitate. 'China teacups and a great big range. And two enormous serving dishes in blue and white with proper lids. And a big pot of stew.'

'Stew, is it? That's all right for a weeknight, I suppose. Beef on Sunday.'

'Yes and after the beef we'll sit down for the evening in those chairs there.'

'Well now,' William continues, 'before you go spending my time for me, I'm the sort of fella that has various hobbies. I have a library full of big books and a couple of hounds. And I have a train set upstairs that I lay out on one of the landings. I have a smoking chair.'

'Smoking jacket, you mean.'

'I do not,' he says. 'I mean a big old chair with a couple of rips from the coins that bulge in my backside pocket. No one sits in that chair but me. Of course the dogs keep it warm and that but when I've finished a day's graft at the office, you know, signing cheques and what not, I come home, the dogs run up to me at the door and I fill my pipe by the fire. I have to have a pipe. A pipe is obligatory. And I sit my bones down in that chair and you can sit on my lap.'

'Some lucky people really live in that house, William.'

'Ah, they do, but not with you,' he whispers. 'It's a lucky man that lives in there with you.' He kisses her hard and she kisses him back. She feels the hardness of his chest and the strength of his arms around her. He pulls her in so close she can barely breathe and she's swamped by her want of him. When he pulls back, he stares at her and squeezes her hand into his pocket.

From then on it becomes their new game, to detour past the big houses and imagine who lives there, what's going on in the different rooms, which one of the mansions they would pick if they won the pools. Nine times out of ten, the game ends the same way with Mona laying the table for dinner, two children – a boy and a girl – playing on the carpet. Mona rearranges the furniture, rehanging the curtains and making everything better or more modern or just different. Even when the houses get smaller as they make their way home, the game continues and Mona begins to wonder how much those houses really cost and whether she might live in one and whether their dreaming might one day come true.

If it's not too cold or wet, Mona and William walk far away from the Irish areas, up to St Agnes' Church or Chantry Road, where vast villas sprawl behind wild front gardens, mansions with turrets and timbers and little coach houses that on their own could house a family of six. They snuggle hand in hand, or hand in pocket, playing their game and talking all the way back along Springfield Road and then up to the College Arms public house.

They sit close together on the velour banquette and Mona tells him about the death of her mother.

'Same for me,' says William. 'No mother, just the aunts and my father, and he's what you might call an unwell man.'

'What's wrong with him?'

Mona notices how he takes a long gulp of his pint before he speaks. She knows all about painful talk and fathers and trying to find the right words. William keeps his hand on his glass, turns it round, picks it up and puts it down again, straightens the little cardboard coaster, pings the side of the metal table with his fingernail.

'He's not well and he's been to the hospital more than once. He has a devil in him. A melancholy devil, that's the word for it all right. He has an ugly sadness he cannot shake off though he tries his best with drink. And then that brings his tempers. Moods. Meanness. He's all right if you keep him busy around the house or he has a little job in the garage where he can be left alone. That's when he's well enough to work. But you wouldn't want to be near him when he's in his temper or stoked like a boiler with whiskey. No. He can be cruel and dark. And he's made me cruel and dark in the past. We don't get on and that's the truth of it, even when he's well and that's not often. We don't see eye to eye and I wouldn't want to see eye to eye with that side of him.'

He swallows six or seven times, gulping at the lip of the glass, and wipes the corners of his mouth with a knuckle.

'But, then again,' he continues, 'he can be a right joker. At Christmas or whenever the drink takes him the right way he can be something like normal. Not exactly the life and soul, you'd never say that, but right enough. Right enough. We know how to deal with him now. You have to let him alone. Don't speak to him, don't ask him any questions, don't trouble him, and he'll cause no harm. So that's what we do, leave him to it.' He took another mouthful. 'Me and the aunts, that is. Pestilence and Famine.'

'What?'

'Well, it's Teresa and Margaret really, but I have other names for them.'

'Famine and . . .'

'Pestilence. Father Hanson gave me the idea. He whispered it to me once when Margaret, that is Pestilence, gave him a tongue-lashing. He'd come to enquire after my father after he'd offended a neighbour and there had been a bit of a row. I have no idea why the good Father got involved, we're not what you might call a holy family by any stretch of the imagination. So Father Hanson knocks the door and, well, my Auntie Margaret has never tolerated interference. She has a tongue that would scythe down thistles. So, she let him have it, both barrels, close range. Father Hanson stood on my doorstep and said, "William, my boy, that woman is a plague. Good luck to you."'

Mona smiles.

'And my other aunt is Teresa Mary according to her birth certificate. But she's no stranger to the baker if you catch my drift. So that's the two of them.'

Mona giggles into her glass.

'You'll meet them,' he says with a nudge. 'They'll come over for the wedding.'

He hasn't spoken of weddings before. Mona sucks her cheeks together in case she squeals.

'Though getting an outfit for Famine could be a bit of an undertaking,' William continues. 'Yards of cloth you'd need. Yards.'

Mona says nothing. She doesn't want the subject changed to dresses for old ladies. She sips at her cherry brandy. It reminds her of the cough medicine of her childhood. It stains her lips and teeth.

'I'll need a suit,' he says and rubs his hands together. 'And a new pair of shoes. I can't wear these old things. Flowers, they always have a great show of flowers at weddings as I remember. What else? Cars? Do people have cars these days? They do, don't they? A cake, of course. That'll be Famine's department, if you can trust her around butter and sugar. Better buy one and bring it in at the last minute. Book a church, I suppose, and a priest. And a ring, definitely a ring. Two rings actually, if you think about it. That's it, I think. That's everything.'

Mona stares at the barman, then she stares at the jukebox, then she stares at the frosted lantern over the door. She pulls her fluffy jacket tight over her chest and rearranges her fringe. She watches William take three consecutive swigs of his pint, putting the glass down between each one. She will not speak first.

Suddenly he slaps his forehead. 'Jesus, Mary and All the Holy Angels!'

'What?' she says.

'A bride! For Christ's sake! I hadn't thought of that!'

His face is beaming, his eyes sparkling in the soft light. He pulls her towards him and kisses her on her brandied lips.

'God, Mona. You'll have to step in.'

She might cry.

'Say you'll marry me and let the search be over.'

Even before she's finished nodding, he stands up, brandishing his glass to the old men in their seats.

'She said yes!' he shouts and then drops down next to her.

'Oh, William.' She hooks his arm.

'As soon as possible.'

William and Mona walk along Corporation Street looking for a ring with an agreed budget of three pounds. William says an engagement ring is a band of promise and a wedding ring a band of belonging. He has a thousand little faery sayings like that. Mona thinks they should save the cash but he won't be talked out of it and, in the end, she's as excited as he is.

Mona's earning seven pounds a week at the factory, good money, plus a little extra from the rent on her father's house. Bridie O'Connor banks the bulk of it on Mona's behalf but sends over a little 'walking money' as she calls it. Poor William is still an apprentice with one more year to go. After he has paid his rent he has two pounds a week left over and yet he insists on the ring. She gives in.

They stop at the first jeweller's shop, frowning at the ugly stuff, huge onyx rings, gaudy bracelets made of silver kittens. They move to the side window where it's less chaotic and there's room to see what's what. And there it is. They both see it together, nestled amongst the creamy vintage pearls and pill boxes. A square-cut dress ring made of a pale-blue stone with a simple claw setting. William points and all Mona can do is nod.

There's no price on it so they have to go in. The shop is half full. It's a little intimidating, all that silver and gold and diamonds and shop assistants in suits and ties.

'Will we come back later, William?' says Mona.

'No.'

'We don't know how much it costs.'

'No.'

He edges her forward and they wait their turn. Someone's collecting an engraved tankard and someone else wants a present for a christening and suddenly William is pointing the ring out to the manager and Mona's mouth is dry. They could be terribly embarrassed. She's ready to say she doesn't like it, that it's too small for her finger and too plain after all.

William doesn't even ask for the price. He takes it off the red cushion and kisses it right there and then with everyone watching. He picks up Mona's hand like she's a lady and slips the ring on to her third finger, slips it on like he's had it weighed and measured and all prepared. Then he kisses her face.

'It's the one,' he says.

Mona blushes and the other customers start to clap and cheer. Mona doesn't sleep that night in her little room in the boarding house on Bradford Street. She can't rest for thinking of William and turning the ring on her finger and wishing there was a telephone line that would stretch as far as her father and crying for missing him.

In the end, less than a month later, it's just a Register Office affair. William telephones his aunts to come over. One of them weeps on the phone and William talks soft to her to bring her round and almost cries himself. The other aunt is a different matter entirely and after explaining himself five or six times William says he can't feed any more money into the telephone unless she wants him to be bankrupt so he'll have to hang up. He comes out of the phone box and does a little dance.

'They're coming!' he says. 'And my father isn't and that's good news altogether.'

So there are four of them in the Prince of Wales plus a handful of boarders. They're wished well and somebody makes a toast to the happy couple and the aunts pay for roast beef sandwiches and a cake. They can stay a week more in Bradford Street and then they'll move into a little flat on Alcester Road, ground floor with a scratch of garden at the back. Famine and Pestilence have paid for a double bed and Mona shopped for brand-new sheets and blankets.

At the end of the afternoon, Pestilence passes William a white envelope. 'This is from all of us, your father included.'

William frowns.

'Now, now,' she says. 'He's only coughed up some money. You'll have your wedding night in a good hotel. The Grand. I've visited it myself yesterday and you're both to have a nice room to begin your new life. You have the reservation details and everything in that envelope. You'll start your new life in style. There now.'

There are kisses and hugs all round and by five o'clock Mona and William are on the bus into town.

The Grand Hotel is grand all right. It dominates Colmore Row with its lavish Victorian facade, rows and rows of huge sash windows set deep against pale stone. Mona and William stand just beyond the marble portico and look at one another.

'Will we just go in and say our name or what?' says William.

'She's paid for us so, yes, I suppose we do. That's what they do in films.'

'Films?'

Mona shrugs. She has a new dress and new shoes. Her hair is pixie short, as bright and white as the sun. She ran a slick of frosted pink gloss on her lips before she left the Prince of Wales and her feet shimmer in patent-leather kitten heels. She's been whistled at once or twice. William hasn't even heard because he's so nervous. He's completely and utterly gorgeous in a new suit and tie. His shoes are polished and he smells of soap and aftershave but ah, his face, all jaw and cheekbones, too good to be true, all man, her man. His hair is freshly washed and dances a little in the wind, and because he is clutching their overnight case with one hand and Mona's hand with the other, he can't tidy it up. If love is butterflies in the stomach, Mona has a thousand wings beating inside.

Mona wipes the pink off his cheek where she's kissed him. 'Well,' she says. 'What's the worst that can happen?'

'I don't like to imagine that,' he says and as they walk up to the huge marble columns, a doorman steps forward and opens the door. He touches his hat and gestures across the thick carpeted lobby to the broad, polished sweep of the mahogany reception desk.

'Yes, sir?' says a man who has a phone to his ear.

'We have a reservation,' says William. 'Mr and Mrs MacNaughton.' William takes the envelope out of his pocket and pushes it forward.

The man holds a finger up and whispers, 'One moment.' He's French or something. 'Of course, madam. Yes, madam. Very good. Of course. Twenty-seventh through to the twenty-ninth. We have that reservation, yes, madam. Of course. Goodbye.'

He scribbles on a pad, adjusts his tie and opens the envelope. 'Very sorry, sir. Mr and Mrs MacNaughton, you said? Allow me to check.'

Mona can't see what he's doing behind the desk but the longer the wait goes on the more she can see William fidgeting. He's thinking what she's thinking. Has Pestilence got the right date? Has she actually paid? Are they going to have to walk the long walk out of the lobby with their little suitcase and watch the door-man smirk as they leave? The receptionist straightens up suddenly and claps.

'Ah, yes! May I offer my congratulations? Welcome to the Grand Hotel!'

He leans forward and shakes hands with both of them. 'Madam. Sir. You are in Room 340, a Superior Double with private bathroom. Here is your room key.'

Before William can put his hand out, a porter who's appeared from nowhere plucks the gold-tasselled key from the receptionist and picks up the suitcase.

'Breakfast is from seven thirty to nine thirty and is served in the Mallory Room, just to your right there, sir. Will you require a newspaper or morning wake-up call?'

William shakes his head. Mona does the same. 'We'll wake up in time,' she says.

They follow the porter, a young man, no older than William and half his height, into a creaky old lift with a metal grille across. The porter stands in front of them and presses the buttons. The boy has a short jacket and a big bottom, his trousers straining across the expanse. Mona can see the stitches in the seam. She wonders how strong the thread is. Will it hold if he bends over? The boy could be an organ grinder's monkey with his braided suit and tilted round hat. Mona dares not look at William. If he even coughs she'll burst out laughing.

They follow the monkey along wide corridors with carpet so thick and so new that the whole two-minute journey is entirely silent. Mona watches the bottom sashay from side to side, while her suitcase swings from the porter's arm. She steals a look at William. His face is red. He makes a winding motion. She looks away and bites the inside of her cheek.

Suddenly the boy stops at a door and flourishes the key like he's a magician. He slides it into the lock and pushes the door open. 'Sir,' he says.

Mona's never seen anything like it. The bed is huge with pillows and cushions in velvet and lace with a little eiderdown billowing down either side. There are two lamps and two bedside tables and two chairs and two big oil paintings and a sumptuous rug at the end of the bed with long silver fringes. And the bathroom! Gold taps on the sink and bath, more towels than you could use in a week, little bars of soap and a real marble floor.

William is closing the door when she comes back to the bedroom.

'Thought he'd never leave,' he says and wipes his hand across his brow. 'He was hanging around the front door, showing me how the bloody key worked. Does he think I'm an eejit or what? Then he tells me again about the breakfast like the fella did downstairs. "All right, mate," I said, "I've got it," and he plonked the key in my hand.'

'Maybe he was angling for a tip?'

'I've got a tip for him,' says William, unlacing his shoes. 'Lay off the bananas.'

Mona starts to giggle. William grabs her round the waist and she squeals.

'Is it too early for bedtime?' he whispers.

'What if he comes back?' They fall together on to the bed.

'Who?' says William.

'The porter.'

'Jesus! He'll be swinging himself downstairs by now, surely to God. Or sitting clapping his hands to his master's tune.'

Mona's laughing.

'Or he's found himself a soft chair for that arse. Or a hard chair come to think of it. Who needs cushions?'

Mona shakes her head. 'Don't, William.' She can't breathe.

'Anyway,' he continues, 'we don't have to open the door. We have the golden key.'

William springs up and locks the door. He goes to the window and looks out on to the street.

'Come and look,' he says, parting the thin white nets.

Mona stands next to him and he puts his arms round her. The lights are just coming on along Colmore Row. St Philip's Cathedral is lit from inside, the stained glass shining in rainbow colours. All across the city, the shops and department stores are bright and alive, people sauntering to their bus stops with bags of shopping on their way home.

'Merry Christmas,' he says.

'It's not Christmas yet, William.'

'It is for me.'

Mona can't believe how messy and awkward it is to make love. They've come close so many times before in her room at the boarding house when they've had five minutes to themselves but they've always been conscious of other people in the house, on the other side of the wall or creeping up the staircase. This is their first time alone, husband and wife, uninterrupted, legitimate sex.

She wants him and he wants her. But there's a lot of fumbling and misdirection and William manages to elbow Mona in the eye halfway through.

'Jesus,' he says. 'This is no good. I'm no good at this.'

Mona can't say anything. She's holding her breath and waiting for all the wonderful things to happen. 'Fireworks' the women at work called it. 'Bells will ring.'

Then it's all over. William rolls on to his back and groans. 'I'm sorry,' he says. He gathers her up and they lie together in the dark.

When the morning comes, things are altogether different. William reaches for her, drawing her nightdress off her shoulders. He kisses her mouth, her neck, her breasts. He kneads her shoulders, squeezes her so close to him that she gasps. He makes love to her slowly, saying all the time how he loves her and needs her and saying her name over and over. 'Mona, Mona.'

The pealing from St Philip's Cathedral wakes them at ten o'clock.

'We've missed breakfast, William,' says Mona, counting the bells.

'Never mind,' he answers, stretching his arms. 'Would we want to be sitting down with all them posh ones watching us cut our sausages?' He sits up and pulls his vest on. He lights a cigarette and picks tobacco strands off his tongue. 'Let's go to the Hasty Tasty. Do you know it? It's right in the middle of town. I went there once. They do a massive big breakfast with white pudding. We'll treat ourselves. You only get married once.'

'I hope,' says Mona, looking up at him from the pillow. His face is different and because she's slept hers must be too. She checks her eyes for grains of sleep, pats her hair where it must have flattened in the night. Maybe she has creases on her cheek. William looks down.

'You're beautiful,' he says as though he knows what she's thinking. He stubs out his cigarette. 'Come on, I'm starving.'

He stands up suddenly and she sees his bare behind. It's firm and white and she thinks again of the squat little porter and she begins to laugh. He turns round and puts his hand on his hip. His vest hardly covers his private bits and she laughs again.

'What?' he says.

'Nothing, nothing,' is all she can say.

He shakes his head and parts the curtains. He peers through the sheer white voile. 'Lovely day,' he whispers. She watches him find the hooks for the big sash window and jerk them upwards. But everything at the Grand is smooth, even the ropes in the wheels of the Victorian windows, and the bottom half of the window flies up at terrible speed, dragging William's vest with it.

'Jesus Christ!' he screams. He stands with his arms raised, his naked belly, his cock and balls all on show to the street, to the Sunday worshippers of St Philip's, to the passers-by and even the bloody doorman if he stepped off his perch. 'Help me, Mona!'

But she's naked as well. She scrabbles around for her nightdress while he writhes at the window trying to free his trapped under-garment. She mustn't laugh.

'Ah, for Christ's sake, will you help me?'

'Take it off, William! Take your arms out!'

Yards of billowing voile lash out wild in the breeze and she watches as he tangles and twists, loses his vest altogether and gains a shroud. He looks like a chrysalis. In another moment, the voile is ripped from the rail and he crashes to the floor.

'God,' he pants, kicking, ripping at the material like a madman. Mona gives in and heaves with laughter.

'Calm down, William! Look what you've done!'

He stamps on the torn cotton and stands panting with his hands on his hips, a wild look on his face, his naked body covered in sweat. 'What happened?'

Mona puts her arms round him. 'You won,' she says. 'That's all that matters.'

They tuck the curtain into their suitcase and click it shut. Mona takes one of the miniature bars of soap and puts it in her handbag. She tidies the bed and folds the towels. She rakes the tassels on the carpet with her fingers until the whole place looks nearly as good as new. She draws the heavy drapes closed and they leave the key in the door. They walk back along the corridor and slip out the back way on to the street, hand in hand.

12

On Wednesday, Mona takes a detour to walk past the Viennese cafe. She's wearing her red coat with the black buttons. It still fits and gives her a good shape. She has black suede heels with a matching handbag and a bright patterned scarf. It's not too much, but just before she gets there, she loses her confidence, wishes she could turn back home and get changed. She looks like she's gone to a lot of effort, like she's off to the bloody theatre or something. She's gone and got all dolled up. What if he was just being polite? What was she thinking? But there's no time. There he is, Karl, at the cafe door reading a newspaper. He folds it in half and tucks it under his arm as soon as he sees her.

'Ah,' he says. 'We meet again.'

And now with their small coffee cups between them, they are both silent. He is immaculate in a grey suit, a pale-pink shirt with mother-of-pearl cufflinks. He has a lovely knot in his tie and a proper gold tie pin. He's taken as much care as she has. He smiles and his elegant hands rearrange the salt and pepper then turn a single flower in a little vase round to face her. He taps the table when he's done it as if to say 'That's for you'. So she smiles back and feels for the crucifix round her neck, makes sure it lies flat, turns her wedding ring round, turns it back, and as she is about to speak he clears his throat.

'The first time I saw you, I wondered how tall you were. I thought you would be taller.'

'I'm five foot five,' she says. 'You must be six foot four.'

'Well, nearly,' he replies, 'depends on the occasion.'

He adjusts his tie and Mona can see creases at regular intervals, like steps, all the way down as though he folded it up and squashed it in his drawer. He must live alone.

He's watching her closely. 'We do not sleep, you and I.'

'Oh, usually I do. Well, sometimes. Depends on the occasion.'

'Ah.'

He has a lovely smile that runs from his lips all the way up to his eyes but there is so much in the silence between them that Mona can barely lift her cup.

'Where is your name from?' he asks. 'Desdemona, I have heard it before. Your mother gave you that name?'

'My father really. He was an unusual man.'

'Shakespeare?'

'Yes, Desdemona was Othello's wife. But everyone calls me Mona, everyone.'

'Ah, yes. I am Karl. So everyone calls me Karl.'

'Pleased to meet you again, Karl,' and she puts her hand across the table. He squeezes it and makes the same bow, a tiny incline of the head.

'So, Mona, the coffee isn't terrible. But you're not drinking it.'

She looks at her cup. The coffee is strong, bitter and lukewarm. 'Well, I like mine with a little more milk.'

'Oh, yes, English people like the cappuccino and the latte. In Italy this is something for breakfast and in Hamburg we don't have those things. Well, yes, maybe now, but when I was a boy, hot milk was for children or grandmothers. We are not so young and not yet so old, you and I.'

'Hamburg,' says Mona, 'so that's the accent.'

'You know it?'

'I only know hamburgers, I'm afraid. No, but I wasn't born in England either.'

'Oh?' He leans forward and scans her face, cups his chin. 'You're not French. You're not Dutch, not Swedish. These people I know. Scottish? The Scottish people are very insulted to be called English.'

Mona leans towards him, close. 'Even more so the Irish,' she says. 'We turn into banshees, little devils, if that happens.'

'Oh, Irish, yes, yes,' he says, closing his eyes and shifting his head again as though he's listening to music. 'Irish. Yes. I hear it now. But you've been here a long time.'

'Yes, I came looking for someone and decided to stay.'

'You found who you were looking for?'

Mona looks at her cold coffee filming over, the shimmer of a skin on the surface. 'No. I never found him.'

'My condolences, Mona.'

Mona nods. 'And you, Karl. What are you doing here so far from Germany?'

'Ah, well, I have been coming here on and off for many years, since I was a young man. I had a friend who was somewhat of an Anglophile – he liked everything about England, as I do. Eventually, he invested here so naturally we would visit often. And I am in the process of selling some property. But tell me, what do you do? I know where you live but that's all. Tell me something of yourself, who you are.'

'Who am I?'

He is still. His listening is more like reading, like he's rifling through her memories and the secret things she has locked away. She can't trust her voice or the answer she might give. His stare turns into a frown and he speaks softly as though he's telling her a bedtime story in a half-whisper.

'I, for example, am in exile.' He looks left and right. 'Well, to be precise, I am marooned here.'

'Shipwrecked?'

'Washed up.'

'All alone?'

'All alone.'

'Ah,' says Mona. 'Well, it's the same for me then, shipwrecked is as good a word as any, but we've found ourselves a lovely island, haven't we?'

Karl turns in his seat and looks over at the counter. 'I must have another cup of coffee if we are to sit here telling our secrets. I need fortification.'

He gets to his feet and speaks to the girl behind the counter. Whatever he says, it makes her chuckle as he returns to his seat.

'She will bring them over,' he says, tapping the side of his nose.

'I have my ways. I asked her about the ring in her nose and if it might suit me. It's a curious adornment, is it not?'

'I have an assistant,' says Mona, 'who has one right here in her eyebrow. I asked her if it hurts and she said no but it must, surely.'

Karl shakes his head. 'One wonders about the future. Fashions change beyond our recognition. Fortunately, good taste does not. That goes for good food as much as anything else.'

He tells her about the cakes in the glass cabinets and what cakes he used to have in Germany when he was a boy, cheesecakes and strudels. His voice is gravelly but soft like worn pebbles on the beach, like the voiceover to a documentary about foreign travel or haute cuisine. She is still staring at him when she realizes he has stopped.

'I said, do you cook?' he asks her.

'I do, yes. Well, I like to now and again. I like to make the odd recipe, when I'm in the mood. I've had my fair share of disasters, I can tell you, when I've been too adventurous or my skill doesn't reach my ambition so to speak.'

'Me, I am always cooking. In the days of my youth there was no fast food. You catch the fish, you eat it the same day with vege-tables from the market, with tomatoes from the hothouse, with oil. Or there is a local butcher who knows you, your grocer who gives you the food that's in season. Nowadays everything comes in plastic or cardboard. Life was simpler then, was it not?'

'Well, it might have been simpler but my mother was always at the stove. At least now we can have a ready meal now and again.'

'Ready meal?' He lifts his hands in horror. 'This is what comes of eating alone. No food that smells of plastic and chemicals, please!'

He's handsome and he wears a lovely signet ring and a nice watch and he cares about his clothes. The waitress puts Karl's cof-fee on the table and he downs it in one like a shot of vodka and taps his chest.

'Ah,' he says. 'Good.' He places the little espresso cup on the saucer and turns the handle. He's a gentleman all right, a little older than he looks from a distance but there's something young about him, something alive.

'You've finished? Would you like to go for a walk?' he says.

Mona picks up her handbag and takes her purse out. 'Well, just let me –'

'No, no,' he says and stands so quickly that his chair wobbles on its back legs. He goes to the counter and pulls money from his pocket. He waves away his change and is back next to Mona in a moment. She fiddles with some notes in her open purse.

'I'll owe you one,' she says but he puts his finger to his lips.

'Ssshh! That is not gallant, Mona. I could not permit it.'

Outside, he looks up at the sky and squints. 'It is fine and a little warmer I think. Shall we walk this way?'

Mona falls into step with him.

'Why not?' she says and notices him slow down and make little adjustments so he's not ahead and not behind. At the busy junction he takes the road side of the pavement and steers her by the elbow when it's safe to cross.

They walk away from the tourist area uphill, deep into the upper part of town, through the terraced streets towards the church. There is nothing to see on the way but right at the top there is a lovely view, the spire of St Gregory's punctuating a spiral of crooked Georgian houses in faded pink and blue, and beyond that, a wide stretch of pewter sea.

They are both panting by the time they reach the top and Karl takes a deep breath. 'Ah!' he says. 'The blood in the veins. Good, isn't it?'

Mona nods. 'I should do this more often. Haven't been up here in years.'

'Maybe we would sleep better if we did this every day.'

Mona laughs. 'We'd be taking the long sleep if we did, all right.'

'The long sleep?'

'Death, the long sleep. It's giving my heart a workout, I can tell you.'

'It does no harm. It's surprising what a heart can take.'

Mona keeps her eyes on the sea, on the smear of silver light at the edge of the horizon. 'I know,' she says.

Karl touches her shoulder and points. 'Look there.'

A red-and-yellow kite is flying up between the black roofs, weaving left and right, dancing in the breeze. The kite is shaped like an exotic bird, with long tail feathers of blood red and gold, its wings fringed with black ruffles that flutter and spin. It arches higher and higher until it's framed against the sea, straining and buffeting against the wind as if it's trying to break free of the cords that anchor it.

It's so high now and so close that Mona can see its huge body and its beak and the blast of colours, the determined climb in its eyes.

'It's too far away,' says Karl and suddenly Mona realizes she has reached out to touch it, that she has stretched her arm out towards the kite.

'I'm silly,' she says. 'What was I thinking?'

He takes her hand and squeezes it. 'A beautiful gesture, if I may say. We are all still children, Mona.'

He keeps her hand as they walk slowly downhill, through the grounds of St Gregory's, through the winding lanes. His clasp is warm and strong and the silence gathers between them until they reach the corner of the main road. He gently lets her hand drop. 'And here you will go left and I will go right,' he says.

'Thank you for a lovely walk. I'll sleep tonight, I think.'

'If you don't . . .' he answers.

'I know where to find you,' she says.

'Perhaps next week we could meet again. It's not too soon? I would like it.'

'It was my birthday a few days ago.' She stops suddenly, surprised she told him, surprised that it matters that he knows. 'I was sixty. I am just sixty.'

He puts his palm to his chest. 'Ah, my congratulations. Then we surely must have a belated celebration. Perhaps next week is too far away then . . .' and he inclines his head as if to say 'Well?'

She thinks of the men she has known in the past twenty years, the dates that came to nothing or petered out after a few weeks, the love affairs that turned out not to be love after all, the flirts and the hints and the winks she's ignored, and she wonders will this be any different? 'Next Wednesday's fine, Karl. I look forward to it.'

'At the same place?'

'The same place.'

He has to bend to kiss her cheek; his lips linger on her skin and when she walks away she knows he's watching.

13

Mona and William share their house with two other tenants. The man on the top floor works nights at the biscuit factory and Mona only ever sees him at the weekend. He leaves bags of broken biscuits at the door of each flat every couple of months and Mona makes him soda bread in return. The flat on the middle floor is Tom's. Tom is from West Cork with an accent so thick that even after two years in England he still sounds like he's juggling balls in his cheeks. Mona often sends William up to ask him to come down for his dinner or they take him up a meal on a plate. And in return, Tom stands William a pint on a Wednesday night.

Each flat has its own electricity meter just inside the front door. It's William's job to feed it every day on his way home from work. Mona hears his key in the door and watches him with obvious pride fish enough coins out of his pocket to appease the iron-grey beast.

The whole house shares the bathroom on the landing, so every night when William comes in from work, he boils a kettle for himself, strips down and washes from head to toe in four inches of water, humming and smiling at her. He throws the water down the sink, rinses the bowl and starts again, a new bowlful for his face and hair. He flicks the fire on, both orange bars sizzling bright. Singeing socks, burning dust, shampoo and damp clothes. It's a smell Mona will remember for the rest of her life.

When he's finished, he wraps himself in a towel, and more often than not Mona ends up on his lap, her arms hung round his neck like a sleeping child. They are often silent, basking in their togetherness, listening to the quiet hiss and murmur of the glowing bars.

Afterwards, if the weather's fine, William opens the back door and sits on the concrete step to have a cigarette. Mona snuggles next to him and they stay like that, smoking and talking until they're hungry. And then the nights are all lovemaking and sleeping and the mornings are lovemaking and hurrying off to work, and because Mona has a little extra money they buy a second-hand television set for their evenings in.

On Sunday mornings neither of them has work. After a half-hearted stab at churchgoing they only go for the occasional mass and holy day. Mostly they wake up late and talk, Mona makes toast and tea and scurries back to bed before she gets too cold. The gas grill is temperamental and she has to be careful lighting the flame. As she waits for the bread to brown, she puts everything on a tray: two mugs of tea, jam, a knife and then a big plate of buttered toast. To make a home is a joy. Little things make a big difference. A proper potato peeler instead of a knife, matching tea towels, enamel saucepans with a green ivy design around the edge, a bedside table and a small three-piece suite from a shop that was closing down. There's a lot yet to buy but all that will come.

Mona tightens the belt on her robe, grips the tray handles and carries their breakfast to the bedroom at the front of the house. She snuggles back under the covers beside him.

'Right,' she says. 'I'll go first.'

'For a change,' says William under his breath.

'Air, clean air,' she says, 'and almonds.'

'Beautiful Mona,' he says and kisses her. 'Babies.'

'Cotton sheets and Christmas.'

'Deep blue eyes,' he says and kisses her again. 'Drowning in them.'

'Electric blankets and egg soufflé. I don't even know what egg soufflé is but I like the sound of it and it begins with an "E" so I'm having it.'

' "F",' he says. 'Flying through the air like Peter Pan.' He flaps his toast above his head. 'And for ever.'

'Giraffes . . .'

'Giraffes?'

86

'I like the pattern on their fur.'

'Their skin you mean.'

'It's fur, isn't it?'

'Not strictly speaking, no, it's a skin, like a goat skin.'

'Well, you're the country boy,' she says, 'you should know.'

'I am that. Although there are no giraffes in Galway, Mona.'

'Really?' she mocks. 'No need of the wildlife out west there, no? Enough of the home-grown variety? That's what I've always heard. Anyway, I'm having giraffes and Galway, so there.'

'Heaven,' he says quietly after a few moments. 'And here. And now.'

'Now begins with an "N", William,' she jokes but he's staring at her. He takes the plate of toast and the mug from her hand.

'Where was I?' he says. 'Oh yes, "H". Here.' He kisses her cheek.

'And here.' He kisses the very tip of her nose.

'And here.' He kisses her lips and they slide down into the bed together.

'And here.'

In the evenings they go to the Bear in Sparkhill. It's an Irish pub and a man's pub full of labourers who want a break from their rented rooms and their own company, and middle-aged husbands let off the leash after mass. Nicholas Doyle is always in the corner with his accordion or violin and a couple of drinks lined up on the table to his right. That's where William likes to sit, right near the music, near the musician's elbow jerking his bow through the air or folding and unfolding the accordion that sits in his lap like a baby. Talking is almost impossible.

Inevitably, Mona ends up on the other side of the snug with the few people she knows from the boarding house or the Irish Centre, women from the area keeping an eye on the housekeeping money. There is the occasional fight and marital row, there are drunken speeches about the English and quieter ones about the Irish Republican Army, but the best nights are full of music and singing and old rebel songs about love and freedom, martyrdom and oppression. Mona doesn't know them all but William does. She watches him follow along, tapping his foot or looking down into his pint glass as though he could cry. He mouths the words and sits with his head on one side, his eyes closed, drinking every note, and when finally he comes to, he winks at Mona and raises his glass.

One night completely out of the blue, when Nick Doyle stops, William stands and clears his throat.

'I sat within a valley green,' he sings out. A few of the old-timers murmur something and a woman next to Mona shouts, 'A good song, boy. Go on.'

So he begins, clear and deep and rich and round, cutting across the noise and the babble of the pub. Mona can't believe the sound that comes out of him.

> 'I sat there with my true love.
> My sad heart strove the two between,
> The old love and the new love.
> The old for her, the new that made
> Me think of Ireland dearly
> While soft the wind blew down the glade
> And shook the golden barley.'

No one joins in but old Nick Doyle, who swaps the accordion for his violin and sways as he strains the strings and follows William note for note. The pub falls quiet and Mona puts her hand to her throat. She might cry for the love of him. He is a different man, one she has never seen. He sings verse after verse until, at the final chorus, his voice gives out, he is almost whispering. The same woman belts out the last words and then the whole pub is alive, stamping and cheering, and William has pints and chasers lined up along the bar for the rest of the long night.

They hold hands for the walk home. He is quiet and Mona can feel him weaving a little on the pavement. She kisses him suddenly.

'I never knew you could sing, William.'

'Ah,' he says.

'What else haven't you told me?'

He would laugh usually or tell her that he had forgotten everything that happened before he met her. That nothing else mattered. But this time, he simply shrugs.

'It was my grandfather that brought me up. Not my father. My father couldn't hold a job and it was my mother that had to keep our family together. My grandfather, her father, who held my hand and took me hurling, or sometimes sat me between his legs in a little wooden skiff, just us two. I used to love the smell of him. He wore a bottle-green waistcoat, a thing that my mother knitted him. Maybe he had more than one, I don't know, but all I remember now is him in that waistcoat and the way the buttons strained across his chest. I remember that waistcoat and the smell of him in it. It's my first memory. I must have been a baby.'

'Shall I knit you a green waistcoat then, William?'

'And he used to toss me high in the air and catch me and just at the last moment I would feel the whoosh in my belly like he would miss but he never did, never.'

There is a break in his voice as he faces her.

'What I mean to say is I want to be like him. Only like him.'

'Why wouldn't you be?'

William shakes his head and Mona folds the lapels of his coat over his chest.

'You've inherited a beautiful singing voice from somewhere, that's all I know.'

'My grandfather's song, that was. He would put me to bed and sing me that song while he read the paper. I used to watch his lips move and I used to hear the paper rustle and it would send me to sleep.'

'You were the star turn in there tonight, William. I was so proud of you.'

But that night he winds himself in the sheets and blankets and Mona has to wake him up. He throws up eventually and goes

89

outside for a smoke. Mona hears him pacing around, muttering to himself. When he comes back to bed, he whispers to her.

'Are you still awake?'

'Yes,' she says.

'I'm nothing like my father. I won't be like him.'

'Ssshh,' she says. 'Go to sleep.'

14

The doorbell rings at five minutes to four that afternoon and Mona is ready.

'Come in. Christine, isn't it? Come in, come in. I take my shoes off but you don't have to. I don't impose that on anyone but it's just a habit for me. But I'll take your coat and hang it here.'

Christine slips out of her mackintosh and moccasins and pads along the hallway, following Mona into the living room. Mona has moved an armchair next to her own. The curtains are half drawn against the bright afternoon sun and the room is warm, as it would be in a hospital, and freshly cleaned. The woman hovers in the doorway.

Mona stands behind the armchair and motions to it. 'Sit you down, love. Sit here. Now will you have tea or coffee before we start? You don't have to have either but you'll want a drink of something as we go along. Water's there on the side so you can have that if you need it.'

'Nothing, thank you,' says the woman as she sits. She puts her handbag at her feet and knits her fingers together on her lap. She has her hair swept up on top of her head in a sloppy bun, ringlets falling on her face. She looks around the flat and Mona lets her settle before she sits down herself and begins.

'I'm going to talk to you now, Christine, and you're going to listen.'

Christine has her pooling eyes fixed on Mona. Mona can hear her shallow breaths and all the things she wants to say. *Stop. I've come to the wrong place. I don't want this. I'm scared.*

But Mona continues. 'Listen with your heart,' she says and taps her chest. 'In here. You'll be safe with me. We'll do this together.'

Mona gets up and before she leaves the room she turns at the door and says, 'Get yourself comfortable. Take a few moments. Relax.'

She comes back with the baby wrapped in Christine's white lace shawl. The baby is cradled in her arms, the tail of the shawl drapes down. Mona makes sure that the little baby won't be visible as she re-enters the room because she needs to take Christine by surprise. And she does.

Christine starts and a moan escapes. It's a wounded noise that Mona's heard before. 'Yes,' she says. 'It's a beautiful shawl. Beautiful. I've kept the paper and the velvet ribbon. You can have them back, don't worry.'

But the woman recoils, pressing herself back into the armchair, turning her head but not her eyes as Mona approaches with the bundle. Mona stands over her, leaning down but shielding the baby so it can't be seen.

'It's a beautiful shawl, Christine, isn't it? Take a look. Ah, it's lovely. Fine linen and lace. Who bought this for you? Was it in the family?'

Mona leans closer and closer until she has the bundle almost on the woman's lap.

'It's so soft. And it smells of lavender. Someone went to a lot of trouble for you. Was it your mother?'

Christine whispers. 'It was mine. When I was born.'

'Ah,' says Mona, 'of course. Lovely,' and as she speaks she lays the baby in the woman's arms and the woman sees what it is, a lump of wood. She looks up at Mona, her mouth trembling.

'Ssshh,' says Mona. 'Close your eyes. Ssshh.'

Christine hasn't taken the baby yet, not properly, but she will.

'Now,' says Mona, slow and quiet. 'Feel the weight.'

The woman's eyes are squeezed tight.

'It's a good weight,' says Mona. 'Five pounds seven ounces. Can you feel it?'

The woman closes her arms round the shawl.

'Feel the weight, Christine.'

The woman brings the baby up to her chest and down again. Up and down.

'That's the weight of your baby. Sometimes, we don't want to remember what we saw or what we felt but we remember the weight. Don't we, Christine? We remember the weight of the baby inside of us and the weight we felt in our arms. Can you feel the weight?'

She nods. 'Yes. I can feel it.'

'It's a good weight. Do you remember what your baby felt like?'

Christine's head is on one side. Her face is softening. She has her tears still.

'Yes.'

'Is it a girl, Christine? Or is it a baby boy?'

'Girl.'

'So, they put your baby in your arms and you held her just like this. Just like this now. Remember?'

There are sounds a way off. There are people calling out to one another on the beach. There are roadworks somewhere and the horn of a car. The bus is just turning off the main parade and the driver is changing gears. Mona can hear them but she knows Christine cannot. Mona is sitting now, close enough to touch, but she doesn't need to any more.

'What have you called her?'

'Faith,' whispers the woman. 'Faith Anne.'

'Faith Anne,' repeats Mona. 'Beautiful. And she's a beautiful baby, isn't she?'

Christine frowns and touches her mouth. 'She had no, no . . .'

'Ah, she's beautiful, Christine, love. Isn't she?'

'Yes.'

'And you thought about her growing up, didn't you? Of course you did. She'll grow up to be a beautiful little girl. Will she look like you or her father? Maybe she'll have your eyes, will she? Or something else?'

'My husband's eyes. My hands.'

'So, there we are. Your husband's eyes and your hands. And she'll be tall, won't she?'

'Yes.'

'You're tall and I'll bet your husband's tall so Faith Anne will be tall. That's the way of things. And she'll have lots of birthdays. What will you do when she's one? What will you do for her birthday, her first birthday? What will you do, Christine?'

But Christine is sobbing. She's quiet but her chest dances in her shirt and little scraps of breath carry her pain out into the room. 'She's dead,' she says.

'Yes,' says Mona.

'She's gone. I can't bear it.'

'Do you remember thinking of all the things you would do with your daughter? Before she was born you were thinking about all the lovely things you would do together. Remember? Did you think about her first birthday? What will you do for Faith Anne's first birthday? Will you do something at home? Have you made a cake?'

Christine says nothing but clutches the bundle to her chest and weeps into it.

'Cakes are a terrible lot of work, aren't they? You could buy one for all the trouble you go to but you'll make one for her first birthday because that's what mothers are like. You'll ice it, will you, and buy her a big candle for the top?'

'A candle? Yes.'

'Who's coming to the party, Christine?'

'I don't know.'

'You'll want people to come, won't you? Who would you ask?'

'My mum, my dad, my sister and her twins. My granddad. Vanessa from next door.'

'Oh, you've a houseful. Lovely. What else?'

'I would have bought her a . . .'

'You bought her what, Christine? What did you buy?'

Christine looks hard at Mona. 'What did I buy?'

'You bought something for Faith Anne's first birthday.'

'I did. I bought her a silver bracelet like the one I had when I was little.'

'And you had it engraved, I bet.'

'Yes, her name and the date.'

'So that's grand. Is she in nursery now?'

'No, no. Not nursery. I wanted her at home with me.'

'Of course you do, Christine. Of course you do. We do when they're babies. What else?'

'I would have made all her food from scratch.'

The woman cradles her baby with one hand; the other is pointing and describing.

'I've got an allotment up on Chesford Lane, you know, near the new estate. I grow everything organically. I'd use my own vegetables.'

'That's grand, Christine, you used all your own vegetables.'

'Yes, I did. I didn't want chemicals and insecticides in my baby. Why do people do that when they have the choice?'

Mona shrugs but says nothing for a few moments, then she starts again. 'Did you take Faith Anne on holiday, Christine? Where did you go? Abroad, was it?'

'Walking. We both like walking. We bought a G3, that's the best baby carrier. We've already done the research on that. It's got a metal frame and a padded backrest. Expensive but they're best for newborns. But we'll have to change it when she gets older.'

'How old was she when you changed it?'

'Oh, we went through three or four before she got too heavy to carry.'

'And she started school, Christine. Which school did you choose?'

'We would have sent her to St Catherine's. It's the nearest.'

'You sent her to St Catherine's. She was a bright girl then?'

'My husband's a biologist. I teach history.'

'Oh, well,' says Mona with a shake of her head. 'She's a bright one all right, there's no worries on that score.'

'She might have struggled with hand—eye coordination because both of us do. Crap at sports.'

'She was in the school play, I bet.'

The woman lays her head on the back of the sofa and Mona lets her be. When she speaks, her voice is calm and even.

'We took her walking in Scotland once. My dad's from Dumfries. It's damp and cold but the scenery . . . she loved it. She walked all the way round Castle Loch like I used to, through the nature reserve. It was wet but she didn't complain.'

'How old was she then?'

'Oh, I don't know. Six maybe.'

'And she's a serious girl, is she, Faith Anne?'

'No, no. Not really. Not as serious as her father, certainly. She's got a wicked sense of humour and she likes to play tricks. She has no interest in dolls though. No, she's more a reader. I'd always find her sitting by the back window where the sun comes in and she'd be reading. And I'd have to tell her off at bedtime.'

'Did she take any notice?'

Christine is smiling now and it won't be long before Mona can sit back and let her live her baby's life. The shawl has fallen from around the wooden doll. The woman has it in the crook of her arm, resting peacefully. She'll be thinking it's asleep because she'll feel the weight of it on her lap.

Mona helps her along. 'She was headstrong, then, was she? Faith Anne? A reader and tall and headstrong and a good walker. Did you buy her a bike?'

'A bike?' The woman sits up with her eyes wide. 'Oh yes, definitely, we bought her a bike when she was ten, a proper bike I mean. Pete, my husband, he goes mountain biking, trail riding, the whole lot, and Faith went with him. I wasn't that keen but the two of them . . .'

'They loved it?'

'Oh yes!'

'Can you remember them? Can you see them, Christine? Riding up the hills on their bikes?'

'Yes, yes I can.'

'And she'll be eleven soon. Where did she go to secondary school?'

'Well . . .'

Mona listens and nods and guides her and asks questions and laughs when she should and when Faith Anne has her first boyfriend they're both relieved when he goes off to university and forgets to write. And Christine tells Mona how Faith Anne falls in love properly when she goes to Durham to read theology like her grandfather but because she's doing her PhD they wait and wait and eventually she's married, not a grand wedding but it wasn't running away to a Mexican beach either. Christine and Peter and the other parents who are both GPs paid jointly for a civil ceremony in a London hotel and afterwards there was a big meal for all the guests in a little bistro next door. It was beautiful and Christine cried, of course.

Faith Anne fell pregnant quickly. Being a grandparent was lovely and Christine got to hold the baby after it was only a few hours old. Perfect. Christine felt sorry for the two GPs who were on holiday at the time of the birth and didn't get back until the baby was a week old. Christine wouldn't have dreamed of booking a holiday so close to the due date but then it's different when it's your daughter's baby, you're somehow more involved. And that's how it was for years and years, Christine always on hand for her grandchild, helping out while Faith went back to work as a lecturer, filling in when necessary in all sorts of ways. Too many to mention.

And Faith Anne goes on to have two more children, both boys, three years apart, and the whole family are involved in looking after Christine and Peter in their old age, sheltered accommodation not too far away. Faith Anne is always there. And then Christine is quiet.

The two women sit together as the shaft of sun moves across the carpet and up the wall, the room becomes darker and the afternoon ends.

15

The temptation, of course, is for Mona to make Joley an outfit for her new job, one that would combine the tartan, black and untidy-looking elements of Joley's style with something stylish, fitted and smart enough for the staffroom. Something feminine and contemporary without the rips. Maybe a little red dress with a velvet collar.

Mona is supposed to be paying attention to her computer lesson but she's fascinated as usual by Joley's expertise in cigarette rolling. She hardly looks at what she's doing, her little fingers with a delicate hold on the rolling papers, her nails bitten to the quick and two thousand bracelets clicking like castanets.

'So, go on then,' Joley says. 'Let's see if you can do it on your own to that new order.'

Mona clicks on the file. 'I open this,' she says. 'Here. Then I add "send acknowledgement". Right. Then, I . . .'

'Print.'

'Yes, print.'

'Then I go back to file. Save.'

'Number?' says Joley, licking the cigarette paper.

'Yes, number it. Like that. Then save.'

'As?'

'Save as customer name and date. So that's "Son Ye-Jin". Do you think Ye-Jin is the surname? Oh well, I'll put it under Y. Right, okay, and today's date.'

'Where does the order go?'

'The printed one? Blue folder for international and red folder for UK.'

'Then?'

Mona squeezes her eyes shut. 'Then add reminder to calendar.'

Joley sticks the cigarette in the corner of her mouth and claps. 'See!'

Mona has a sheen of sweat on her brow and realizes she hasn't been breathing properly for a full five minutes. She blows all the air out and shakes her head. 'This isn't my comfort zone, Joley. Not one bit of it.'

'We can do "close orders" next time. You're doing great, and anyway, Turk says comfort zones are just for Zoners.'

'Zoners?'

'People that just go along with whatever. You know, people that let things happen to them and don't, like, make any personal progress. I've got loads of friends who are Zoners. They're, like, living at home watching game shows and eating meat.'

'I forgot you were a vegetarian.'

'Yeah, I'm not saying that everyone has to be or anything but, like, just be passionate about something.'

Mona, as always, marvels at the little rolled cigarette tucked in and wobbling at the corner of Joley's purple lips.

'I agree, love,' Mona says, walking away from the computer. 'Now, as far as I'm concerned, Turk is right. I'm a great fan of personal progress so today we're going to shut up early and go to Danny's for a treat. God knows, we've done enough work here today. Come on. We can sit outside and you can puff away.'

No one calls Danny's cafe by its new name, Vinegar & Oil. The heritage paint and industrial seating, the black-and-white photos and hessian mats have only ever looked temporary and out of place and poor Danny, despite his best efforts, has bought himself the local egg and bacon cafe. He saunters over in his bandana and faded T-shirt, bringing their cakes and drinks to the courtyard table.

'You're looking natty, Danny,' says Mona, kicking Joley under the table. They watch him scratch his greying beard and hike up his low-slung jeans.

Joley draws on her cigarette and whistles. 'Hear you're in a band, Dan?'

Danny smacks his imaginary cymbal with a flourish. 'White

Horse. Resident tribute. Come down, both of you. It's a good night. I'll get you in.'

'Festivals, Dan. That's where the money is,' says Joley with the wink and whisper of a market trader.

'Yeah, yeah, I know,' he says. 'But I've got this place now. Time I was putting down roots. Anyway, art for art's sake.'

They watch him slouch indoors, his stubby plait bouncing on his shoulders.

'Now you couldn't accuse him of being a Zoner, Joley, could you, God bless him? At least he's trying to outrun middle age. Now, will you look at the size of this cake?' Mona cuts her Danish pastry in half and shares it with Joley. 'Have that after your doughnut, you'll burn it off in no time. And just wait till you're running around a classroom after thirty little ones.'

'Half of me doesn't want to leave, you know. It's just, like, a really, really great opportunity.'

'Joley, love!' says Mona and she makes sure her voice is light and firm, motherly. 'You can't stay working in a shop your whole life! This is what you've always wanted. And I don't want you to leave either, of course I don't, but my little enterprise is not your future.'

'I know but . . .'

'You're not going to Thailand, are you? Or New Zealand? You'll come in on a Saturday and check up on me, I know you will. And give me a few more lessons till I have that computer licked.'

Joley is smoking and eating at the same time, and drinking her coffee in between. 'Mona, listen, why don't you get someone else in so you have some company?'

'Ah, they're big boots to fill, love. I mean, literally.' And Mona kicks her again, under the table.

Joley laughs and blows smoke up into the air. 'Did I tell you that Turk's had four of his photographs chosen for an exhibition? Yeah, we're really pleased. They're all of me. One on the beach and the others were posed. A gallery in London.'

'That's fantastic. He has the eye, all right.'

'The first exhibition, that's all it is. There'll be others.' Joley goes on, her plans and her life and her boyfriend and their future, everything with the ring of love in her voice, the certainty of good things to come.

'. . . and then, like, get our own place. Turk can't stand it where he is and I've got to move out sometime . . .'

And the smoke curling and dancing in the late-afternoon light, the special time, just before it gets dark. A whole cigarette would be too much but Mona wouldn't mind a drag.

'. . . so we could go up when it opens in March. Why don't you come? There's other things on apart from photography. Paintings and stuff. And textiles. You should, like, you know, go out and do things, see stuff.'

'Oh, I'll come, yes.'

'And there's really interesting people there. Like, older people. People you could meet.'

'Yes, lovely. Let me know the exact date. I could do with a run up to London, get myself some new clothes or treat myself to something. Maybe I'll get Val to come up, make a weekend of it.'

'You should.'

'I will.'

Then suddenly there's a mist of rain, cold and persistent, settling and beading on Mona's coat. They say goodbye and Joley gives Mona such a hug, such a hug she can hardly get her breath.

'What's that for?' she says.

Joley shrugs. 'I'm going to miss you, that's all!'

'Go on with you,' says Mona. 'We've weeks yet. Weeks. Go on, you'll catch your death with your midriff on show like that, catching raindrops in your belly button. Go on, love. Bye.'

Mona walks home, her head down against the wind, her hands shoved in her pockets. Tobacco on Joley's jacket, tobacco in her hair, on her skin, on her breath. Such a hug, like the ones William gave her, a hug and a kiss when he was just as young as Joley, younger even, young and alive. Like the one he gave her right there in front of all his friends, in front of the boarding house on Tipton Terrace, in front of the whole world because he loved her and because she followed him from one end of the country to the other.

He'd been sent away for work, two hours on the train, and he'd be gone for a week he said, or more, working on a new-build housing estate with ten other men, all sharing rooms in a boarding house.

'I'll come back at the weekend if they don't offer us the overtime,' William says, stuffing his boots into a carrier bag.

Mona sits on the bed watching. 'So it could be two weeks?'

'Well, it could be. I can ring you at the same time every night so you won't worry.'

But she did worry. And she missed him before he'd even left. They'd only been married six months and nineteen days, every one of which they'd spent side by side, heads and bodies together. Now here he was leaving her, his absence threatening like black clouds out at sea.

The first couple of days were purgatory. She spoke to no one all evening and paced the hallway for a full ten minutes before his call. He plied the payphone with money until it became too expensive, blew kisses and promises into the receiver and then left her with the burr of the dialling tone. She cried alone in the flat. She knew she was being ridiculous. She didn't care.

By Friday morning she was on the train to him. She took a day off work with considerable difficulty and didn't even bother to lie. She said there was a family emergency, that she had no choice but to go and someone was in trouble. The somebody was herself. The foreman, a huge West Indian with a thin moustache, took his time and looked hard at her.

'Homesick?'

'Sort of.'

'Is Ireland you goin'?'

'No.'

'Where?'

'I'm going to my husband and I'll be back on Monday. Eight sharp.'

'You sure you comin' back?'

'I am.'

He lodged a toothpick between his bottom teeth. 'Don't tell the others. Go.'

She told William nothing. She took his phone call that night with a happy heart and after a few cunning questions about the address of the boarding house, she could hardly wait to get off the phone in case she blabbed. She packed enough clothes for two days and bought mints at the train station then daydreamed out of the window for the whole journey south.

It was a beautiful day. She found the house with no bother and was sitting on the front garden wall when he came ambling up the street in a gang. One of the men whistled when he saw her and another shouted something she didn't catch. But William broke from the group, ran to her and dropped his sandwich tin. He held her and hugged her and kissed her and then did it all over again without the least embarrassment while his mates cheered and tumbled past. Such a hug, she could hardly get her breath.

'How did you get here?' he said. 'I mean, why? Is everything all right? You're not at work.'

'I missed you,' she said simply. 'I really missed you.'

His smile was all she needed, his smile and the smell of him and the weight of his arm on her shoulder and the feel of his face on hers. He took her bag and they walked to the corner of the road where there was a little park with swings and slides.

'There's four of us in one room, Mona. We'll have to find somewhere else to stay tonight. You are staying?'

Mona patted her case and raised her eyebrows. 'You don't get rid of me that easily. I thought you might have another woman down here already.'

He looked at her. 'I would not.' He took his cigarettes out of his pocket and lit one. The smoke made her eyes sting. He waved it away.

'It's all right,' she said and threaded her hand into his pocket. 'I like it.'

Two children, a boy and a girl, were chasing each other on the grass. The boy was small, maybe only six, but the little girl was eight and getting the best of the game.

'There's you and me,' he said, 'when we were young.'

'You've been a pest all day,' said Mona, nudging him, 'you've stolen my sweets and broken my doll.'

'I'm chasing you for a kiss.'

'I'll let you catch me, William. Always.'

Tobacco on his jacket, tobacco in his hair, on his skin, on his lips.

16

Wednesday again. Mona closes the shop at half past one. She walks into town towards the cafe. As she stands at the kerb waiting for a gap in the traffic she sees Karl standing by the third bench, his back to the sea, looking up and down the esplanade. He's in a navy linen suit, creased as linen will but tailored beautifully. And he's wearing a cravat of all things. He holds himself tall and upright, one hand in his jacket pocket, the other shielding his eyes from the sun. He has a cashmere coat over his shoulders, impossibly elegant, and Mona wonders if she has dresses enough to keep up.

A little boy scooters up to Karl, bumping into him, shoving him backwards. Karl pretends to fall then squats down and talks to the child, who laughs and shakes his head. Mona watches the mother, relieved and proud, sees Karl hold his hands up. 'It's all right, it's all right.'

When he sees Mona, he makes his little bow. 'Good afternoon,' he says, 'we meet by coincidence. I was just on my way to the cafe. How are you?' He takes her hand and squeezes it tight, better than a kiss.

Mona undoes the buttons of her gabardine coat. 'We're both in navy blue today, Karl. We must be in sync.'

'The classic colour,' he says. '*Klassiker.*'

'*Klassiker,*' Mona repeats and looks up. 'We're even matching the *klassiker* sky. Look, bright blue.'

'Yes,' he says. 'The seasons are indecisive this year. Shall we walk?'

They climb down on to the shale and away from the pier where the walkers thin out.

'Is it cold in Hamburg?' she asks after a while. 'I don't know my geography very well. Is it north of here?'

He doesn't answer straight away as though the question is a difficult one. 'Wet, cold, yes. Harsh winters. But yet, it's warm in the summer, of course, and sunny days like here. And, naturally, it is a port and it is therefore windy sometimes. Spring is beautiful and we have many parks and gardens. There is a quality to the light just along the coast, outside of Hamburg, a long stretch of beach and a little island . . .'

She's talked about the weather like an Englishwoman. She's made him feel awkward.

'But I spent most winters abroad. I used to travel a lot until quite recently in fact.'

'As a girl I lived by the sea,' Mona says, 'in Wexford. It's on the east. I think about my childhood more and more these days. I used to play on the sand. Me and my father. That is to say, I used to play and he used to have his face in a book. I could have drowned and he wouldn't have noticed.'

'Ah, I was rather spoiled I'm afraid, by my mother at least. My father was not so indulgent. He had very high expectations. He wanted the best for me as I suppose all parents do. I can't say. I have no children of my own but I have a sister and she has children. Of course, I don't see them often and they are grown now with their own children. I am a great-uncle, that most ancient of things.' Karl stops speaking suddenly and raises a finger. 'However, one thing my father did get right is he showed me what it is to eat and drink well.'

'You love your food then, Karl?'

'I do, I'm afraid. I'm rather a food snob if you will. I have become over the years a competent cook, perhaps better than competent, and yes, I have eaten wonderful food all over the world and enjoyed it.'

'What's your favourite thing?'

'Ah, too difficult a question. Too difficult.' He nevertheless closes his eyes and turns his face to the sky. 'It depends of course on the weather, on the hemisphere. So, let me see. If I were for example in Paris or Moscow and,' he holds up a finger again, 'and it is wintertime then I think something involving roasted pork. Yes, perhaps roasted pork with cabbage, simmered in wine and garlic. Beautiful.'

'Oh, delicious!'

'In hot weather it is a different matter entirely. Not pork. If it was hot then one would naturally think of seafood, grilled lobster perhaps with a herb butter, wine, a good white burgundy.'

Mona looks out across the water, dark grey now as the early evening approaches. 'I wish I had been to Paris.'

Karl touches her face, brings it round. 'Mona, you speak as though the city has disappeared. It is still there.'

'Yes but.'

'But?'

'Well, I don't know really. I haven't really travelled, something always got in the way. I suppose there's nothing stopping me really.'

'Perhaps we could go together. I have been many times and I speak the language a little. We could enjoy ourselves. What prevents us?' He stops suddenly and pulls the collar up on Mona's coat. 'Are you warm enough, Mona?'

She nods and pulls the belt tight round her waist. Karl gives a little laugh. 'Something occurs to me. Come,' he says as he threads her hand through the crook of his arm. 'I will tell you a story about Paris as we walk. Andreas and I were on a train. We were travelling from Deauville where we had been staying, at the coast . . .'

'Andreas?'

Karl covers her hand with his own and is quiet for a moment. 'We were brothers almost. We played together as children on the same estate. We did many things together, travel mostly. We had a taste, both of us, for good living and, forgive me, for the company of women. He was ill from time to time and, well, I took care of him.' Karl coughs. 'Andreas died recently. I must say it has shaken me somewhat. In fact, more than shaken me. I had known him all my life. I am adrift somewhat.'

'I'm sorry, Karl. Really I am.'

'Yes, yes. It was quite sudden, you see, although he had had epilepsy since he was a child. Quite, quite severe.' He takes a deep breath, adjusts his cravat and shivers. 'It's quite cold actually, now that the evening approaches.'

They reach the barrier where the beach disappears under the cliffs and Karl turns them round to walk back the way they have come. 'Anyway, where was I? Yes, on the train. Andreas was invited by some friends to a grand dinner in Paris. Naturally, there was a lady involved. Two, actually. I confess, we were both keen to go. Paris and Deauville are not so far apart and the railway service is excellent, not even two hours. We dressed for dinner and took a taxi to the station, leaving our luggage in the hotel.'

'That sounds exciting.' Mona looks up. The windows to the carpenter's workshop are open as usual. She can hear the *zizz* of the circular saw, imagines what he's making. Not dolls, certainly, but cutting something down to size, making a piece of fine furniture or repairing an antique dresser for a dealer.

'Unfortunately, Andreas had eaten rather too much at lunch. There had been a banquet and not only had he drunk to excess but fish had been served. If I am a gourmand, Andreas is somewhat a glutton.' Karl stops. 'Was. He was a glutton. Though that is quite unfair. No, I can't say that. Anyway, he was ill and despite my advice he had no intention of missing the occasion. I, of course, was fine. I always am. So! We are in the taxi and he is groaning, like this.'

Karl puts both hands round his stomach, pulls his tongue out. 'He is in agony and as we cross the bridge on the way to the station, he, how should I say, embarrasses himself.' Karl puts his hand to his backside and wafts away a smell.

Mona laughs.

'Yes, it was quite remarkable. I opened a window but I'm afraid things had gone rather too far and there had been an accident. "Oh my God, Karl," he said. It was quite disgusting and yet hilarious, of course. Even Andreas is laughing. We ask the taxi to stop at a department store and I dash in. We are late, naturally. I have to find new trousers on the first floor, I have to find undergarments on the second floor, I have to pay, find my way out, I go to the wrong exit, there are women in my way, I drop the bag, I pick it up, we are late, we are late. I get back into the taxi, the taxi speeds off, we get to the station, I walk behind Andreas all the way to save his embarrassment. We make the train with seconds to spare.' Karl puts his hand to his chest. 'At last!'

They reach the pier again and join a long queue for ice cream.

'So Andreas takes the bag and goes to the restroom. I wait outside. He peels off his clothes and opens the door and passes them to me. Really, what can I do? I open the window and drop them out. Disgusting. He washes himself carefully.'

Karl gives a little cough. She can see the skin crinkling around his eyes. He's trying not to laugh.

'He dries himself with paper towels, opens the bag and pulls out a pink cardigan. A lady's pink cardigan. With little sequins!' Karl holds his hands twelve inches apart. 'This big!'

As Mona laughs, Karl shakes his head.

'The train has started. He is trapped. Inside I can hear a noise. "Andreas! Andreas!" I call. He opens the door and cannot speak. He has forced his legs into the sleeves which have ripped and he has buttoned the rest around his private parts. He is weeping with laughter. Weeping.'

'Look,' says Mona. 'A bench. And one the birds seem to have forgotten. Let's grab it while it's still clean.'

They take their ice creams and sit. The beach is almost empty.

'You miss him,' says Mona after a while.

'Oh yes, very much. We had much in common and, of course, we had our differences. I helped him to manage his affairs.' He speaks quickly with his face away from her as though he doesn't want her to hear.

The gulls scream overhead and people amble past with their pushchairs and children, some with windbreaks and folded chairs. Mona sees herself through their eyes; they look like a couple, so long-married that all the words have been said.

When he finishes, Karl takes a folded handkerchief from his pocket and hands it to her. 'For your fingers,' he says. Mona dabs her lips and wipes her hands. He thinks of everything.

'Now you,' he says. 'Your turn. Tell me something about yourself.'

Mona roots around for something to say. 'I don't know what to tell you, Karl. There's nothing remarkable about me really. I'm an only child. There weren't many only children when I grew up. In Ireland a small family used to be looked on with suspicion as though you'd been practising birth control on the quiet but there must have been something passed down through the ages like an heirloom because my father was an only child too and my mother's relatives all live in America. But I was never spoilt. My mother died when I was really little but my father more than made up for the loss. I had his love and his disapproval depending on my behaviour and I was never really what you might call a wild child. I was well behaved.'

Karl turns to look at her. 'Go on.'

'My mother tried – that's what they thought in those days, that the woman had something to do with her non-pregnancies. I do remember once she thought she was pregnant or maybe she was pregnant but I was too young to know what happened. Anyway, I was never really lonely because I was a solitary child, always at the shore on Kilmore Quay or Ballyteige where the treasure washed up and I could play for hours on my own, sing as loud as I liked. You only miss a sibling when you're standing at a graveside and there's no one to understand or say "Me too".' Mona folds the handkerchief and passes it back to Karl. 'Thank you. Anyway, that was a very long time ago now.' The wind comes in off the sea and blows Mona's hair around her face.

Karl stands up. 'Come, it's growing cold.' He holds his hand out and she takes it, soft and warm and strong, and she knows that if she looks at his nails they'll have little manicured half-moons.

'Oh yes,' she says, 'I was in a car accident once.'

'Oh dear. Were you hurt?'

'Well, I wasn't driving but I was thrown left and right as we swerved across the carriageway and we dropped into a ditch. There were three of us and we all had our seatbelts on so we scrambled out a bit shaken but no bones broken. A motorbike and a small lorry had collided as well and two men started a fight. The motorcyclist kept his helmet on the whole time and the van driver kept trying to get at him. In the end, the motorcyclist head-butted the other man and knocked him out cold. It wasn't funny really but we were all crying with laughter. Standing on the hard shoulder with tears in our eyes.'

They walk back towards the main road.

'We'd been to the Royal Craft Makers Conference in Southsea,' she continues, 'and when I opened the boot, all my stuff had tipped out all over the place, a couple of dolls were broken, but we had ages to wait for a tow truck so I sorted everything out. Took us three hours to get home and I didn't realize until the morning that I had whiplash.'

'Dolls? You collect dolls?'

'Make them. Well, I don't actually make them, I get them made by a carpenter. He lives not far from here actually, just down there.'

Mona points towards the workshop. 'He'll be up there now. He's a proper craftsman, an artist. I order the dolls and he makes each one by hand. They're beautiful already when I get them, dark mahogany or cherry or blonde wood, nearly white or teak or pine. Little articulated joints, like this.'

'Like a marionette? A puppet?'

'No. They're dolls.'

'For children?'

'No. Well, sometimes. The dolls I make are the sort you collect and keep. I make their clothes by hand, little outfits and accessories. I get a lot of my business from abroad, Japan and Korea or America.'

Karl stops and looks at her, squeezes her hand. 'I am very impressed, Mona. I had no idea.'

'I have someone who helps me with the online business. Well, when I say online, I advertise on a sort of a specialist website. I'm no good with a computer but my assistant is leaving and I've got to learn. It's not as easy as it looks.'

Karl shakes his head. 'I have never thought it looks easy.'

'Well, she's giving me lessons and I'm getting the hang of it. I have no choice. Or I could try and get someone in to take her place.'

'No, no. If you can do it, then do it! We must always keep learning. It keeps us young, no? Maybe when you learn you can teach me. Men are a lot slower than women in these sorts of things, I believe.'

'It's funny but the male dolls always bring customers to the shop and get picked up the most but I never get a foreign order for a man, always a girl. And if men come to the shop they make sure they say it is for a present and they try to avoid handling anything at all. I think they're a bit embarrassed. Little boys always try to move the legs and arms and then look up the skirts.'

'Naturally.'

'Anyway, I'm good at it, I suppose, I paint them and bring them to life. Sometimes it's too dark and miserable to paint faces. I don't paint then. No. Whatever it is you're feeling is right there on the doll's face so I paint on sunny days with the window open. I got the carpenter to make me a sort of harness on a frame. I stand it on my workbench like this, and it holds the doll's wooden body up straight at eye level.'

'I see.'

'Then he made another contraption that holds the magnifying glass in front of the doll's face for really close work, for the features. He's very clever, knows exactly what I want. And I've got an Anglepoise lamp on my left-hand side. I have a special brush, a Kolinsky, so soft, so fine that you could tickle your eyeball and you wouldn't blink.'

'Hmm, I have never had my eyeballs tickled. We must try that sometime.'

He is watching her. There's a lovely silence about him with only the dragging sound of the sea, its endless shushing and sighing, and

Mona feels like she's been talking for ever, like she could tell him everything about herself and he wouldn't be surprised and she could tell him even about William and the terrible time she had and he would just listen with his lovely eyes and his polite restraint.

'Well, it's been grand, Karl. I have to go now.'

'Of course, of course. I have a few things to do this week, some affairs to sort out and some obligations, but perhaps next time we can carry on where we left off?'

'Yes, that would be nice.'

'Yet it is only still early, perhaps we might take a small drink on the way back?'

'Oh, I'm not going home. I've got a collection to fetch. I've ordered something from the carpenter. I'll walk back that way.'

Karl leans down and kisses her twice, once on each cheek, and gives his little bow. He smiles his crinkly smile on his handsome face and says, 'Then I'll say *au revoir*. Next week? Would that be too presumptuous?'

'No, I'd like that,' she says. He kisses her cheek again then touches it lightly with the back of his hand, and as he walks away Mona feels a little lurch. A week is suddenly a long time to wait.

The carpenter is standing at the window with a mug in his hand. She walks towards him, her steps loud on the wooden floor, but he doesn't turn.

'I saw you just now,' he says. 'On the beach again.'

Mona sees the eight-pound baby on the side. He's made it out of yellow pine, waxed and polished it, spent more time than usual. His jumper has frayed cuffs and the neck is gaping. Loose threads could catch on his saw, he could lose a hand or an arm, but if she says anything he ignores her, or worse still he gets annoyed.

'I was out for a walk,' she says. 'With my new neighbour. Just showing him around.'

He drains his mug and points it at his bench. 'It's been ready since yesterday. Eight pounds two ounces.' He puts it in her arms.

'Thank you,' she says. 'Was there something else?'

'Such as?'

'I just thought you had something to say about the beach or . . .'

'No.'

'Okay then. I'll take this and go.'

'Right.'

And after all, Mona needn't have rushed to get the baby. The horsewoman didn't turn up, as Mona expected.

But the following Monday morning, as soon as the shop opens, she walks in with a young girl, nine or ten, carrying a doll that wobbles at the neck. The child places the doll on the counter. Her mother stands behind her.

'Well, now,' says Mona, 'who is this?'

'My doll,' says the child. 'My mum gave it to me. It was hers and now it's mine.'

'And she's sick, is she?'

The girl nods.

'Well, we don't really do repairs here. Some dolls are made differently to the way I work. I only make wooden dolls and some dolls are made of cloth with springs inside, or sometimes plastic. And some of them are best handled with care for the rest of their lives. Maybe put them on a shelf or in a drawer so they don't get any worse.'

But as Mona speaks she picks up the doll and lifts its dress. Feels for the body underneath. 'You've had her a while,' she says. The wood is sound but the joints are stiff with age, the articulation is all but gone and the clothes are falling to pieces. The lacquer on the doll's face has cracked like old skin and the way it falls to the side makes it look sad, forlorn.

'Lovely workmanship,' Mona whispers and winks at the child. 'I think we can do something with . . .'

'Annabel,' says the girl and she looks up at her mother. But the mother only nods.

'Annabel. That's a grand name. Well, let's see what we can do with Annabel and see if we can't lick her into shape. Now she might need a new outfit as well as a bit of attention to her arms and legs. Are you all right if we give her a change of clothes?'

The girl smiles and turns round. 'Can I, Mum?'

'Yes,' she says.

'And how old is Annabel?'

The girl beckons her mother. 'Mum, Mum. She's thirty-nine, isn't she?'

The mother comes back to the counter. 'She was mine when I was a baby. Given to me by my grandmother. A christening present. I gave her to Polly – this is Polly – a couple of years ago. Thought we should get some use out of it.'

The girl picks the doll off the counter and kisses it – 'Bye, Annabel' – and goes off then looking at the other dolls, picking them up and rocking them. The mother stays looking at Mona and starts, twice, to say something.

'It shouldn't be more than five or ten pounds for the carpenter but the outfit will be more expensive. Shall I ring you and give you a price before I start or do you want to pop back say in a week?'

'I'll come back when it's ready,' says the woman. 'And sorry about last week. Something came up.'

'That's all right.'

'Okay, then.'

She takes her daughter and leaves so quickly Mona doesn't have time to say goodbye.

17

When the power cuts start right after Christmas, Mona and William buy a box of candles, a little paraffin heater, two boxes of matches, a couple of hot-water bottles and a supply of batteries for the radio. Mona washes out two jam jars to use as lanterns and they put everything where it can easily be found if things happen without warning.

They sit together one January evening in the flickering half-light with the local radio station on low in case of any announcements. William has brought their blankets in from the bedroom and they're hunkered down on the sofa to keep warm.

'Well,' says William, 'there's no strikes in Ireland. But then again, there's no jobs.'

'They're talking about a three-day week at Canning's,' says Mona, 'and I had to join the union because they're talking about going out on strike.'

'Gallagher's won't be laying anyone off,' William says, draining a small bottle of beer. 'I asked the foreman already. He told us not to worry. There's more than enough work on that new estate in Bartley Green. We've two hundred units on second fit. It will be all over by the time we've finished that job. They'll have made an agreement by then, surely to God.'

'Good,' Mona says and a little ragged breath escapes her.

'What's up?'

Mona watches the flame dance in the jar before she speaks. 'What if I got pregnant?'

It doesn't seem to come as a surprise to him. His voice is even and light as he answers. 'And what if you did?'

'Could we afford it?'

'What? Babies don't eat much, do they, for the first couple of years? I think I could stretch to an extra potato.'

'William, you know what I mean. I would have to give up work. I can't be bending over on the assembly line with a big belly in the way. And then afterwards, there'd be no one to look after a baby but me. We've no family here, nothing. We can't ask favours and I'm not paying a childminder. There'd be nothing left of my wages. And anyway, I wouldn't want to. I don't believe in having children and farming them out to anyone else. That's a mother's job and I would want it to be mine.'

He sits up. 'Come on. What's got you all upset, Mona? What is it?'

'Nothing.'

He touches her chin and she brings her eyes up to meet his. 'Are you pregnant?'

'No.'

'You sure? Are you trying to tell me something here?'

'No. I thought I was but I was wrong and it made me think, that's all.'

'Really?'

'Really. I just said, what if. That's all.'

'Well,' he says, and snuggles back down with her. 'Sounded to me like you were giving me a warning or something. And for your information, missus, no wife of mine is going to work with a baby left at home. No child of mine, for that matter, is being brought up by strangers. I don't believe in it so you can stop losing sleep over things I've already decided.'

Mona smiles. He sounds like a headmaster or one of the men who stands at the bar with a pint and his belly stuck out.

'And another thing,' he continues, pointing into the distance as though there was an audience standing by the cold fire waiting for an argument, 'I'm a man who provides for his family. What you need as my wife and what any child of mine needs, he will get. Or she will get. Or whatever. If I have to work a sixty-hour week for the rest of my life. I don't believe in handouts and I don't believe in wet nurses and I don't believe in beggary.'

'Well, I was only saying . . .'

'There's too many men drinking their wages at the Bear. You've seen them, staggering out penniless while they've children at home in rags. That's not the life for me and mine.'

'No,' says Mona. He's in full flow, swearing a lungful of promises, countering imagined slurs.

'My father was no good. We had a hot dinner every night and there was never a Sunday without money for the plate but that was my mother's doing and my grandfather when he was alive. I know what a good man is and I know what a good man is not. I had shoes for school and another pair for church. The point is, the care of the family, that's a man's job – no, it's his responsibility, his duty. To put food on the table, a roof on the house and a coat on the hook. A coat for everyone.'

Mona has to purse her lips together in case she giggles. 'Where did you get that from?'

'What?'

'Those ideas.'

William shrugs. She can tell he is proud. 'Just decent living, Mona. It's nothing I've heard, it's what's right and what I feel in my heart.'

'Well, I like it,' she says, threading her arms round him. 'I like your heart.'

'Good. And you're sure?'

'I'm sure.'

But only six weeks later, she knows. February is freezing. Mona leaves the oven door open for a bit of heat in the kitchen and always has a hot meal ready as soon as William comes home. She puts his dinner in front of him, three slices off a gammon joint, boiled potatoes and carrots.

'So, William, when did we meet?' she says.

'Come again?'

'The date.'

'Oh, I don't know now. November. Maybe the fourteenth, something like that. Before Christmas at any rate, I'm sure of that. Have I missed something?'

'Eighteenth,' she says. 'It was the eighteenth. We might be lucky.'

'We are lucky,' he answers, his mouth full of meat. 'You know we are.'

'Luckier then.'

'How?'

'We might have an anniversary present. An anniversary to remember.'

'You've sold the house in Kilmore?'

'No.'

'You've been saving? Pass me the pepper.'

'No.'

'What then? November's a long way off.'

'No, this is from me to you.' She places the plastic drum of pepper in the middle of the table and takes a deep breath. As he reaches his hand forward she covers it with her own.

'I've got some good news.'

'What?'

'I think I'm pregnant.'

He goes quiet. He eats his dinner without saying more than 'Oh', and by the time she has cleared the table and poured the tea, she is furious. She sits down and folds her arms.

'Is that it then? Oh?'

'I was just eating my dinner, that's all.'

'I'm playing second fiddle to a bit of boiled bacon, am I?'

He says nothing.

'William!'

He looks up, petrified. The life has drained out of his face, his eyes are huge.

'I thought you'd be happy,' she says. 'I thought this is what you wanted.'

He nods.

'Are you all right?'

'I'm delighted,' he answers, 'absolutely delighted. A hundred per cent.' But his mouth is slack and the colour has gone from his skin. His hands lie on the table, open and still.

'William,' she says. 'What is it?'

She can hear the quick breaths between his words.

'It makes you think, Mona. Makes you think about things.'

She gets up and wraps her arms round his neck. 'What things?
A roof on the table, a coat on the house and food on the hook. Was
that it?'

But he's not laughing. He lets his head drop on to her chest.

'I'll do my best,' he says. 'I swear to God.'

18

Even though Mona's busy, the week seems to drag. Joley is rehearsing her new role as a teaching assistant and is very much in charge. She comes in and sits down, and if there are no customers she has Mona buckled into the office chair while she explains in what she calls 'easy language' how to manage the export business and paperwork. Except that there's not a piece of paper to be seen.

'Would it not be easier to print some of these out so I could go over them and just make sure I have it all right, Joley?' says Mona, knowing already what her answer will be.

'No. Close that file now. That's it. Save. Always save.'

There's whole galaxies and black holes and constellations and solar systems inside the flat face of the computer screen where something could get lost. With just one rogue click or slip of the mind Mona could wipe out all her orders and customers, the phone number of her paint supplier, her billing account with Simply Freight. All of it in the tiny bite of a mouse. If she could just print off one or two pages, she would feel a lot safer. Mona slumps in the swivel chair and Joley pats her on the back as she goes into the kitchen. 'Don't go backwards,' she says.

'No, miss,' calls Mona. 'Can I have a gold star?'

Joley puts the kettle on. 'That's it, you know? You've done everything. I could leave now and you've got it down. Told you it was easy. You just need the confidence, that's all.'

'Yes, miss, but I've done no sewing for a fortnight, miss, and I'm behind with my homework, miss,' says Mona. And it's true. With Joley on her case, some of the export orders are a bit late and Mona's been staying up till the early hours in her workroom. But at least she sleeps.

★

Wednesday comes eventually. As Mona approaches the Viennese cafe, she sees Karl standing with his hands behind his back looking in a shop window. He doesn't stoop at all and his hair is very sleek, curled neatly over the collar of his shirt. He is always early, but then, so is she. He's wearing flannel trousers and a tweed jacket with a white shirt and a red tie, a matching handkerchief in his breast pocket. He looks even more distinguished than usual and Mona wonders exactly how old he is. Not ancient. He greets her with his bow and when he moves aside she sees he has an old leather satchel.

'Come,' he says and looks at his watch. 'We must hurry.'

He steers her by the elbow away from the shops and down the hill to the promenade.

'Where are we going?'

'Packington House.'

They take the special bus straight there. Half the passengers have guide books and leaflets from the Tourist Information Office. But Karl chats all the way there about the house and the grounds and the special paintings and grand rooms. Some of the passengers are eavesdropping, turning in their seats to see who has the lovely accent and the inside story. When they get off the bus, Karl puts his satchel across his chest and bottles inside chink together.

'Oh dear,' he says, 'I have given the game away. Come, let's not go with the others, there is a little footpath here, over the bridge and near the river. Not so well known and quiet.'

He takes her hand. She feels the nearness of him. He has changed his shoes from sleek leather soles to old leather walking boots. He's been walking before, proper walking probably, up real mountains, perhaps in Switzerland or Spain, and Mona wishes she had boots to match and the memories that would go with them. She's wearing trousers at least and a fitted blouse with short sleeves. She has a light summer jacket because the sun has shone like a demon all morning and she would have felt a fool in a winter coat.

She follows him up a track between the trees that becomes a bridge over a shallow river that becomes a wide, dusty path that leads to a sort of meadow overlooking the town. They're so high up that she can see the sea and if she tried she could probably see her house and even the lane where the carpenter lives. But Karl walks quickly on towards a grey wooden bench facing the view.

'This,' he says as he sits down, 'is my secret. Ah.'

He takes off his bag and jacket and places them on the long grass. 'We will have to eat soon,' he says, looking up at the sun, 'or our meal will spoil. On second thoughts . . .'

He squirrels the bag under the seat of the bench and puts his jacket over it. 'The shade is better and it will keep everything cool.'

Mona copies him, takes her jacket off and walks away towards the view. 'It's beautiful, Karl. I'm ashamed to say I've never been here before. They say you don't appreciate the things on your doorstep.'

'Everything is beautiful from a distance, even our memories. Even the memories that were not once so good can be appreciated over time, don't you think?'

'Some of them,' she says.

He speaks still sitting on the bench. She can hear him catching his breath, hear the slight strain in his voice. 'From here you can see the whole of the town, the good and the bad, the electricity towers, there, look. And the industrial park to the right, see it?'

'Yes,' says Mona.

'And look by the bay, there. See, the cranes and the towers they are pulling down. We have to be thankful. We have only found one another because they destroyed the building that was between us.'

'Yes,' says Mona but she keeps her eyes on the horizon. Karl comes and stands next to her, puts his hand in the small of her back and points. 'Look there,' he says, 'you see? Elizabeth Gardens? Close your eyes. See the old black-and-white buildings in the old town and the cobbles and the pink houses, the terraces and lanes, this field and the brush of yellow flowers, I don't know their name. And the smell of the sun on the dust. And it makes us feel we are, at least, here on earth. We are alive.'

Mona keeps her face to the view. She doesn't trust herself to turn round and smile, doesn't trust herself not to look moved, so she says nothing.

Karl gives a little laugh. 'There is a small village in the south of France, spoiled now. We were young, Andreas and I, when we went there. He had some relatives there, an uncle I think, I'm not sure, but it was hardly a visit he wanted to make. His father had insisted. There was nothing there. Nothing. Sheep, old women in black. It was many years ago, Andreas and I were barely more than children. Anyway, Andreas went to pay his respects and we agreed to meet later. I found our hotel and unpacked and when he came back we took our boots and went walking up into the hills. No, they weren't hills, they were cliffs and we climbed with our bare hands. Where were we going? I don't know. Anything was better than the old people, listening to their terrible stories. You know what it is to be twenty.'

He looks down at her and shakes his head. 'You must have been beautiful then.'

She raises her eyebrows.

'Yes, I know. You think I don't know how that sounds but I do. You are beautiful now, of course. If you weren't, you could not have been beautiful at twenty. You could have been the girl from the village that we saw strip off in the bay. We climbed, Andreas and I, right to the top of a hill and sat down. She came from nowhere. Andreas put his fingers to his lips. Say nothing. We watched her pull her dress over her head and underneath? Naked. My God, the sight of her in the sun. She turned round with her arms raised overhead and made some kind of dance. No one was around. She couldn't see us in the trees. We were just boys.' Karl puts a hand over his mouth and gasps.

'Oh, it was like a moment for me. A moment when I grew up and knew something about the world. A naked woman with breasts. Not like the magazines I'd seen which made a boy feel bad inside but like a fairy tale or a film. She turned round in the sun, round and round, and then without any warning she flipped like a mermaid and dived into the sea.'

Karl is speaking to her but she can see he is still there on the cliff in the south of France.

'When she came out of the water, we watched her dress and had to wait for a long time until she went so we could climb down and go back to the village. And, of course, on the way back we got lost and returned to our hotel too late for dinner.'

He touches her on the cheek. 'The sight of that woman has never really left me. I have known many over the years but that one has stayed with me. After my marriage broke down I went back to that place. What was I hoping to see?'

Mona looks at him. 'What happened?'

'To my marriage? It lasted six months. It was a mistake and I was young. We both were.'

He claps his hands together. 'A toast!' He pulls the bag from under the bench. 'Warm white wine. And a screw top. *Je suis désolé.*'

'I don't mind,' Mona says. 'It's lovely of you.'

He opens the bottle and pours. They touch paper cups together. 'To what?' he asks.

'Memories,' she says, 'and dancing girls.'

He pulls his cup back. 'Memories? No, no. We are here. I am here with you. To us. On the top of the hill.' He has his eyes on her. 'Drink.'

Karl pours himself another inch of wine and quickly brushes her cheek with his lips. 'You drink and I make lunch.'

There are jars of things in oil and vinegar, pots of pâté, cheese and salami, spreads and dips and seeded crackers, things she's seen in supermarkets and never bought. There are paper napkins and plastic knives but no forks and all of it spread between them on the bench, enough for four.

'Eat, eat,' he says. 'It's hot and will spoil. Really we should be sitting at a long table under an arbour of jasmine with the juice of lemons on our fingers and crumbs on our laps. And a little dog snuffles around between our legs. We feed him and we shouldn't.'

'He will get fat.'

'That's it. Yes. He will get fat and we will get fat and that is as it should be, no? There are, in fact, several dogs at Packington House. They hunt. Or should I say they used to hunt. There is no hunting any more.'

'You've been to the house?'

'Many times, yes. Andreas knew them. Of course, the family have moved on, moved away. It was too expensive to maintain and too large, naturally. But when they lived there Andé had many invitations and I used to go with him. We stayed, oh, twenty times. Although no hunting, it would have been too dangerous for Andé should he fall. Andreas's family eventually bought property in this area because he was so enchanted with the Downs and the sea. They were very clever, very clever. They have many investments in this part of the world but, alas, not Packington. Yes, it's a beautiful house, many fine pictures, and the grounds, of course, as you see, immaculate. This is the best place though for me. Up here, now, with you. The very best place.'

They walk back down the hill and Karl guides them towards the house, talking about the architecture and the gardens. Wide stone steps lead up to the grand entrance and Mona stops at the bottom.

'Come, come,' says Karl and as they go inside a woman at a desk smiles and stands.

'Karl!' She wears a tailored dress in brilliant amber and a matching streak in her steel-grey hair. 'We hoped we might see you today.' She stares at him and turns slowly to Mona. 'Good weather, you see, it does bring them out. We were quite busy.'

'Mona,' says Karl, gesturing to the woman, 'this is Yvonne. Yvonne, this is Mona, my friend.' Her handshake is brief. She takes a few steps towards Karl and brushes non-existent dust from his shoulders. 'Have you been walking? Up the hill? Lovely view.'

She wears nail varnish, amber again. 'I put Max on this morning. He was good as gold and I did the afternoon myself. Wasn't too bad.' She leans in closer to Karl. 'But you were missed.'

Karl removes his satchel and stows it behind the woman's desk. 'We'll be quick,' he says and then grabs Mona's hand. 'Come on.'

He guides her towards the curving staircase. 'We only have fifteen minutes before it closes.'

'Karl!' Mona whispers. 'Where are we going?'

'Come.' They hurry along a long hallway, take another staircase up and then along a narrower corridor, blue swirls on the carpet, white swirls on the ceiling. They walk all the way to the far wing of the house and stop at the last door.

'Here,' says Karl, 'look,' and he opens a wooden door. It's a nursery full of toys and antique furniture, a little brass bed and a little wooden cot, little chairs painted in eau de Nil tucked under a little wooden table with turned legs. There's a rocking chair for the nanny and a rocking horse for the child. There is a miniature tea set on a nightstand and crocheted blankets folded at the end of the bed. And there are dolls propped up on the bed and on the mantelpiece and sitting on the window seat.

'I thought you would like to see this room,' says Karl, walking in. 'It is as the family used it during the war. The first war.'

Mona follows him in. There are photos of children on the wall, sepia, black-and-white, colour. There are rag rugs on the carpet and sticks in the fireplace waiting to be lit.

'Very few people come in here. It is only when there is a special tour.'

'You do the tours, Karl?'

'Occasionally, yes. Since I moved here I have had the time to do some voluntary work and, well, as I knew the house . . .'

'We shouldn't touch anything, should we?'

'No,' says Karl. 'We shouldn't, but, well . . .'

Mona would like to feel the cloth on the old dolls and examine the seams, peer at the stitching on the undergarments. She touches the dolls' faces with the very tips of her fingers. One of them has blue eyes with heavy lashes, another has paint worn on one cheek where a child has kissed it night after night. Still another has pigtails and a blunt fringe and is wooden, just like the carpenter makes, and is dressed in white cotton broderie anglaise and velvet with leather boots and white stockings.

'Oh, Karl, isn't it beautiful? Think of the children that lived in here.'

'Ah yes, fortunate I think.'

'Oh, it's very grand. What a lovely place to sit, a lovely place to look after children. And it overlooks the gardens and that little lake. Imagine it.'

'I thought you would like this room. The dolls,' he says again.

'Yes, yes I do, Karl. It's lovely. Very much, I do.'

'I'm afraid the house is closing now otherwise I could show you the bedrooms. Some of them are extraordinary.'

'That was so kind of you, Karl. Very thoughtful,' Mona says as he closes the door. 'Let's go before we get into trouble.'

He takes her hand as they walk along the corridor and down the stairs. Yvonne watches them from her desk. 'Your bag, Karl,' she says. 'I have to lock up now.'

She chivvies them through the door. 'And I think it's Tuesday next that we're expecting you, Karl. Bye now, bye.'

Mona doesn't turn and doesn't wave but slips her hand into Karl's as they leave and they have to hurry for the last bus from Packington House. He walks her to the door of her building and kisses her cheeks again.

'Next week?' he says.

'Next week.'

19

Mona told the women at the factory she had fallen pregnant. They were all middle-aged Brummies, a couple of young grandmothers, crude, outspoken and affectionate. They used her news to punctuate the monotony of their piecework, the jibes and jests flying across the assembly line.

'How long you been married? Didn't take him long, did it, love?'

'Length isn't everything, Dot.'

'You Catholics don't believe in the pill, do you, Mona?'

'Bet the Pope has got a few bastards toddling around the Vatican, though, eh?'

But eventually giving advice became irresistible to them. They began comparing notes and circulating old wives' tales. They kept asking her about dates and morning sickness, about pains in her back and cravings.

'It's a girl, then,' one would announce.

'First one's always late. You'll go two weeks over.'

'I wanted gherkins all the time,' said another, 'and I had twins.'

And then afterwards they talked about the equipment she would need and the best place to get it. The list went on and on. They asked her what she had in her bottom drawer but Mona had no bottom drawer and had no relatives to ask for anything. So when they got to clothes and linen, Mona spoke up.

'I'm making my own. I'm going to night school.'

'Oooh! She wants handmade!'

She had offers of second-hand stuff and some of the grandmothers wanted to bring in nappies and bibs that they said were hardly used. Mona had to be careful not to offend but she was firm.

'My mother used to make everything,' she said and because

they knew she was an orphan they relented. They began encouraging her and talking about the old times when there was nothing cheap and imported, no nylon and manmade fibres, when every baby had its own antique shawl, handed down from the nineteenth century.

Mona signed up for weekly night school at the community centre. She sat in front of a sewing machine there with a bundle of material, a pattern and a spool of yellow thread. The teacher was an exacting woman with a nasal Scottish accent. She did very little teaching but walked up and down the aisles between the students, adjusting tension and seams or raising an eyebrow at a piece of garish cloth. Mona tried to avoid her attention and just got on with her work. Not knowing the sex of her baby, Mona first concentrated on a two-piece suit, a smocked and embroidered top and little elasticated knickers edged in white lace. She thought of spring colours when the baby would be three months old and because by then she would know if she had a boy or a girl she planned a dress in pastel pink or a pair of dungarees in sky blue. She raced through the first outfit and after a couple of weeks the teacher picked up Mona's work and gave her a nudge.

'You have a definite flair,' she said. 'Undoubtedly.'

Mona blushed. She had no sewing machine at home so began hand-stitching every evening, often sitting by candlelight during the power cuts while William read the paper or snoozed in a chair. She found herself humming and daydreaming, losing track of place and time, thinking only of the next stitch or the next outfit or the match of one colour against another.

By the time she is eight months pregnant Mona has made, in various shades of yellow, lilac, cream and white, seven romper suits, two cot blankets, four bonnets, a quilted coat, a christening gown, two pairs of linen dungarees and three sleepsuits. Then she gives up work and begins to knit as well. She sits on the bus to and from the community centre and works on a cardigan or shawl, she knits while she watches television with William in the evening and knits and knits until her fingers ache or her eyes close.

She keeps everything in a wooden box under the bed. The box is also handmade, painted white with a little rocking horse engraved on the side. Later, she will paint the baby's name and date of birth on the top.

One Thursday before she leaves for her class she pulls the box out and examines the stock she has built up. Everything is perfect. Now Mona can say she has a bottom drawer. Yes, she has a bottom drawer and she has beautiful things that can be passed down from her children to their children, handmade garments, heirlooms that, one day, someone will touch and say 'My granny made this in 1974'. The thought fills her with joy and peace.

As she shoves the box back under the bed she feels a sharp pain in her side. It's gone as quickly as it arrives and Mona wonders, not for the first time, what the agony of birth will be like. The women at work spoke about it all the time and made no secret of the horrors of labour and how their skin ripped and was stitched up again without anaesthetic, the hours and hours they screamed on their hospital beds. But afterwards, they swore, it was all worth it.

20

Mona's premonition comes quick and hard on 1st November 1974. She's washing up, her hands deep in the hot water, bubbles tickling her arms. She's so big she can't get close to the sink any more so she has to lean forward and press her belly, not too hard, against the cold metal. She's humming a tune and staring through the window at the square concrete yard that leads to an alley behind the terrace. It's late afternoon and she's waiting for the right time to start the dinner. She has a couple of pork chops to fry and some potatoes to boil with carrots and cauliflower, things that will spoil if she starts too early. She's tidied the kitchen and half filled a saucepan with water, put it on a low flame.

She didn't wash up after their breakfast that morning. She just sat around all day, dozing and knitting. She had several cups of tea, a sandwich for lunch and then lay down again. Unable to stay still at night, her days have become one long, lovely rest after another. She has a day's worth of dishes to wash up before William comes home.

So she hums and watches a little brown bird land on the back gate, watches it fly off again and quite suddenly she knows. She puts her hand on her belly and feels the life drain away. Her breaths come shallow and quick. She pulls out a kitchen chair and sits down. She will not panic. No. She will wait it out. She will stay where she is until the baby kicks, until she knows it's fine. Until everything goes back to normal, back to the way it was five seconds before. She will wait for hours if she has to. Days. For the whole two and a half weeks before their baby is due. Her father told her that there was nothing good in trying to see into the future. Hadn't he said that? She's been spooked by nothing more than a sparrow. She has only to sit down and wait for the baby to kick and when it does she'll get up, put a flame to the frying pan and start the dinner.

Everyone in Kilmore went to see Peggy Slattery at some time or another; pregnant women, farmers with a poor crop, the parents of a sick child, a new widow. Father Byrne would periodically say something from the pulpit, his thin and savage voice pronouncing soothsaying, sign-watching, tea-reading, star-gazing and the like as the work of Satan. Everyone tried to look innocent and meet the eye of the priest. Some would look away and wring the hands that the night before they had laid palm up on Peggy Slattery's kitchen table. Others, women with stretched bellies, would glance down and remember the kneading of Peggy Slattery's fingers on their skin and her comforting whisper, 'Ah, you're not to worry, he's grand in there.' But right at the front of the congregation, Peggy Slattery herself maintained a blank and guilt-free face.

One night, according to Mona's father, Peggy Slattery sat straight up in her bed at ten minutes after ten. She dragged a shawl over her nightdress and headed out barefoot up the low lane to Bridie O'Connor's big house. She hammered on the door until it opened. Bridie asked her what she wanted and Peggy Slattery stared at her, shook her head, said nothing and slunk away. It was all over the village the next day with the conclusion that the fortune teller had finally lost her mind.

When Bridie O'Connor got the news that her only son had fallen off the scaffolding in New York on his birthday one week later, to the hour, Bridie went running down to Peggy Slattery's cottage and the two women fell to the floor crying, holding on to each other, inconsolable.

Some called it a coincidence. Mona, who was fifteen at the time, called it magic but Mona's father frowned at her.

'There's no such thing as magic, Mona. Nor is it coincidence as such. Nor is it the work of the devil or guesswork or witchcraft or hocus-pocus. It's none of these things. Is everything explainable? No. Is it from God?' he said as he put his hat on at the front door. He was off for his evening walk down the lane to the beach with his stout rubber boots and walking stick.

133

'Ask yourself this. Is it good? That would be my advice. Ask yourself, is it a good thing to know the future, Mona? Maybe so.' He kissed her before he left. 'But.'

He would be gone for half an hour or so. She would make the supper, brown bread, butter and jam, cold apple pie and a pot of cream, some ham if there was any left. When he came back they would eat together off their laps in front of the fire and take up the conversation where they left off.

'She could bet on the horses, couldn't she, Dadda?'

'Who?'

'Peggy.'

He looked at her over his glasses. 'Do you mean gambling, Mona?' But he was smiling. Everyone in the village would have a wager on the Irish Grand National every Easter and crowd around the television and radio to see who won. Mona never did.

'Maybe we could take the teapot round when we've finished.'

'For the leaves? You've no need to go that far. I know what she'll say, pet,' he said, draining his cup.

'What?'

'That whoever made this tea has homework to do. Mathematics homework for her exams. And let me see, now.' Her father squinted and looked up to the sky. 'Oh yes, and somewhere just dimly I can see the promise of a trip with her old father. Yes, a trip to the cinema on Sunday.'

Mona got up and hugged him.

'Really?'

'Really.'

So Mona couldn't recall what conclusions they came to about the future and Peggy Slattery's premonitions. She only remembered Peggy Slattery's funeral that same year and the huge wreath that Bridie O'Connor laid on the coffin.

William finds Mona on the chair at six o'clock, sobbing into a tea towel and the kitchen full of steam.

She convinces him after five full minutes.

'Are you positive?' he asks.

'Yes, William. I just had a funny feeling, that's all,' she says, wiping her face. 'And then I felt a kick and I just, you know, I just was so relieved.'

He puts a mug in front of her and takes her hands. 'You're sure?'

'I'm sure.'

'We could get a taxi to the hospital. Get everything checked out.'

'No, no. I'm being stupid. I was thinking about when I was a little girl and there was this woman who used to predict things and then I saw a bird and then I just imagined something going wrong. I feel stupid now.'

William closes her fingers round the mug and makes her drink. 'What have you eaten today?'

'It's not that. Honest to goodness, I've had a sandwich and biscuits and I'm not even tired neither. Remember, William, the midwife said that just before they're born they go quiet and keep their energy for the birth. And anyway, the baby just kicked so it's all right.'

'Yes,' he says after a while. 'She did say the baby would be quiet. Yes.'

She watches him struggling with his fears. She knows he's thinking the worst, wants the ambulance called and a doctor on standby. She knows she keeps him awake at night, twisting and shuffling in the bed, and that every morning he can hardly wake up. And after all Gallagher's promises, they're laying people off right, left and centre. One late morning and William would be out of a job. They'd both be unemployed. He mutters in his sleep, doesn't eat, stares off into space, and no wonder. He's exhausted with worry. And now this.

'William, come on, it's nothing. Have your tea,' she says, holding on to the table to get herself upright. 'Then later pop out for a drink with Tom. Didn't he say you were to call for him? Go on. You go out and let me lie down on the sofa. Yes? Good.'

He stands behind her while she peels the potatoes, his hands cradling her belly, his head on her shoulder.

'I think I will go out,' he says, 'just for an hour.'

21

Tricia is standing behind the reception desk pouring sweets into a big glass bowl when Mona pushes the door open.

'Hello, Tricia. Anything for me today?'

'Only some white curls. We had a bloke in the other day, old bloke with a big head of hair who wanted a number one all over. He went from farmer to farmhand in about ten minutes if you know what I mean.' She winked. 'Took years off him.'

'Oh, white curls are great. I can use them.'

'Adele! Adele!' Tricia raises her eyebrows, fills her lungs with air and bellows. 'Adele!'

The Whippet saunters in from the back. 'Yeah?'

'Bag of white curls. Drawer near the fridge. And two coffees, please.'

As soon as the girl has gone, Tricia puts both hands on top of her head. 'I will definitely, definitely swing for that child before the week is out. She's either deaf or canny. If I find out she's canny, she's out. I tell myself she's deaf out of the goodness of my heart and a legitimate fear of industrial tribunals. Anyway, how's you?'

'I was thinking of having a haircut.'

Tricia jerks forward. 'Come again?'

'A haircut.'

'A trim?'

'No.'

'A proper haircut? With scissors?'

'Yes. Short. Very short. Really short.'

'Short like that?' Tricia points to a huge poster on the wall.

'Yes.'

'You sure, Mona? You won't regret it but I don't want you doing it just because I say so. It's your choice,' but as she speaks she peels Mona's coat from her shoulders and sits her in a chair. 'At bloody last.'

Mona keeps her eyes closed all through the cutting stage. She clutches her coffee cup and sips from time to time but she cannot look up. At last, Tricia says she's finished.

'You can look up now.'

'No, I'll wait, I'll wait.'

'No, come on. Be brave.'

Mona's head looks smaller but her face looks better. Her eyes seem too big for their sockets somehow and her neck has grown three inches.

'We're not finished. Blow-dry now and you're done. Finger-dry, actually, you've still got a good bit of natural wave. Just you wait. What changed your mind?'

'Oh, just wanted a new look, that's all. A birthday makeover.'

'You did right, love. You look fabulous or you will in a minute. Don't worry.'

But Mona's not worried. Trish was right all along. 'I love it, Trish.'

'Did you see next door?' says Tricia over the hairdryer.

'The burger place? Is it open?'

'Oh yes, it's open all right. Fried chicken, burgers, kebabs. Chips with everything. Does deliveries day and night. My flat upstairs stinks like an abattoir the amount of meat going in and out of that place. He's got boys dressed in red and white on motor-bikes and pushbikes and a bloody great van.'

Tricia tugs at Mona's hair with her fingers, raking it forward and back, and curling it again and again.

'Keith, the bloke's called. Wide as you like but there's something wrong with him if you ask me.'

'Oh?'

'He's got a big sign on the front. Three big red letters on a white background with a big red rooster at each end. Can't believe you didn't notice. Anyway, it won't be up for long, he's going to have to change it.'

137

'How's that?'

'Well, when I asked him about the sign he said he'd only called it after the name of the shop. Keith's Kebab Kabin. I said, "You can't do that, Keith, love. They'll have you in court." '

'Why?'

Tricia turns the dryer off and puts her hand on her hip.

'KKK.'

Mona laughs and Tricia turns the hairdryer back on.

'Bloody idiot. Anyway, he did tell me a good joke.'

'Go on.'

'This couple are in bed. It's their wedding night.'

When Mona walks in, the carpenter is cleaning ash from the wood burner. He turns when he hears her and drops the brush. He stares at her and opens his mouth but nothing comes out.

Mona's hand flies up her neck, all that new exposed skin, the cold wind on it.

'Fancied a change,' she says and walks to the far side of the workshop and picks up one of the five dolls he's made since she was last there. It's been a week, longer than usual.

'I've got an old doll that needs repairing for a little girl. I keep meaning to bring it down for you. Can you take a look?' she says, keeping her back to him. 'Oh and I've had a couple of orders from the States. Rush jobs, the same client wants two for Christmas presents. She wants varnish instead of paint and she wants teak. I can't decide if that's a good idea. On the other hand, I do that for the black dolls so we can see the wood. So I might start doing varnish on a lighter wood. You'd have to do it for me though, the varnishing I mean. I'm too busy these days.'

She knows he's watching, can feel his eyes on her.

'I've been taking the odd afternoon off. Thought I might try and have a bit of a social life for a change. All work and no play isn't good for anyone. I went up to Packington House the other day. Have you been?'

He says nothing but he's watching, she can feel it. She sees then that there's a lump of milk-white wood on the bench. Even in its roughness, there's the beginnings of his handiwork; it has a pale beauty, an even grain in white circular lines like they were drawn by hand, like the contours of a face. It will shine when it's oiled, it will glow. She strokes it.

'This is special,' she says across the room. He's sanding the armoire now with short, rhythmic, sifting strokes, scratching at the wood. 'This will be nice when it's finished. It's different,' she says and moves to pick it up.

He's quick beside her, moves it out of her way and stows it under the bench. He turns his back to her and his voice is sharp. 'Teak, oak, ash, yew, varnish, oil, light wood, dark wood,' he says. 'I can make whatever you want.'

'Sorry? Whatever I want? That's not quite right, is it?'

He bangs the door of the wood burner. 'If you want big ones, I'll make big ones. Small ones, I'll make them too. And I'll make the babies but that's it.'

Mona picks up two of the finished dolls and puts them in the carrier bag with the white curls. 'Right. I'll tell you what, just make the two dolls. Teak. Varnish. I'll bring the little girl's doll for repair and you can do that as well. And don't say you make whatever I want because that's not true. And you know it.'

'I make the dolls for the women and the dolls for the shop and the toys. Whatever you order for the business, I'll make it.'

'Yes, I know. I remember. You said. You've made that very, very clear right from the beginning. I heard you.'

She pauses at the door. 'Do you like it? My hair?'

He won't speak. She walks down the stairs and takes the long way home.

Mona rings Val that evening.

'How's your mother, love?'

Val starts crying halfway through the telling and Mona's heart aches for her friend.

'So, it's not Alzheimer's then? Parkinson's? Really? Oh dear.'

Mona listens until Val has recovered and is making light of it as usual. 'There's no shaking. No, they don't all shake. You would think I would know it with all my years of nursing but I've never seen anyone with such a rapid decline. She's a pain in the bloody arse as you know but I'd rather have that than the silence and the mumbling. I mean, a few months ago she was still telling me about my grey roots.'

'On the subject of roots,' says Mona, 'I've had my hair done.'

'Cut?'

'Short.'

'No.'

Mona giggles. 'Short short!'

'About time. Aren't I always saying how it suits you short? Bet it looks great.'

'You'll see when I come up. And I've had a date. Three.'

'You're kidding me?'

'No. Karl, that's his name.'

'Bloody good for you,' says Val. 'Not before time, Mona. I'm happy for you, love.'

'I'll tell you all about it in November. But listen, let's do something, Val. Take a holiday. I want to go somewhere hot. Somewhere with great food and music and lemon groves.' Mona looks out at the flats opposite and the grainy light behind closed curtains, at swirling spits of rain caught in the street lamps, at the sea disappearing into the night. Karl isn't there. She closes her eyes. 'I want a bit of heat in my bones, a bit of luxury. I want to stay in a nice hotel and sleep with the windows open in the south of France.'

'Yes, yes! Count me in, I could do with a break. I'll get Mum sorted and then we can plan something. I'll get some brochures. You all right otherwise?'

'Me? Grand, grand.'

'Okay, bye, love.'

'Bye.'

22

On Wednesday, outside the cafe, Karl surveys her front and back. He takes her arm.

'It suits you very much, Mona. Chic. Sophisticated.'

'I used to have it like this when I was young,' she says, touching the back of her neck and caressing the wisps that Trish has left around her face.

'You are still young, Mona. And very attractive. You must know this. Come, I thought this afternoon we might go to the antiques fair on Stanley Street. Did you see the advertisement? It says it opens at eight in the morning until eight o'clock in the evening so we have plenty of time. But with antiques fairs, you have to expect that the best things will have gone immediately. Still, as we are only looking . . .'

He takes the outside of the pavement and never lets her go, taking a step back to allow another pedestrian to pass, smiling always and chatting as they go.

'You never know what you will find in these places. I have been to many auction houses, to the best, all over the world, New York, Stockholm, London, of course.'

Karl guides her out of the way of a gaggle of children coming up from the beach. They aren't children really, more like mini adults, the girls in short skirts showing too much bare skin, the sun bright in their eyes, the boys gangly and awkward, showing off. They take up the whole pavement with their loud loveliness.

'One can spend too much with only the blink of an eye or a slight movement at the wrong time.' He nudges her and when she looks up he is smiling.

The antiques centre smells of beeswax and old houses. Some of the stallholders have arranged the furniture into mock living or dining rooms with aspidistras and table runners. Everywhere are Tiffany lamps and oil paintings in gilt frames, silver cutlery in the open drawers of maple dressers, vases and pitchers in porcelain and glass, rings and necklaces locked away in pretty display cabinets at the front of the stalls. They meander through the aisles together, Karl pointing out the things that catch his eye, Mona running her fingers over the polished desks and cabinets, over the fur stoles on headless mannequins. She has long wondered about a little real fur jacket for one of her dolls but her good sense tells her it would be a mistake, that her customers would think she sanctioned hunting and killing and that, no matter how beautiful it looked, she would always be in the wrong.

They come to a stall where the furniture is arranged like an Edwardian sitting room; two battered leather chesterfield chairs, an open book face down on one arm, a low table of polished oak with two silver coasters, a cut-glass decanter, all of it sitting on a worn Persian rug. There is a standard lamp in one corner and a brass coal scuttle. With a squint of the eye, you could half expect the master of the house to walk in and take up the book where he left off.

She moves slowly through the room. It becomes quieter the further in she goes and because there is no window and no daylight, it could be evening time, just after dinner. Mona sits in one of the chairs and runs her fingers over the curve of the arms and the cool, brass studs. She looks at the one opposite and is surprised to see Karl sitting in it. He rests his head against the back with his eyes closed.

'Ah,' he says. 'Imagine it.'

'What?'

'We have just come in from the opera – no, the theatre. Something by Oscar Wilde perhaps. We had a wonderful evening and now we have come home. In a minute, the girl will come in and light the fire.' He opens one eye and whispers, 'We have servants, naturally.' He closes his eyes again and Mona laughs.

'So,' he continues. 'She has lit the fire. She leaves but wait!' Karl holds up a finger. 'Who will bring the whiskey?'

Mona is about to speak.

'Oh dear, it must be my turn. Very well.' He gets up and takes a decanter from the display. He carries it casually, swinging it from the neck. He sits down and pours into two empty glasses on the table.

'Chin-chin,' he says and motions for her to pick up her glass but before she can move the stallholder appears.

'Beautiful chairs, aren't they?' he says and stands behind Mona. 'So comfortable. 1930s. Notice the marbling in the leather. Well-worn but without cracks. I think these have been well looked after. Probably from a gentleman's house.'

Mona catches Karl's eye and he raises one eyebrow. 'Oh, a gentleman,' he copies.

'Yes, these are in fact European, maybe French, a pair.' The man runs his hands along the leather. 'Deeply curved barrel-shaped backs, sprung seats. Loose cushions which can be restored. Quite handsome and capacious as you can see.' He taps the side of the chair with the flat of his hand. 'Traditional design, standing on squared tapering legs with the original brass and brown ceramic castors. Beautiful examples. A pair.'

Karl gets up and walks over to Mona. He lifts the open book on the arm.

'Was I reading this?' he says to Mona. 'Or were you? We seem to have been interrupted.'

'I think it was your novel, dharlink,' says Mona. 'Do continue.'

Karl holds the book in one hand, picks up one of the crystal tumblers and pretends to swill his drink and gulp it down. He holds it up to the stallholder and says, 'Same again, would you?'

The stallholder's smile is wide and indulgent. He takes the glass and puts it back in its cabinet. Then he picks up a champagne saucer and hands it to Mona.

'These are my personal favourites. Again, simply beautiful examples. Not quite the same period. Circa 1910, one of almost a complete set. Tumblers, port and wine, red and white. Extremely rare to find such a collection. Heavy cut. Circular facets on the side, ten-sided base, star-cut underneath. Beautiful.'

'Oh, they are,' says Mona, holding the glass to the light. It sits heavy in her hand and she can just faintly smell the remnants of something, feel the trace of another hand and another evening with this glass, in this chair in front of a fire. She wants to drink. She holds the glass to her mouth and stops. Karl is looking at her.

'Go on,' he whispers. 'Imagine.'

She looks at the glass but sees they are being watched. 'They are beautiful,' she says. 'Aren't they, Karl?'

'Well,' he replies. He selects another glass and examines it like a jeweller. He runs his fingers round the rim and pings his fingernail against the side. 'Good quality, certainly.'

'In my opinion,' says the stallholder, 'champagne should not be drunk from a flute but from a saucer.'

'A coupe,' says Karl.

'Sorry?'

'A coupe or a bowl. It allows the champagne to lose its carbonation, bubbles. It is also best for aroma although not everyone would agree.'

The stallholder keeps his smile wide and constant. 'We'll split the set,' he says and points to the other four glasses in the cabinet behind Mona's chair. 'These would make quite a gift. Or something for a special occasion.'

Mona stands and looks in the cabinet. The stallholder opens the door and gestures to the tumblers on the top shelf. 'Like I said, we can split the set. Any set. These tumblers, set of eight, are one hundred and seventy-five pounds.'

Karl gets to his feet and joins them, peering into the cabinet.

'Do you drink champagne, Mona?' he asks.

'Oh, it depends on the occasion.'

'Ha!' says Karl and taps the side of his nose. 'Occasions can be created.' He leads her from the gentleman's study and back into the aisle.

'Shall we have champagne this evening?' he says. He squeezes her fingers, draws her in close and drapes his arm on her shoulder. He smells of herbs, of cologne, like it's deep in his skin, in his blood.

'This evening?' she says. 'Where?'

'Wherever we want, away from whispering salesmen. On our own. I would like to eat with you this evening. Just the two of us. Would you like that, Mona?' He comes closer with every word until his lips brush the side of her cheek.

'I'm not sure, Karl.'

He runs the tip of his finger against her cheek. 'This hairstyle has changed you, Mona. You look different. Even more beautiful.'

Mona feels the burn on her cheeks, wonders if the salesman is watching, if they look daft, like two young lovers who can't wait to be alone.

'It's too early to part, I think, Mona?' He curls his arm round her. 'Do you agree?'

She can feel his body through his suit, through his shirt, wonders what his skin would be like to touch. Her breath comes short and she speaks in a rush. 'Maybe,' she says.

His hand is firm in the small of her back; it moves by inches into the curve of her waist. 'Let's go,' he says.

Outside on the street, the lights have come on, it's almost evening, people hurrying past them to home, to children, to relaxation. They walk down towards the pier.

'An early supper perhaps,' says Karl. 'Maybe the new fish restaurant, you know the one?'

Mona looks ahead and sees a light on in the carpenter's workshop.

'Or maybe not fish,' says Karl, trying to see her face. 'We have all evening. Perhaps a drink first.'

Karl talks on and on about restaurants and bars she's never been to. He seems to know them all. Mona hasn't seen the carpenter for two days. She's been too busy. She would have gone today but for Karl. She should have told him she wasn't coming. He might have something for her.

'Cocktails,' he says. 'Although not on an empty stomach. No, I think –'

Mona stops suddenly. 'I've just remembered, I've got a couple of orders from America. They're very particular, the Americans.

And I've got to collect some dolls from the carpenter and get them finished.'

'Tonight? Now?'

'Yes, sorry, Karl. I should have said earlier.'

He steps back and for a moment he says nothing. 'The carpenter. I see,' he says. 'A pity.'

'I'm really sorry. I didn't remember until just now. I should have said.'

Karl nods slowly. 'Of course,' he says. 'No matter.'

Mona hurries off. She forgets to kiss him goodbye. She forgets to turn and wave.

23

Mona knows something is definitely wrong when she goes to the toilet towards the end of her sewing class.

The same pain in her side, like a period pain but not as bad. A bit of an ache in her back, like a period pain but not as bad. A slick of blood in her knickers, black-red and heavy. Exactly like a period.

She flushes the toilet, washes her hands and her heart turns over. She walks back to the class and makes an excuse. Backache, tiredness, something she ate. Everyone waves her goodbye and tells her to get some rest. She wonders if she is as pale and sick-looking as she feels. She picks up her handbag and the shopping basket with her sewing inside and closes the classroom door behind her. Her coat no longer buttons over her belly and outside the cold wind dances her dress up and down as she waits for the bus. She can feel the warm blood between her legs; if there was any more it would start to trickle down her legs. William is out in town but he's never late. He will be back soon.

She climbs on the bus, gripping the metal poles as she inches into her seat and squeezes her legs together. She's so near her due date and lots of babies come early so she repeats like a mantra over and over, 'You're worrying about nothing, Mona. Calm down. Calm down. Calm down.' But the tears force their way through and the worry coils round her chest like a serpent. The bus is half empty. She balances her bag on what bit of lap she has left and slips her hands down her knickers. Oozing, sticky, warm and wet. She draws her hand out and looks at her fingers. Blood is never a good thing, is it?

William isn't in when she gets home. She goes straight to the toilet, takes her knickers off and wipes herself with toilet paper. She wipes again and again and then takes a sanitary towel from the bathroom cabinet and puts on a clean pair of knickers. Her hands are hot and shaking, her legs barely take her weight. She has her hospital bag packed. Two brand-new nightdresses, a dressing gown, a toiletries bag with Lily of the Valley talcum powder, a new bar of soap and a white flannel, a toothbrush and a mini tube of toothpaste that was more expensive than a proper-sized one. All ready. She doesn't take off her coat because as soon as William comes in they will be off. This is it. The baby is coming. She hasn't had a contraction but any minute now her waters will break. It's started.

She can't stand and she can't sit still. She knows without looking that she's still losing blood. She goes to the payphone in the hall-way and lifts the receiver. She dials 999 but before it can ring she puts the receiver down. William will be very annoyed if she goes without him. In the living room she writes on the back of an envelope 'Hospital! Hurry up!' She picks the phone up again and dials.

It's funny what the woman says, 'Is this an absolute emergency?' Mona hesitates but says, 'Yes, it is.'

'Do you have any other means of getting to hospital?' says the operator.

Mona looks at the receiver as though she can see her down the curling wire.

'I'm having a baby!' Mona shouts.

The operator tells her there has been a major incident and that all available ambulances are involved but she must hang on, one would come as quickly as possible. Just hang on.

Mona puts the receiver down and goes back to the mantelpiece. William, William, come home. Her knickers are soaking and something is wrong. Where is the pain and the doubling contractions the women at work spoke about? Where are the breaking waters and the baby's kick? She picks up the envelope and puts a kiss at the bottom of the page and writes 'Please'.

She'll wait outside. Either William will come first or the ambulance but if she's outside it will save time. She picks up her handbag and her little case and she stands outside the gate. The squalls of

148

drizzle are welcome on her hot face and when she looks towards town the wind buffets her hair, swirling it around her face so she can hardly see. She'll look terrible when the ambulance comes. And when she remembers there's no hairbrush in her overnight bag, she suddenly begins to cry.

'William, hurry up,' she whispers. 'I'm frightened.'

A siren in the distance sounds like it's getting nearer but then it whines away and disappears. A rivulet of blood pools in her shoe. She walks to the kerb and strains to see as far as she can down the wide road. Nothing.

'Come on! Come on!' she shouts. 'Where are you?'

Her legs are sticky and wet and when she sees a car coming she walks out into the middle of the road, waving with both hands. 'Help me!' she screams.

24

William, William.

Mona's lying on a narrow hospital bed with wheels. 'There are no wheelchairs,' one young nurse says to another nurse and they both start crying. An older nurse comes and tells them off. 'Be quiet,' she says. 'You have a patient. Control yourself, Archer.'

Nurse Archer has an afro with a little white starched hat perched on top. She steers Mona through swinging doors and on to a ward.

William, William.

There is screaming somewhere. The ward is dim, like everyone's asleep. Nurse Archer speaks to the Sister behind the desk.

'We haven't got any paperwork. It's chaos down there. Thirty-eight weeks, vaginal bleed, heavy. We've got no wheelchairs, she's on a bed. Name's Mona MacNaughton, twenty years of age, date of birth –'

'All right, Archer, all right.'

The midwife holds her hand up like she's directing traffic. She comes round to the side of Mona's bed and leans down.

'When did this start, the pain and the bleeding?'

'Early on today. Is the baby all right?'

'That's what we're going to find out. You're not to worry.'

Then the midwife starts ordering people around and telling them where to put the bed and pointing at the end of the ward and saying, 'Get Dr Blake,' and, 'Curtains, curtains,' and asking all the time where her auxiliaries are and someone needs to get the mother undressed and get the mother cleaned and now, now, now. And Mona realizes that she is the mother.

Nurse Archer is only the same age as Mona but she does everything at top speed and Mona thinks it's a good job that her hat is secured with two black grips because it bobs and shakes all the time. In fact, the more Mona looks, the more Nurse Archer seems to be spinning and then moving in slow motion, her face up close to Mona, saying, 'Stay awake, stay awake.'

It feels lovely to have somebody in charge, tugging her wet tights off and taking the dead weight of the handbag off her chest. Somewhere there is a radio on but no music and outside the window the whoop and wail of ambulances and police cars as though everyone knows there is a disaster going on, everyone knows that Mona is bleeding to death and her baby is hurt.

Three people stand round her bed. There is Nurse Archer, the midwife and a doctor in a white coat. They're talking so fast that Mona can't follow what they're saying. 'Emergency' is the only word that she understands. If she wasn't made of concrete with a head as heavy as a cannonball she would sit up and ask questions and she would scream at them to do something, or if William would come he wouldn't let them stand around saying things like 'placenta' and 'foetal distress' without explaining anything. No, William would be all, 'Help my wife! Help my baby! Do something!' But Mona can hear herself groaning and crying like a child that's fallen over and cut her knee.

The doctor puts a metal trumpet on Mona's belly and keeps saying, 'That's the maternal pulse, wait, no, that's the maternal pulse. No.'

He stands up and turns his back so Mona can't see his face.

'Get it out,' he says. 'Induce immediately.'

'Yes, doctor.'

'I have to go. Downstairs is hell. I've never seen anything like it. Call me if you need me.'

More nurses rush in with blood and drips and sometimes the curtain is left open and there's whispering and nurses saying, 'I'll go down, I'll take over,' and the midwife all the time saying, 'I can't spare anyone else.'

It hurts when Nurse Archer puts a needle in the back of Mona's hand and straps it down and Mona wants to cry all over again with the pain but when she remembers what the women at the factory have told her to expect she knows that this is nothing. She's got it all to come.

'Sorry, sorry,' says Nurse Archer and she puts her cool hand on Mona's forehead and strokes her hair. 'It will be over soon.'

'Is William here?' Mona mutters.

'Who?'

'When William comes, I want to see him.'

'Okay.'

'Tell him to hurry up.'

'I will. Ssshh now.'

'Is something wrong?'

'Don't cry. It will all be over soon.'

But it isn't soon. It's forty-nine minutes. Pain comes slowly like huge crashing waves, breaking over her, breaking and breaking until there is no space between them, until she's in the eye of the storm. Nurse Archer keeps count and goes off all the time to tell the midwife. 'I think she's ready,' she says eventually and just outside the door Mona hears the midwife hiss, 'She's Irish, isn't she?'

'I think so,' says Nurse Archer.

'Irish! There's police downstairs saying it's the IRA. Two bombs.'

Nurse Archer gasps.

Then the curtain is ripped back and the midwife bustles in. She has a white mask on and so does Nurse Archer now. Mona's legs are lifted into stirrups and the midwife places her hand on Mona's belly.

'You'll need to push it out, I'm afraid.'

'Mona,' says Nurse Archer. 'Her name's Mona, Sister.'

'Thank you, Archer. You'll need to push it out, Mona.' She's as cool and precise as Bridie O'Connor but her eyes are not bright and searching, they are still and black. They hold Mona's a long while. 'There is no other way,' she says.

But pushing isn't as easy as it sounds and Nurse Archer has to hold Mona's head up and grasp her hand and keen with her and tell her to keep going, keep going, that's it, keep going, bear down, one more, keep pushing, and Mona does because she wants to do everything right for her baby and because they are trying their best to make it all right and isn't she in the right place after all, with nurses and doctors all around and hasn't she got a drip of blood in one hand and a different drip in the other and the nurse is right, it will soon be over and it will all be all right.

Mona grinds her teeth and drives her life-force into the big muscles in her legs. 'Get her chin on her chest.' Right into her backside. 'Keep going.' Deep down into her bowels. 'Bear down.' Her groin. 'That's it.' Her gut. 'That's the head.' Her throat and head and face and teeth and then she feels the give and the tear and the letting-go. And she sees the midwife making short quick movements, careful and precise.

'Lie her down,' she says to the nurse. 'Get her head down.'

Nurse Archer lets Mona's head down on the pillow and she's too tired to lift it up again. In a minute, Mona's baby will cry and they will hold it in the air and say 'A girl!' or 'A boy!' In a moment, they will wrap the baby in a pure white towel and lay it over Mona's heart just like she's imagined. Mona will see its little face, tiny hands curled over, William's black hair, her blue eyes. In a second, Mona's baby will cry. The midwife will say 'Seven pounds five ounces' or 'Five pounds nine ounces' and she'll say 'Ssshh' to the baby because it's shocked at being in the world. Any second, Mona's baby will cry.

Somewhere far off there is the most horrendous screeching. 'She's torn.' Some poor woman is bellowing and crying and has lost her mind. 'Clean her up.' She is crying for her baby. 'I want my baby!' 'Stitch her up.' 'Where is my baby? I want my baby!' Mona is still made of concrete and her head is still as heavy as a cannonball and she is still lying down, rolling from side to side, but her mouth is working all on its own, screaming and screaming, and the terrible noise is not far off, it's coming out of Mona's own throat.

A different nurse parts the curtain and brings her a glass of water. 'Here you are, bab, drink this. Come on now, love. Have a sip of water. Come on, sit up. Ssshh, ssshh.'

The nurse has to hold the cup and Mona can't swallow because of the words in her throat that are trying to come out.

'Where's my baby?' she says but it comes lumping out all ragged and bruised.

'I'll get the Sister. Wait a minute.'

Mona's mouth starts working on its own again, crying and calling for her baby, and it only stops when Nurse Archer comes in with her fingers on her lips. She comes straight over to Mona and puts her arms out.

'You have to be quiet. You have to be.' She gathers Mona up and holds her close. Mona sobs.

'Listen, ssshh,' says the nurse. 'Ssshh, listen. Mona, isn't it? Mona, ssshh. I'm Val. Listen to me. Your baby was a little girl. And your little girl is gone.'

Mona's wails are muffled against the nurse's shoulder.

'Ssshh,' says Nurse Archer. 'Ssshh. Listen, you have to be quiet, you have to be. If you keep screaming they send for a psychiatrist and they come and give you a drug to put you out. You don't want that. You have to be quiet.'

Mona holds on to the nurse and bites down on the noise. 'Where is she, please? Can I see her, please?'

The nurse says nothing for a moment. She strokes the back of Mona's head and takes a deep breath.

'They've put the baby in a special place. She's gone now.'

'I want her back.'

'Ssshh, she's gone now, Mona. She's gone, that's all you have to know.'

'I want her.'

'Don't shout. Stop shouting,' but Mona can hear the tears in the nurse's voice.

'Please.'

The nurse moves back. She wipes Mona's face with a corner of her apron. She wipes her own. She holds Mona firm and strong on her shoulders.

'Wait. All right? Just wait and be quiet. Can you be quiet?'

Mona nods. The nurse disappears through the curtains and Mona lies down on her side. When William comes she will never, ever, ever be able to explain how the baby died. He will go mad when he knows. He will ask that doctor how they let the baby die and what it died of and why they didn't slap it and make it cry. Her. Her. Why didn't they slap her and make her cry?

When the curtains are parted, Nurse Archer comes in with a white bundle. She puts her fingers over her lips and says again, 'Ssshh.' Mona sits up and holds her arms out. Nurse Archer puts Mona's baby in her lap. 'She's a good weight, isn't she? Seven pounds two ounces.'

Mona's baby's eyes are closed like she's fast asleep, as perfect as you could wish. She has two tiny perfect little fists and in one of them Nurse Archer has slipped a white flower, a daisy.

'She's brought you a little present,' says the nurse. She peeps out through the curtains then walks back to Mona. 'Now listen,' she says, 'you have to be quiet. This isn't allowed. You have to be really quiet. I'll come back in a few minutes. You're not to move. Don't make a sound. No one must know.'

Mona doesn't see the nurse go and doesn't hear the radio any more or the sirens and whispering and ambulances coming and going right under her window. She wraps her baby up tight in the blanket because wherever they took her it was too cold and her skin is mottling, turning blue like she has a bruise underneath.

'We have to keep you warm,' says Mona. 'Yes, we do.'

She nestles her baby against her breast. They are both still. A memory of her father comes so strong she looks up for a moment and expects to see him striding across the sand, calling her name. She looks again at her baby and knows what to do.

'Hello,' Mona says. 'Hello, Beatrice.'

25

Mona hurries away from Karl towards the light in the carpenter's window. She rarely visits in the evening. She opens the big metal door, climbs the stairs and calls. Nothing. The windows are open and the overhead light swings in the breeze. The place is freezing. The stove is cold. He's gone out.

She walks around the room, sees one doll is made and another is on the bench. And he's fixed the doll for the little girl. She closes the windows and goes to the sink. There is a plate with a smear of grease on it, two hard crusts and a curling rind of bacon. His standards are slipping but it's none of her business. Has she just walked off from an evening with Karl for someone that couldn't even bring himself to say something nice about her hair? She's a bloody fool. She marches to the shelf, picks up one of the dolls and then she hears a moan. She runs to the alcove, pulls back the curtain.

'Hello?'

He's lying on his cot under a thin blanket. His hair is wet, plastered to his scalp, and his face is red.

'Jesus,' she says. She smells the sickness, his bitter breath chugging out in quick damp squalls.

Mona takes her coat off and folds it on to the floor. She forces the curtain behind a nail and fills the kettle. While she waits for it to boil, she tips the filthy water from the bowl, squeezes in some washing-up liquid and scrubs it clean. She finds the three-legged stool and drags it up to his cot. His eyes are closed but she knows he is awake.

'Can you hear me?' she asks and he makes a noise.

She sits on the stool and peels off the blanket. The smell is terrible, two days of stale sweat. She fills the bowl with hot water and tests it as you would for a baby.

'That'll do,' she says. 'Up, up, up,' she says, holding his clammy hands and pulling him towards her. He sways and swoons, his head lolling on his chest.

'Shirt off, shirt off.'

She unbuttons it slowly, talking all the time. 'You've got a bad flu is my guess. Don't think it's food poisoning or you would have messed yourself. Have you messed yourself?'

He shakes his head.

'Good. So you've got the flu and while we take this shirt off I'll tell you what we'll do. First,' she says, pulling his arm up, 'a good wash. That'll immediately make you feel better. Second,' she slips the other arm out of the shirt, 'change the disgraceful sheets on this bed that might have walked off on their own at any time.'

She sits him on the stool, hunched over and shivering. She dips a dishcloth in the warm soapy water and begins to wash him. She lathers his neck and his face first. Wets his hair and eases it back. She soaks his beard until it curls and drips. He keeps his eyes closed and his head down. She scrubs his chest and notices the pallid skin and how, like hers, it has lost the rosy plumpness of youth. But he has a good shape underneath it all, wide shoulders and no fat at all. She dips the cloth again and wrings it out, soaps his back and under his arms, down to his wrists and his strong hands. She washes his fingers one by one and covers his waist with her own coat.

'Stand,' she says. 'Up, up.'

He holds on to her shoulders and she sees his legs tremble under the strain. She turns her head.

'Drop your pants. I'm not looking.' When she's sure he's naked she puts the cloth in his hand and points at the bowl. 'Use that on yourself and don't skimp.'

She turns her back to him and strips the grey, damp sheets off the bed, pulls the pillowcase off. She bundles them into a heap and looks around.

'Where are your spares?' she asks, turning to him. He is clutching the stool and crouching over the bowl, water dripping on to the wooden floor. 'Never mind,' she says and she unhooks the velvet curtain and lays it over the thin mattress. She covers the pillow with a tea towel and shakes the old blanket straight. It's better than it was before. That's the most she can say.

'Have you finished? Back into bed now.' She takes her cardigan off and hands it to him. 'You can cover yourself with this. Quick now. Into bed.'

He nods and lies down and she puts the blanket over him then adds her own coat. He turns on to his side to face her and when he puts both hands together and tucks them under his cheek she has to stop her tears.

'There, now,' she whispers. 'You'll sleep until I get back.'

She runs up the road with no coat and no cardigan and with her purse in her hand. She remembers the other times she has found him ill, the times when he had taken himself to bed and turned his face to the wall, coughing and heaving. And another time he half fainted right in front of her and admitted eventually that he had eaten nothing for days and days. Each time his illnesses seemed to go deeper and last longer and she worried that one day, when she hadn't called for a while, she would find him dead on his little bed and she would feel responsible.

At the shop she buys two tins of soup, orange juice and a fresh loaf. She buys butter and grapes, three bananas and a packet of dry biscuits. She lets herself back into the workshop, climbs the steps quietly and peeps in on him. He opens his eyes, looks at her and closes them again.

She tidies around the sink, washes up, lights the pot-bellied stove and the little cooker and puts the soup on. She butters a piece of bread and puts some orange juice in a tin mug. She watches him resting and shakes her head. He will be a long time getting past this.

She feeds him. He eats. She makes sure the windows are locked and won't fly open in the night. While he sleeps she sweeps around his living area and stuffs the stove full of logs again. She swills the sink and cleans around the toilet. She puts her coat back on and lays his own over the blanket and, because it's nearly black outside, she leaves the light on above the sink so if he gets up in the night for the toilet, he won't trip over.

Just before she leaves, she bundles his sheets and pillowcase together, fills his mug with orange juice and puts it next to the bed. She touches his shoulder but he doesn't stir so she watches him for a few moments.

'You'll be all right now.'

She doesn't call too early in case he's sleeping. She works all morning then after lunch she hangs a little sign in the shop window – 'Back in an hour' – and walks to the workshop. He is up. She takes his clean sheets from her bag and lays them near the sink. He's kept the stove going and one of the windows shut. He's wearing her cardigan round his waist and she remembers Karl's story. She smiles.

'I'll tell you a funny story about a cardigan. These two men are on their way to Paris . . .'

'Don't tell me, an Irishman and an Englishman. Anyway, look, two big dolls finished,' he says to her. He doesn't raise his head. She walks slowly over and when she's quite close she touches his arm.

'Feeling any better now?' she asks. 'I didn't expect you to be up so quick.'

He's sanding the top of a little chest of drawers. He keeps his head down, his hand sweeping, stroking the wood in a smooth arc over and over.

'Used a nice bit of yew. They've come out lovely.'

'I know, I saw them yesterday. Shall I make us a cup of tea, then?'

'Just had one,' he says, 'but you go ahead.'

'How are you feeling?' she asks. 'You still look a bit pale.'

'Good. I'm good. There's nothing wrong with me.'

She watches him a moment. She sees the effort he's putting into his work, into not looking at her, into not saying thank you. She could take her cardigan back and let the cold draughts creep back under his skin, let him shiver and shake all over again.

She picks up the dolls, stuffs them into her bag and walks away.

'Mona,' he calls but she doesn't turn.

26

Nurse Archer is gone for a long, long time. For weeks and months and years. Beatrice feels warmer. Mona holds her baby so close and wraps her so well that she isn't freezing cold any more except when Mona touches her face. That hasn't changed. Beatrice's eyes are still closed and her lips, just barely open, are still grey and silent.

'You're beautiful, aren't you?' Mona whispers.

'Mona!'

It's William. He's holding one of the curtains open and standing there, grinning from ear to ear. Except one of the ears is bloody and torn and his grin is red, his teeth are stained and he has more blood on his face, his jacket is ripped, one eye is half closed and the state of him makes Mona gasp.

'William!'

He walks over slowly, carefully, wiping the dirt and the sticky red from his hands, dragging them over the mess of his clothes.

'What happened to you? Where have you been?'

His eyes are shining and bright and he shakes his head. 'Doesn't matter. Let me see her.' He kisses Mona's head. 'Her. It's a girl then. Knew it was.'

He touches the edge of the blanket, folds it back and peers close.

'She's sleeping, is she?' Mona can see the horrible thought worming the back way through his brain. She can say nothing.

'Is she all right, Mona?'

William moves the blanket off the baby and exposes Beatrice's body. He stares at it a long while and then looks at Mona.

'Mona?'

Mona touches his arm. 'It's all right, William.'

William puts his hand on the baby's chest and draws it back like it's burnt. Mona quickly covers their baby up. She leaves a little opening for Beatrice's tiny face and tucks the white flower behind her ear. She swaddles the baby and lifts her up.

'Hold her, William.'

But William holds his hands up. 'What's going on?'

'Hold the baby.'

'Stop it, stop saying that! Get a bloody doctor!'

As he turns, the midwife rips the curtains apart. 'What is going on in here? What's the noise?'

'We need a doctor!'

She looks from William to Mona and the baby and points. 'Who brought that on to my ward? Archer!' she shouts and she makes that name long and sharp as a spear. 'Archer!'

Mona would like to ask them all to be quiet, the nurses and the radio that has come back on and the talking patients and the babies that are crying. But the midwife turns her savage face on Nurse Archer and points at Mona's baby.

'Did you do this?'

'She was upset, Sister.'

'Was she? Was she upset?'

'Yes, Sister.'

'You took a dead baby out of the sluice room with whatever diseases or bacteria fester there and brought it on to my ward?'

'Sorry, Sister.'

The midwife grabs Nurse Archer by her arm and pulls her outside of the curtain. Mona cradles her baby close with one arm and pulls William with the other.

'Hold her, William. Quickly. She has no diseases or bacteria. I've checked.'

'Dead baby?'

'William, look at her. She's perfect.'

'She's dead?'

'She's seven pounds two ounces.'

'She's dead.'

Mona doesn't really want the dirt and the blood that's on William to soil Beatrice's clean white blanket but she hasn't got time

161

to ask him to get cleaned up. She hears the midwife's words as they fly and spit.

'Upset was she? As upset as the grieving parents of them kids blown to pieces that we've got bits and pieces of downstairs? Have you been down? No. You've been up here breaking every rule in the book. You're a student nurse, Archer, and not a very good one at that. Seventeen dead and more blood and missing limbs than I've seen in twenty years. Upset? Upset? Save your pity. And if you've got time to pander to patients I suggest you go downstairs and make yourself useful. Now get it off her and get it to the mortuary. Now.'

Mona has so little time. 'William, remember we said Beatrice for a girl. Here she is. Beatrice.'

But William is turning round and round in a circle like a dog looking for his tail, one hand on his hip and another tapping his forehead.

The midwife and Nurse Archer come and stand either side of the bed.

'Now, sir,' says the midwife. 'Your baby was born dead this evening. We're very sorry. Your wife requested to see the child and that has been done although it's strictly not allowed. The baby will now be taken away. It's for your own peace of mind. Nurse Archer.'

Val Archer steps forward and puts her arms round Beatrice. Mona holds on. Nurse Archer slips her hands right round the body and tugs but Mona holds on.

'Please, Val,' she says. 'Let William hold her. William, take her. William! Take her!'

'No.'

She watches him step back and back, watches his hands claw the air like he's fighting a beast, watches him tangle in the curtains and drag them down.

'No, no, no.'

The last she sees of him is the blood on the back of his coat as he strides the length of the ward away from her.

27

Mona isn't sleeping again. She stands at her window looking out at a black morning, ten minutes past four. No Karl. No Karl for three nights. Mona makes a cup of tea and takes it back to bed. She picks up a little cloth doll she has been hand-stitching. She makes one every November, every one a little bit different but always made with undyed linen specially bought, stuffed with little brown lentils or beans to give it some weight and all natural fabrics for the doll's clothes. It will get cold and wet, dried maybe by a weak winter sun, nibbled and slithered over, cold again, wet again, and eventually rot away to nothing.

There's only the face left to do, cross-stitch for the eyes and neat, pink backstitch for the mouth. It's as close as she can remember to the doll her mother made. Mona has a photograph of herself, taken in Cork when she was a baby, maybe nine months old. There she is all studio-tinted in a hand-smocked dress the same colour as her eyes, blue violet. There are small yellow roses around the hem of her dress. Her mother must have sewn them on, one by one.

There are so few memories of her mother but Mona can see her on the beach with a picnic, in an apron in the kitchen and hanging out washing in the garden. Mona passing a peg or a sock from the basket and her mother humming and frowning against the sun.

If Mona's mother had lived to be an old lady then Mona would know if she took after her. She would have known to expect the downturn at the side of her mouth and the beginnings of heavy lids, that she would have a crease between her eyebrows and more recently unaccountable palpitations.

She remembers. She's not done it for a while. She lies back down and holds each breast in turn, kneads around it, up into the shoulders and under her armpits. She squeezes each nipple as she's done so

163

many times. She gets up out of bed. Turns on the bathroom mirror and, raising her arms, examines her breasts from every angle, pokes them again and finally lays the palm of her hand over her heart.

She goes back to the window, looking out towards the sea and then at the window where Karl lives. He is sleeping. She holds the hot cup to her chest and feels the burn on her skin. This is what it is to age alone. There's no one to say, 'Don't be daft, Mona. Will you listen to yourself? You're fine.'

At eight o'clock she rings Joley.

'I'll be late in, love, if I come at all. I have a touch of something, I think.'

Joley, good as gold and twice as precious, will open up and see to the customers and take the cash and the cheques and the credit cards, she'll be patient with the browsers and keep an eye on the stock and it's impossible to think she'll be gone next week.

Mona thought she might sleep but she can't. She tidies up all morning and then sits down with a cup of coffee and four biscuits on a plate. She doesn't turn the telly on. Nor the radio. She opens the living-room window a bit wider and listens to the traffic below and the chatter off the street that whips in on the breeze.

It wouldn't take much to redecorate. She could repaint the whole place in a couple of days. She could make a feature wall like she's seen in the magazines. She could install wall lights for the winter evenings, give the place a bit of a glow. Perhaps some new cushions. She could make them herself with braid and piping. And accessories can make an enormous difference. A vase. A new picture, something cheerful. Mona knows exactly that all her plans are just the usual November distractions.

Certain things are unreasonable and make no sense. It's stupid to compare one type of grief with another and, in the end, nothing makes it any easier. But Mona wishes that her baby had taken a single breath. She wishes that her baby had been born alive, if only for one moment, for one little cry or gasp. There were breaths being taken and expelled all over the world that night. Whispers and moans and full-bellied laughs, telephone calls and garbled warnings, everyday conversation – 'Where's my dinner?' 'Where's my shoes?' – but not one puff of breath to spare for her baby.

Sometimes she wonders about her baby's last moment. When was it exactly? Was it as Mona waited for the bus to take her to the community centre? Was it while her foot was on the treadle of the sewing machine? Was it while she snipped a loose thread?

It could have been that evening when she pushed the box back under the bed or a different moment, earlier that day, when she was making a cup of tea, washing her armpits, brushing her hair. She would never know and they never told her and it was all so long ago that it's time she stopped thinking about it.

And then she sees the horsewoman. Mona watches her slip between the parked cars and make her way across the busy road towards Mona's building. Even at a distance, Mona can see the set on her face. She looks up and sees Mona watching. She doesn't wave.

When the door opens, she walks straight in.

'Hello, Sarah,' Mona says.

'Hello.'

She hovers in the hallway until Mona directs her to the lounge and tells her to take a seat.

'Thanks.'

Mona takes her coat and lays it over the back of a chair. 'I wasn't expecting you today, Sarah. Did we have an appointment?'

'I went to the shop but you weren't there. I just called on the off-chance.'

Mona picks Sarah's coat up again and takes it into the hallway, puts it on a hook. She comes back into the lounge. 'I usually stick to appointments, Sarah, but now you're here would you like a cup of tea or coffee? Or a glass of water?'

Sarah shakes her head. 'Let's get on with it, shall we?'

Mona sits in her chair opposite and smiles. A word of kindness, a word of reproach, and Sarah's tears would come or her rage.

'It's difficult, isn't it?' says Mona. 'Even thinking about it is difficult.'

'I don't think about it.' Sarah's arms are folded, her legs crossed and tucked out of the way. 'It's actually not my idea to be here. I think I said that before.'

'Whose idea is it?'

'My husband's actually and that woman from the support group, Gayle. She thinks this sort of thing could be beneficial and Hugh agrees.'

'Hugh agrees.'

'Yes, Hugh is my husband. He's the talker in our family. Maybe he should be here instead of me.'

Mona nods. 'Tell me about your baby, Sarah.'

'Well, I will, but quite honestly it was a long time ago. And listen, I'm the first person to admit that I found the loss very difficult but you've met my daughter, she was born two years later, and since then I've had two boys. That is not to say that the lost child is forgotten.'

'Yes.'

'I'm not in denial about anything.'

'No. Tell me about your baby. Was it a boy or a girl, Sarah?'

'I went to the support group on the advice of my husband who read about it in a magazine.'

'Did you go together?'

'He said he found it helpful. I'm not so sure.'

'About him?'

'About its usefulness, this pulling things apart.'

'I agree.'

The woman looks at her hands, examines them for a moment and then looks up.

'What exactly is this? What's this session for?'

'We won't pull anything apart, Sarah, honestly.'

Mona goes to the kitchen. She calls behind her. 'Sure you won't have a cup of tea? I'm making one anyway.'

'No thank you.'

If Mona had her way, it would be the husband they would talk about and how he was when it happened and how he coped and

166

what he did at the hospital bed and how he cared enough about his wife to help her through it. It's the husband Mona would like to meet. But it's Sarah that's come, held together with threads.

When Mona returns to the lounge, Sarah is standing by the sideboard looking at Mona's photographs.

'Your husband?' she asks.

'Yes,' says Mona and takes the photo from her hand. 'William.'

'Have you got children? I mean any more children. I take it you had a stillbirth yourself?'

'We had no more,' says Mona. 'Just the one. What did you have, a boy or a girl?'

'I always think it's harder than what happened to Hugh and me. We at least had three more perfectly healthy children. It does help.'

'I'm sure,' says Mona and sits down in her seat, waiting for Sarah to do the same. Mona is very tired. All this not sleeping. All this thinking about things. The doll she has left on her pillow. Just the face to finish. She thinks of the clean sheets on her bed and the silence that she would have if this stranger wasn't in her home.

But Sarah is strolling around now, looking out of the French windows, running her hand along the back of the sofa.

'We're happy now. That's what matters, isn't it?' she says. 'I don't know if I agree with this sort of thing, dredging up the past. I'm not trying to be difficult but –'

'Sit down,' says Mona quietly. 'Let me tell you something.'

The woman does as she is told and Mona leans forward in her chair.

'How old are you?'

'Thirty-nine.'

'Well, forty years ago, before you were born, I lost my baby. She was born dead.'

Mona watches the woman's face and the slice of the words as they go in.

'She was beautiful. Of course she was, they all are. Full term. Not a scratch on her. Not a deformity to be seen. All her fingers and toes. Everything.'

Sarah is listening. Mona goes on.

'I didn't see her at first. They took her away as soon as she was born. Things were different then. Do you know where they took her?'

Sarah shakes her head.

'They took her off me and put her in the sluice room. I'll tell you what the sluice room is because things have improved a lot since those days. I should imagine you had a nurse take your baby and wrap it up and leave you and your husband with it for a little while so that you could talk together, say goodbye. Yes?'

Sarah starts to answer but Mona goes on.

'Well, the sluice room in a hospital is the room where they stick all the bits of liver and kidney they cut out, the half a leg that came off someone in a motorbike accident, the skin and tissue they will put in the incinerator later. Or throw out in the bins. The rubbish room. Yes, that's where they put my baby, my perfect baby.'

Mona takes a breath.

'It was only the kindness of a stranger that gave me the time to say goodbye. And that kindness gave me forty-five minutes with my child and I turned that forty-five minutes into a lifetime, into all the days and hours and weeks and years that we would never have together.'

The French windows rattle against the frame and Mona stands up to lock them.

'There is a trick to time, Sarah. You can make it expand or you can make it contract. You can make the most of what you have.'

The room is still and quiet with just the sizzle of tyres on the road, the quiet drum of the water on the glass. Mona sits down again. She crosses her legs at the ankle, places her hands together in her lap and waits.

'A boy.' Sarah speaks so quiet and soft that Mona can barely hear. 'A boy,' she repeats. 'We had a boy. Eight pounds two ounces.'

'A beautiful baby boy.'

'There was nothing wrong. Nothing. I was healthy. He was healthy right up until labour.'

Mona sits on the edge of her seat and squeezes Sarah's hand. 'Now I'm going to talk to you and you're going to listen. We'll do this together.'

In Mona's workroom she covers the eight-pound-two-ounce wooden baby with a piece of blue silk. She carries it in and Sarah closes her eyes. Mona places the bundle in her waiting hands. She lets it go and whispers, 'Feel the weight.'

28

Nurse Archer gave Mona something to make her sleep. She swims up to consciousness and hears the plaintive bleating of a new baby. Mona listens. Mothers know the cry of their own baby. Mona screws her eyes shut and listens. Both hands cradle her belly and she listens just in case. But the sound dies. Mona's baby is gone.

Nurse Archer must have gone home. Another nurse wheels the payphone to Mona's bedside, another nurse brings her a cup of tea and a piece of toast and a different nurse wheels the payphone away again.

No one picked up the phone that sits at the bottom of the stairs where Mona lives. William isn't there or, if he is, he's sitting blank-eyed on the sofa, crying about their baby, and he can't face her. Does he blame her? Is that why he ran off? As soon as she knew something was wrong she went straight to the hospital, that's what she'll tell him. And when they said push, she pushed and their baby just came out dead. There's nothing she can do about it. If William blames her it won't be right and it won't be fair. She rings everyone she can think of but that's only three people.

Mona lies down for the whole day. The curtains are tugged shut every time someone comes to make her eat or use the bedpan or change her pads or examine her with their cold fingers and sorry eyes. Something makes her sleep again and in the morning they tell her she can go home. Nurse Archer is nowhere to be seen.

She takes a taxi from the hospital to her little flat. She carefully opens the door and calls for him.

'William!'

A beef dinner and soap powder and old cigarettes is what the house smells of; it doesn't smell of William and a small bottle of beer and work clothes and aftershave and him desperate to see her.

'William!'

He isn't home. Mona puts her handbag on the kitchen table and lights the gas under the kettle. She turns it off, walks slowly to her bed and lies down.

It's dark again when she opens her eyes. Pestilence sits on a kitchen chair next to the bed. Even in the poor light Mona can see the difference in the woman that came to the wedding. No felt hat pinned at an angle, no fur collar on her jacket. Pestilence looks like she's aged, the life drained from her face, her coat, her hair, her scarf all merging into a thin, brown blur.

'You're awake. Good, good,' she says. 'A man upstairs let us in after we were knocking the door off its hinges. And you'd left your front door wide open. Did you know that? It's never safe, Mona, love. You have to be careful. We could be anyone.'

She holds Mona's hand and kisses it. 'Thank you, love, for ringing us. We were half out of our minds with worry about the bomb. We didn't hear from William and no one answered the phone and we thought the worst. But we never imagined this. Never imagined this. This is worse than the worst.'

Mona turns on to her back and feels the tears running down her temples, dribbling into her ears.

'He's not come back then?' says Pestilence.

Mona shakes her head.

'Now, now. He'll be in shock, love. As we all are. His father has been knocked back by this. He's too ill to come. I have one of the neighbours on twenty-four-hour watch, popping in all the time. He's a very unpredictable man at the best of times.'

She covers Mona with a blanket and takes the shoes from her feet. 'What you need is to get yourself well.'

Famine edges into the room still in her headscarf, her round face white and worried. Mona sits up. 'Where can he be? Something's happened, I know it has. He was covered in blood.'

Pestilence raises her eyebrows. 'He was walking, wasn't he? Talking? Yes? So he's living and breathing. He'll come back when he's calmed down. He will,' she continues and Mona can hear the fear and doubt in her voice. Pestilence dabs Mona's face with a tissue and sniffs. 'And I could box his ears for him, leaving you like this.'

Mona shakes her head. 'It's not like him.'

'Oh yes it is,' says the aunt quickly. 'Indeed it is like him. He ran away once when he was twelve because his father told him off. He has a head like an ox. He sets it to something and that's an end to it. But this business?' She shudders.

'And remember when he was seventeen?' says Famine. 'That was weeks he was gone.'

'What was weeks?' says Mona.

Famine has her eyes on her sister as she continues. 'He had words with his father about something just before he left. It wasn't anything important but he got it into his head that he was a failure. Isn't that what he kept saying, Margaret? Or something like that.'

Pestilence narrows her lips. 'It was nothing at all like that, Teresa. Stick to the facts, would you? He didn't pass his driving test and he was unable to tolerate the tutor, who was an idiot in any case. He took it hard as he always does because he wanted to pass his test before he came to England. That was entirely different to this.'

Mona glances from one to the other. 'You think he's run off?'

Pestilence shrugs. 'I'll have words with him when he creeps back here, I will. This is time to be a man, William.'

Famine edges out of the room, comes back with a tray of tea, and Mona is made to sit up in bed. Without her scarf, Famine has a shock of red hair that ripples in flat, concentric waves. It's brushed down neatly and curled under like a bad wig. Mona finds herself thinking that at least her baby didn't have red hair and won't be teased at school, and as quick as the thought comes, the truth follows hard on its heels.

'There, there,' says Pestilence, patting Mona's arm. 'There, there.'

Famine pours the tea and the three women sit together with their cups and their sorrow. Mona can hear children playing in the street outside and the two aunts look at one another. Pestilence puts her cup down.

'Shall I close this window, Mona? There's an awful bite of wind in here.'

She slams it shut and folds her arms. 'Right. In my opinion,' she continues, 'we need to make a plan. Teresa?'

Famine is staring into her cup.

'Teresa?' repeats Pestilence.

'Yes?'

'A plan, we need to make a plan. Right, Mona, love. Who are his friends? What are their names? Do you know where they live? If I have any notion of men he'll have gone to the nearest bar and soaked his pains with alcohol. And there's nothing at all wrong with that under the circumstances.'

She pauses after the last sentence and looks at Famine as though she expects her to say something. Famine inches a biscuit off the plate and dips it in her tea.

'So,' says Pestilence, 'if you have an address and a name for these friends, I will personally go and see them and take William by his ear and bring him home because as God is good his place is here with his wife on this terrible occasion.'

Famine nods and they both look at Mona.

'Mona, love,' says the aunt, 'who are his friends? His local friends?'

Mona shakes her head. 'There's only Tom,' she says, sliding down on to her back and turning away. 'And he's not in. William's left me.'

29

The health visitor comes the following day. Pestilence and Famine take themselves to the corner shop for bread and milk and a packet of biscuits, and come back with the Irish brands Mona remembers from her childhood.

They creep in and peek round the door. 'Are you all finished?' they say and don't wait for an answer before Famine is making her a snack or a sandwich or a mug of tea. 'You're skin and bone, Mona.'

Pestilence takes her hand and gives it a squeeze. 'You'll be grand. You're young yet. You're not to worry. We're here to do the worrying. You get better.'

Mona closes her eyes. 'I'm to have another one as soon as I can.'

Pestilence says nothing and Mona hears the children again outside on the street. It's all she hears now, the voices of children and the crying of babies. She doesn't hear the cars and the men and the women and the banging of front doors.

'She said there's nothing wrong with me. That's what she said. The best way to get over it is to have another baby. Get pregnant, she said, and it will all be forgotten.'

Pestilence kisses Mona's forehead. 'He'll have to come home for that to happen,' she says. 'And we'll see to it.'

They tell her to stay in bed. Women neighbours she hardly knows pop in with 'Get Well Soon' cards, leaving flowers and advice.

'Rest.'

'Try not to think about it.'

'Take your time.'

'You're a healthy girl.'

'These things happen.'

'Rest.'

'Time is a healer.'

'He'll be back.'

'Rest.'

But no one apart from Pestilence and Famine does anything to make her feel better. They sit with her, either side of the bed, and eat their lunch and talk not about waiting for him to come home but going out there and getting him.

Famine chatters with her mouth full. 'Eliminate the possibilities. I keep saying it: it's not where is he, it's where he isn't.'

Pestilence hisses. 'All right, Teresa. Where isn't he, then? Go on. Tell us. We're both waiting to hear.'

'Well, he's not at home.'

'That's a grand bit of deduction, Teresa. Really it is.'

'I mean,' says Famine, between the crusts of her bread, 'in Ireland. He's not gone home to Clarinbridge. Nor to Kilcolgan because we would have heard.'

Pestilence nods. 'We have people there, family. He has an old uncle and a couple of girl cousins. I can't see him in Kilcolgan at all.'

'So to my mind,' continues Famine, 'I think he's gone and got drunk somewhere or maybe had an accident.' She raises a finger. 'Nothing serious, Mona, love, that's not what I'm thinking. I'm just saying he might have had a knock on the head and be sleeping it off somewhere.'

Pestilence stands up and takes the plate from her sister's hand. 'Knock on the head? He'll get one when he reappears, that he will.'

They leave the room together and Mona hears them wittering outside the door. In a few moments, Pestilence calls out to her.

'We're off to see what we can find out. Stay in bed.'

The cotton sheets are rough and cool and the aunts have tidied the little bedroom, hung up clothes, dusted and polished and opened the window a crack. They come at half seven in the morning from the little boarding house on Stratford Road. They make her breakfast and put her back to bed as though she's an invalid.

The house is quiet without them and she slips down between the covers and waits and thinks of William somewhere with a bandaged head and a hangover or a pair of broken legs and crutches and him trying to walk home and she sobs for his pain and for her own.

It's dark when she opens her eyes. They are whispering outside the bedroom door.

'I'm not going inside to that girl, Teresa, until you've got yourself under control. Are you fit now? Are you?'

Famine sniffs and clears her throat. The door opens and they come in. They stand each side of the bed and look at her.

'What?' Mona says. 'What is it?'

'You're not to worry,' says Pestilence. 'Sit up and we'll tell you.'

Famine has a red nose from crying.

'What?' Mona repeats. 'Just say it!'

'Ssshh, ssshh now. We don't know where he is, Mona. That's first. But we do have an idea where we might look.'

'What we've been through, Mona,' says Famine and her face crumples. 'I've never been called a murderer in my whole life. I've never been accused of horrible crimes.'

'Shut up, Teresa. Shut up, can't you? Let me tell her. Go and make the tea.'

Famine shuffles out of the room, a handkerchief to her nose, and Pestilence begins.

'We left here and took the bus into the centre of town. The whole area is destroyed. There are police everywhere still and a big gaping hole in the side of a building and there's blood on the pavements. And people sightseeing, would you believe, sightseeing over death and destruction. We went to the main police station, Steelhouse Lane, and we introduced ourselves. We only wanted information and to see if we could let them know we had a missing person on our hands.'

Pestilence adjusts the sleeves of her cardigan and takes a deep breath.

'The police officer asked us where we were from and we told

him. "You're Irish," he said but he must have known already because he heard us speak. And then he said, so quietly I thought I'd misheard, he said, "Two Irish bitches." There were other people on our side of the counter and I looked at them because I really didn't know what it was I was supposed to answer and one of the men sitting on a plastic chair said, "Why don't you clear off back to your own country," except he didn't say "clear off", he said something else. I took my sister and we left because I didn't feel safe there, Mona, I didn't, and that's the truth. We didn't trust the bus to take us home so we got in a taxi and as soon as the taxi driver heard our voices he asked us what we were playing at. I beg your pardon, says I, and he said he wasn't sure he wanted Irish money in his hands, blood money he called it, and told us to get out.'

The aunt's lips quiver and she raises her chin to the ceiling before she continues.

'We got back on the bus, the number fifty, and it brought us here. Right outside we saw a woman trying to force a key in the door so I said did she need help and she said she was Tom's mother. Oh, I said, that's grand, but she burst into tears all over me and told us that Tom will lose an eye.'

'Tom was with William. He was with William. What happened? Where is he?'

'Mona, Mona, calm down. Sit back. Listen.'

Famine brings in a tray with a teapot and cups. She places it carefully on Mona's lap.

'I don't want any bloody biscuits, Teresa. What's wrong with you? What's going on? What's happened?'

The tray clatters to the floor and the hot tea seeps through the blankets and on to her legs. She flings them off and kneels on the mattress. She feels the thick pad between her legs wet with her blood and the scald of the tea. The whole room is alive with pain.

'Margaret, tell her!'

'All right, Mona, all right. He's all right. He's not injured. Not properly. This is what Tom's mother said. She said they were attacked on their way home from the town centre, walking they were and minding their own business but there were ruffians riding about looking for Irishmen to attack.'

Famine strips the bed around Mona and places her back on the mattress while Pestilence continues.

'She said William and Tom –'

There is a knock on the door. The women all stop dead.

'He might have lost his key.' Mona scrambles off the bed and hobbles to the front door. It's not William. Tom stands there with his bandaged head, with his face a riot of blue and purple, his arm in a sling. She wouldn't have recognized him on the street. His mother stands behind.

'We've come to pay our respects, love,' says the woman.

Famine ushers them in. 'Where's William, Tom?'

Tom's lips are mashed on one side and his words are more garbled than usual.

'Ah now, Mona, I was shocked I was when my mammy told me that you've had a bit of bad news. I'm sorry, that I am, and it's an awful thing to happen to a woman.'

'Do you know where he is, Tom?'

'I don't, I don't. We were attacked and the last I saw of him was when we got ourselves back here. There were no buses from town because of the bomb. We didn't know it was because of the bomb at the time, like, we were in town waiting and waiting and in the end I said, "Jesus, Billy, will we just walk and be done?" and he said, "Aye, we will," so in the end we were coming down by the flyover and we'd had a few pints apiece but nothing out of the ordinary. We're neither of us fully into the drink.'

He looks at his mother. Big Tom, with his mangled voice and baby face. Mona holds one hand with another because she can hardly stop them from flailing up all wild and terrible, and screaming at him to tell her what happened.

'You'll have some tea, won't you both?' says Famine.

Pestilence raises a finger. 'Teresa, could you allow us five minutes devoid of refreshment while this young man gives us the details of the whereabouts of our nephew. Please.' She glances at Mona but speaks to Tom. 'Continue.'

'Ah right, so where was I?'

'You were sober,' says Pestilence.

'We were that. I had had a couple of pints, no more, and Billy the same.'

'William,' says Pestilence.

'Ay, William. Him and me is walking down past the flyover and he was talking about, well, it was me to be honest, talking about why we ever came to England when the beer is so bad and now our jobs aren't safe, and having the craic, you know, high jinks, pushing one another, and he was after telling me to get married and stuff like that and then this car pulls up sharp right next to us and you'd never think so many people could be in one car all together. It must have been eight of them piled out. English boys. One of them says, "You fucking Irish pigs."' Tom shakes his head. 'I can't say what they said to us without cursing, Mammy.' He touches the bandages on his head with his good hand.

'Go on,' says Pestilence, 'I think we can imagine.'

'I don't really know what else happened. I haven't a good memory of it and that's the honest truth. Me and William took a terrible beating. I know I'm a big lad but William isn't. I thought he was all right, like. I tried to protect him but we were outnumbered four to one. Maybe more. I will lose my eye.'

He covers his mouth with his hand. Mona sees it shake. His mother puts her hand on his shoulder. 'There, there.' She looks at Mona. 'We're going home,' she says, 'back to Cork. He should never have come.'

Pestilence nods. 'Yes, good idea. What happened to William? When did you last see him?'

'He was running away with me. Some other cars stopped and the first boys left us alone so we ran off. William was limping. It was a terrible beating but we got away and ran off down the back streets, through Pool Farm, you know, through the blocks of flats and up on to home. We got here at the same time. We were both exhausted. He read your note, Mona. He said, "She's having it," and he ran out again.'

'That's it?' says Pestilence.

'That's the last time I saw him.'

'Then Mona sees him at the hospital,' says Pestilence to the room, 'and then he disappears. It makes no sense.'

Mona gets up and walks out of the living room. Her pad is soaked with blood and it chafes the tops of her legs. She stands at the bedroom window and watches the cars drive past and the people talking and laughing on the street like nothing has happened, like the world is just the same as it ever was.

Pestilence comes in after a few minutes.

'Now, Mona, at least we know. He was attacked, which is why he was covered in blood, and thankfully he wasn't in the bomb. And then he sees you there with your little one in your arms, you said yourself you hardly spoke to him, you said you were beside yourself and who could blame you. No wonder he didn't tell you. He was sparing you.'

'Where is he then?'

'He'll be in hospital, Mona, won't he?'

'It's been four days! Tom said he was all right. He wasn't that bad when I saw him. Where is he?'

'Well, maybe it's worse than we think. Maybe he's having his wounds attended to. Now don't cry any more because we have progress. We have progress, Mona.'

30

Mona has to get out, away from the aunts, so she can think. She puts on her coat and goes off for a walk. Pestilence says she'd like to come for the air but Mona manages to put her off. The woman has a unique version of kindness but is often as angry as a wasp in a jar. And yet, as soon as Mona sees the shops and their little displays, she wishes she had an arm to lean on. Christmas is everywhere. Little baby Jesus in a cradle or his mother's arms or wrapped in swaddling, looking perfect and regal. 'Christ is born!' screams a sign outside St Mary's Church while Mona struggles to walk on account of the huge wad of sanitary towel rubbing between her legs and the creasing of pains.

Only a few weeks ago she had been delighted at the sight of prams and pushchairs and saw herself joining the proud mothers in playgroups and nurseries, pushing swings and waiting with outstretched arms at the bottom of the slide. 'Careful!' she would shout. 'Mummy's got you!'

And now 'Christ is born!' She begins gulping, the tears flowing hot on her freezing cheeks and clouding her eyes, right there on the street with people looking. She ropes her scarf across her face and rushes home. She tears off her coat and climbs into bed. What was she thinking? Did she think she would bump into William with presents in his arms? Did she think he would be getting off the bus in his work clothes on his way home like it was a normal Friday night? Fish and chips and a bottle of beer? Stupid.

Famine brings her a cup of tea. 'You've no business being out in the cold, Mona. It's only been a week, my love. You're asking too much of yourself just now.'

She fusses about the room and Mona knows she has more to say. 'What?'

'You'll be coming back with us, won't you, Mona? Say you'll

come to us for your Christmas. We were expecting you anyway, before all this.'

Mona turns her face to the wall and Famine begins stroking her hair.

'I know, I know, I know. You're thinking about William and aren't we all? Come for Christmas then we can come back, all of us together. We'll bring reinforcements. He has a good lot of family at home, cousins and so forth. Half the village are related in some way or another. We could bring ourselves a regular army. If he's alive, we'll find him.'

Mona gives a start.

'No, no,' Famine says, 'that's not what I meant. It's just a saying, I mean that it's not possible that we don't find him. That's what I was to say. No, no, don't cry. Of course he's not dead.'

Pestilence opens the door.

'What's this?'

'Oh, Margaret,' says Famine, crying now as well and holding her sister's arm, 'I didn't mean it. I didn't.'

Pestilence sends Famine out of the room and sits down on the side of Mona's bed. 'I'm going to ask you some questions, Mona. Stop crying and hear me.'

Mona moves her hair from her face and turns her head.

'I've asked you some of these questions already but you can answer them again so we know where we are. And sit up. Stop crying and don't bother with Teresa's nonsense. Sit up now and we'll get to the bottom of this, you and I, together.'

Mona sits up and gets her breathing under control.

'That's better,' says Pestilence and knits her fingers together like she's about to tell a story.

'We have to take an inventory of what we've done.'

'Yes,' says Mona.

'He's missing but we know two things. First, he has been injured, not badly as far as we know but enough. Secondly, he came here and he came to the hospital so we know he can walk and he has all his faculties. Or he did have.'

Mona nods.

'We have St Anne's and Father Nolan on high alert. We've been to all the pubs you told us about and half of those you didn't. We have that nice Mr What's-his-name saying he'll put up a poster at the community centre.'

'Mr Colgan.'

'Colgan, that was it. And we know for certain we cannot rely on the British police to do anything for a decent Irishman under the present conditions.'

'No.'

'Our next plan of action is to ring the hospitals. But before we do that, which might take us a month of Sundays, I want you to answer some questions.'

'All right.'

'Did you argue? You and William, did you argue before the baby came?'

'No, I told you, it was all lovely between us. Perfect.'

'Perfect, was it?'

'Yes, it was.'

'All right, then. Was he in a pack of friends? Was he out every night?'

'No, no. We had no money to be going out all the time.'

'You're sure about that? Was he straight back to you after work?'

'Straight back and I had the dinner ready.'

'Good.'

'And Gallagher's say he hasn't turned in for work as well.'

'I know that,' says Pestilence. 'Wasn't it me that told you to ring them?'

'Yes.'

'Right, then.'

Pestilence is quiet for a moment, her lips pursed into a wrinkled little rosebud. She screws up her eyes and shoots Mona a piercing look.

'Women?'

'No,' says Mona.

'Hear me out,' says Pestilence, raising a finger. 'He's sleeping somewhere, isn't he? You say he had no friends, which matches what I know of him myself. He's always been a day-dreamer, out on his own or sticking to one person at a time. But, Mona, and you can stop crying, we have to think clearly, make an effort if you can. It's a possibility, is it not?'

Mona nods. 'I know, I know. But I just don't believe he would do that. He came home every night and we were always together. I had to force him out these last few weeks, he didn't even want to go. But I felt sorry for him because I wasn't feeling great, and anyway, I didn't want to be in a smoky pub when I was pregnant, it made me feel sick, so I made him go. It was me. He had no opportunity for other women.'

'He could have met someone lately, couldn't he?'

'No.'

'He could have.'

'I said no. He's dead. I know he is.' Mona clutches the sheet in her fists.

'If you're going to keep crying, we can stop our discussion. I'll come back later.'

'No!' Mona grabs her hand. 'Carry on. I'm all right.'

'He has a bed somewhere, Mona. And that bed belongs to a man or a woman or,' says Pestilence, 'and I must say it, or in a hospital. If that's where he is, then we still must find him. He can't have disappeared into thin air.'

The women shake their heads in unison.

'So then,' continues Pestilence, making a tent out of her two hands, 'my plan is this and I won't deviate from it. You are his wife and you are entitled to feel that you have the greater say, but let me tell you this. That boy is my brother's child and like my own.'

Mona hears the crack in the woman's voice.

'We will attack all the hospitals tomorrow. Each one in turn. We will ring the police again and make them take us seriously and we will ring the mortuary, if such a place exists, to eliminate it, nothing more.' She pauses. 'That's what we will do tomorrow after you have rested and had some sleep. Then my plan is to go home for Christmas and to bring you with us. For all we know he may be waiting there for us and no one has the brain to let us know. It wouldn't be the first time the Irish have been accused of being thick.'

Mona nearly smiles.

'William's father is not well, not grand at all, and not young. He goes off and gets anxious if there's a break in his routine and God knows this has been a break in all of our routines. We have to think about him as well as everything else. There's no one to look after him like Teresa and myself, who know his ways. We have to get home and make sure he's keeping to an even keel. We also have to get you well, Mona.' Pestilence taps the blanket. 'You need rest. You need family around you, our family. You need some decent food as well, lamb and pork, butter and cream. Look at you.'

Mona nods.

'Teresa and myself, we were delighted when we knew he was getting married. It felt like a weight off our hands, someone sensible to look after him. It was a relief to us all.' Pestilence opens the door. 'William will resurface, sooner or later. He'll come home either here or there with his tail between his legs. And when he does, I will kick that tail from one end of England to the other. You mark my words.'

31

A handshake from Sarah as she leaves, and then a kiss on Mona's cheek, and then thanks and thanks again and a different voice, a softer one. Sarah wanted to keep the wooden baby, said she wanted her husband to feel the weight, wanted them to share their memories and the things she had remembered. Mona says goodbye, wishes her well and closes the door. So tired.

Mona sits in her workroom and stands the new Joley doll in the clamp to paint her face. In the end, the patent-leather boots have turned out well. Mona bought a shiny black pencil case and cut it up and, to be honest, the whole doll is perfect. Joley's last day on Friday.

'I'll miss you, love, and that's a fact, but you look splendid if I say so myself.' Deep breath.

Now, should she make an alternative outfit? One for Joley at work, a little teacher's outfit complete with joke mortar board and gown, a pair of half-moon glasses and a cane? Mona eyes across the room a square of amber jacquard that would make a neat cropped jacket she could fasten with a single button around her waist. The single button could be a pearl earring Mona remembers in her box of fasteners and clips.

Almost time. Three more weeks, that's all. November 21st, train to Birmingham, visit to the grave, see Val, train back. She sometimes stays on an extra day but there'll be no Joley to fall back on and leave in charge. She'll have the whole thing on her shoulders, the bookkeeping, stock control, orders to post, shop to mind and all the computer stuff to get right. And extra dolls to make for Christmas.

It's harder than she thought to paint Joley's face, to get her little nose right and the sweet apple of her cheeks. She hears the doorbell. Mona doesn't move because this has happened before when it's been Jehovah's Witnesses or young men selling dusters and cloths from huge holdalls who assure her they've recently been let out of prison and they're doing the only job they can get, going door to door with household goods, and all they need is a leg-up, missus, and would you buy a couple of things so I can be on my way. She never needs anything but her natural sympathy means she always ends up five pounds poorer with a tea towel in her hand. So she pays no heed to the single ring.

To complement the orange jacquard, Joley could have a black corduroy pinafore dress edged with lace or a stiff collar perhaps. Would a petticoat be a step too far? Heavy black liner with a flick at the side for Joley's eyes. And the bell again, two rings and a confidence in them that moves Mona to the front door.

'Hello?' she says to the lock.

'Mona?'

'Yes. Who is it?' But she knows. Her hands fly to her hair, fluff it up at the top. She looks down quickly, what is she wearing? She has no tights on, she has paint all over her fingers, on her face, her wrists and even on the cuff of her cardigan.

'Just a minute.'

She dashes into her bedroom and rips her cardigan off. She pulls another from a drawer and shoves her arms in. She stoops to the dressing-table mirror, licks her finger and smooths it over her eyebrows. She hasn't time for any more, he'll be suspicious and she'll look vain or slovenly. She slips on a pair of shoes and half runs to the door, turns the lock, opens it.

Karl stands there with two carrier bags that he raises in the air.

'Dinner!' he says.

She stands back. 'Come in, come in.'

He bends down and kisses both cheeks. 'You look lovely. It's good to see you.'

'And you,' she says. There is a little dance between them in the narrow vestibule while she tries to squeeze past him, to get ahead and show him the way to the lounge.

'I beg your pardon,' he says. 'You don't mind me coming? We didn't have a plan of course but I thought as I had promised so many times to make you a meal . . .'

'No, no,' she answers, 'it's fine.'

'And then of course,' he says to her back, 'sometimes one must act on impulse. Do something without a plan. Surprise is what keeps us young.'

'Oh, I agree,' Mona says and shows him the kitchen.

He puts the bags on the work surface and draws out a bottle of wine. 'This,' he says, 'we can open now and drink later. It needs a little while to become full, round. Would you like to . . .?'

'Yes, yes.'

She opens a drawer and takes out a corkscrew.

'Allow me,' he says. As he works the cork out, he laughs. 'I went to the wrong apartment, I thought it was next door. They told me you were here. I misjudged.'

'Easily done,' says Mona.

'Now, smell,' says Karl.

Mona puts the bottle to her nose. 'Oooh,' she says.

Karl taps his nostril. 'Vanilla, I think, and a sort of woodiness.'

'Wood?' says Mona. 'Hmm, I'm not sure.'

Karl begins taking items out of the bag one by one and putting them on the side: a cabbage, two polystyrene trays of chicken, an onion, a bulb of garlic, bunches of dried herbs and potatoes.

'Of course,' he says, 'you would know more than I about the smell of the wood. You are always at the carpenter's house. Maybe he would be more specific than simply "wood".'

'I think you can smell a bit of resin or something. I'm not sure. I don't know much about wine.'

'Taste it.' He moves the bottle an inch, while he begins opening Mona's kitchen drawers. The cutlery rattles in its tray. 'Knives?' he asks. 'Do you have sharp knives?'

'Er, yes, here.'

He moves the bottle again. 'Try some.'

'I will, I will. A little later.'

He stands back and looks at the cooker. 'Electric. Hmm. Mine is gas. I want the oven to be quite hot. Not very hot but say a medium, a number seven.'

He takes up a lot of room in the kitchen. He looks taller somehow or the room is a little narrower than before. Impossible. He throws her tea towel over his shoulder like a waiter and discards the two carrier bags in the sink. He sets the wooden chopping board in front of him and plunges the knife into the heart of the frilly green cabbage, cleaving it in two.

'Colander,' he says, 'for rinsing. And the oven, please. Medium, as I say, not too hot.'

Mona opens a kitchen cupboard and points inside. 'Everything's in there,' she says and turns the dial on the oven. 'Medium. There we are. I'll get some glasses, shall I?'

She goes back to her workroom to check on Joley. She has no eyes, her head has dropped to the side. By now she should have small red lips and the hair, wild and black, earrings as well. Karl has begun to sing, low and rumbling, not loud. He clanks a pot on the stove and opens the oven door, closes it again. It has been many years since Mona has heard the sound of a man's voice in her kitchen. She unclamps the doll and realizes her hands are shaking.

She lays Joley on the side. 'Back soon,' she whispers and closes the door. She brings two wine glasses from her cabinet into the kitchen and pours.

'I am a little ahead of you,' says Karl when she returns. 'I drank a glass of Shiraz at home so I will join you as soon as I have finished preparing our meal if I may. But you must try. Go on, go on.'

The wine is rich and strong, it tastes good. She needs to calm down. Stop fussing. Smile, Mona, smile.

She stands at the kitchen door and finishes her wine just as Karl pushes the casserole dish into the oven. He claps twice and picks up his glass. He sips and runs his tongue round his lips.

'Ah, very good. Yes. So! Forty minutes. Time for the chef to relax. Come, let's sit down.'

If he had given her some warning she could have bought a packet of crisps or nuts, she wouldn't be wearing her old brown dress and she would, at the very least, have a decent pair of tights on her milk-white legs. First Sarah calling without any notice, now Karl. If only she'd slept, if only it wasn't November. She sits in her chair and pulls her hem low.

Karl is on the sofa and looks for all the world as if he was born there, one arm slung across the back of the cushion, his long legs crossed at the knee.

'So this is home, Mona. It's very elegant.'

'Thank you.'

'I would have expected nothing less.'

It's hard to avoid his smile, every time she looks up it seems to be there waiting for her.

'Sorry, I'm a bit on the back foot, Karl, with one thing and another, and I've been trying to get a doll finished. My assistant, the one who's leaving, I've made her a present. Well, nearly.'

The smile wavers. 'I've interrupted you.'

'No, no. I didn't mean that, only that I'm not dressed for visitors, that's all.'

Karl shrugs. 'But look at me. I'm hardly dressed for a wedding. Comfortable shoes, a simple shirt and trousers. And anyway, you look perfect for an evening at home and a meal for two.' He leans forward and holds his glass in front of her. 'Here's to comfort and joy.'

She clinks his glass. 'Comfort and joy,' she repeats.

He drinks two glasses to her one. He tells her about Malbec and the making of the meal and he tells her what it's called and that it was Andreas's favourite and he tells her where he tasted it first and how it should be eaten and that really there should be crusty bread for the sauce and that it should be served in a deep dish with a rim or a cast-iron skillet. Mona doesn't have a deep dish with a rim. She doesn't have a skillet. He tells her about the skill of pairing wine with food. He tells her that you can have red wine with fish and dry white wine with dessert and that matching food with people is just as important, no, *more* important than anything else and that in food as in life there are both contrasts and complements and the two things are very different and yet almost the same, and all the time he is talking she watches his mouth and his hands, the way he has rolled his sleeves neatly and the way the heavy gold watch turns and jangles on his wrist. He pronounces German words with a German accent, French with French, and she wonders how many languages he speaks, how many places he has seen, how many women he has loved over his life. She should just get into the bloody spirit of things. Maybe if Sarah hadn't come . . . if she'd been sleeping better . . .

'So, you see,' he says; 'marrying wine with food is an art. It took many years to learn but Andreas was very particular –'

'I might go home,' she says, saying the words before she realizes she had thought them.

'Home? You are already at home, are you not, Mona?'

'To Ireland.'

'I see.'

Mona looks past him to the black outside. With the oven and the central heating on, Mona is sweltering. She wants to scratch her scalp and wipe the top of her lip. She gets up and opens one of the French windows. She pulls her cardigan off, exposing the paint on her arm. She can't remember using perfume or deodorant, and anyway, why should she when she hasn't left the flat all day. She didn't expect visitors. You don't need scent for a night in with a sandwich.

'You're thinking of going soon?'

'Sorry?'

Karl holds on to the arm of the sofa as he gets to his feet. He stands next to her. 'When will you go?'

'Oh, I don't know. Never probably.'

'Good,' he says and walks into the kitchen. 'I was worried for a moment. Would you like to lay the table?' he shouts. 'It's always best, I think, to eat at the table.'

Mona pulls the table from against the wall. She puts the two leaves up and brushes the dust from the top. She goes quickly to the airing cupboard and finds a tablecloth and, because God is good, a couple of napkins. She hurries to put knives and forks and two water glasses down, sweating now, while she hears him with plates in the kitchen, the constant and repeated refrain of his humming, his loud noises and the fear that he might break something. Barely has she finished laying the table than he comes slowly into the living room with two plates, loaded with food, more than Mona has ever eaten in a single sitting.

'Dinner is served,' he says, proud as a schoolboy.

The quiet seems to go on for ages. Mona knows she should speak and she knows he is waiting. He has gone to so much trouble, bought all the ingredients and a good bottle of wine and been charming and witty, thought of her alone on a Saturday night. And the food is very good.

'This is great cooking, Karl. Really good. It's lovely.'

'When food is made with affection, it always tastes good. I made it for you.'

He reaches across the table and lays his hand on her arm. Mona smiles, keeps her eyes on her food. There is only then the sound of their knives and forks on the plate, the sound of his swallow and of hers, and in fifteen minutes she has finished, had enough.

'No wonder you are so slim,' he says. He pours wine until the bottle is empty.

Mona sits back from the table and drinks water. But Karl severs the meat from his breast of chicken, wielding the knife like a surgeon until he has a tidy pile of bones on the right of his plate and a fold of flaccid skin on the left. He has his head bowed to the plate and she watches him, sees the brown spots on the side of his neck and the freckles on the back of his hand. He has no one to tell him that his collar is folded at the back and his hair, a little long for a man of his age, needs a trim. He looks up quickly.

'I'm sorry. I eat quite slowly these days. But I have finished now.'

'Take your time,' she says, 'don't let me rush you.'

She sees that the sauce has gathered in the creases of his mouth, a drip has run on his chin and there is a sprinkling of perspiration across the bridge of his nose. She stands up.

'I'll make some coffee, shall I?'

Mona never takes coffee after six. If she drinks it she will never sleep but after tonight she may not sleep anyway. There will be washing-up to do and clearing away and she prays that he won't insist on helping. Even with the window open, her flat is over-hot and the very smell of the place is different. She has no mints to serve with the coffee which is from a jar, which he with his European palate is bound to find disgusting, and everything, everything is wrong. She should not have answered the door. She knows that now.

She takes the two mugs into the living room and finds him on the sofa reclining.

'Come and sit by me,' he says and pats the seat next to him.

She hands him his drink and sits down. The cushions feel hard and unused and she realizes it is many years since she sat on the sofa, maybe only when she bought it and when was that? She looks at her chair and sees that differently too. It looks like a pathetic throne, taking up too much space with the delicate nest of tables at an angle, with the lamp and the TV remote control just at hand, as if an invalid sits there alone night after night, watching quiz shows and shopping channels. She is ashamed again and wonders if he sees her like that.

'Thank you, Karl,' she says. 'I'm touched that you thought of me.'

'You're welcome,' he answers and he reaches across the space between them and touches her arm so lightly it tickles and she flinches.

'Whoops.' She steadies her mug with both hands and keeps the smile that sets on her face.

He says nothing about the state of his coffee, says nothing about her flustering, nor the paint he must surely have seen on her arm but chats with charm and ease about his day visiting friends and their meal and his decision to come round.

'Now that Andreas no longer needs me, that is to say, now that he is dead, I must make the effort to fill my days.'

Mona nods. 'Yes.'

He sighs deeply, twice, and then passes her his mug. He stands up and rubs his hands together. 'So, I think I have taken up enough of your time, Mona. And anyway, at my age, one needs beauty sleep almost more than good company. Almost.'

He gives his little bow and unrolls his sleeves. He fastens the buttons, slips his jacket from the back of the chair and puts it on.

'I hope you don't think me too rude, leaving without helping with the washing-up and so forth but, if I may say, you seem a little tired. As I am myself.'

'Oh, you're quite right, Karl. Yes and don't worry about the mess. I won't do it now. It can stay until morning without causing a crisis. I'll just leave it be.'

'If you're sure.'

She leads him to the front door and steps aside. 'Thank you for a lovely evening. You've been very generous, Karl. Sorry I wasn't better prepared.'

He leans down towards her and kisses her cheek.

'You must not worry,' he says. 'It was enough to see you.'

She smiles and he kisses her again, the other cheek.

'Goodnight,' she says but his face is close and she can feel his breath. He kisses her again on both cheeks quickly and then on her lips, soft at first and then firm, insistent, while his arm slips round her waist and pulls her towards him. She is against his chest, feels his hand in the small of her back, pressing her in.

'Mona,' he whispers.

She leans back but he follows. She's rigid and taut. Her arm's almost up in surrender. He must not do this. She puts her hands against his shoulders and pushes gently and finds a voice that suits her refusal.

'Karl, it's been lovely. Genuinely lovely. Thank you.'

She pulls away and gives a wide smile. 'Goodnight.' She puts her hand on the lock and turns the knob. His hot hand covers hers.

'You're very beautiful,' he says.

'All right, Karl. That must be the wine talking. You had more than me, that's for sure.' She gives a little laugh and tries to pull the door open.

'No,' he murmurs. 'It's not the wine.'

'Well,' she says and tugs hard at the door, opening it against him so that he has to stand out of the way, 'it's getting late.'

He pulls his jacket closed and raises his eyebrows.

'I see.'

'It's been a grand night, grand, but let's not spoil it.'

'I didn't realize that a kiss would be spoiling anything, Mona.'

She closes her eyes.

'I'm afraid we misunderstand one another,' he says. She feels him move past her and out of the door.

'Yes,' she says, 'maybe you're right.'

She doesn't intend to slam the door but the breeze catches it or the knob slips from her fingers or she just wants him gone, but the noise is deafening, obscenely loud. She stands there in her hallway listening to his footsteps grow quiet and disappear. She stays there a moment longer and turns the key and then another moment with her fingers tracing the outline of her lips and the touch of his mouth on her cheek. She should never have answered the door.

32

It's a long journey out to Rubery Hill Hospital, a long walk, two buses and another walk at the other end, but Mona's determined to go alone. She doesn't want the aunts talking all the time.

Pestilence put a chair in the hallway right next to the payphone and Mona sat there for three days working her way through the Yellow Pages with a bag of coins and a shawl round her shoulders. She had to hold the line, ring back, give a description, prove who she was, which was almost impossible, and sometimes she just got cut off and she had to start all over again. 'Who did you say?' 'No one of that description.' 'No, sorry.' Mona dialled and waited and got nowhere until they answered at Rubery Hill. 'What's his name again? Let me check. Yes. I'll put you through.'

The Hollymoor Annexe looks like a school, blood-red brick and high windows, trees and shrubs all along the drive, but getting in is a different matter. Locked doors and keys and bolts everywhere.

'Dr Wright, left and down the hall.'

Right at the end of a long corridor, an old man buffs the lino with an industrial polisher; another man with a comb-over walks forward and back between the walls with a cigarette. Mona checks every door and when she sees a sign that says Dr Wright, she knocks.

'I'm here to see about my husband, William,' she tells the secretary. 'I have an appointment.' She gets a cup of tea and is told to wait in the doctor's office.

'He's always late.'

This isn't like the doctor's offices Mona is used to. There are posters of waterfalls and sunsets on the walls, two decrepit sofas and four armchairs. There's an old dark-wood desk covered in heaps of papers and two telephones. It smells like the snug of a pub, old tobacco and something metallic. Maybe it's the bars on the window. Mona sits in the middle of a green velvet sofa but the springs have gone and she sinks so low that she has to struggle to look dignified. Nearby she can hear pop music and someone with a wild, untidy laugh.

She wants to put the mug of tea down, she wants to pull her skirt a little lower over her knees and make sure she doesn't look as hysterical as she feels so she can explain why William must be let out, that he doesn't play pop music too loud or roar like a madman, and anyway, she's the one who should say what happens to William because she's his wife. But every time she moves she splashes tea on to her coat and she's all but crying when the door opens.

If he's a doctor, he has no white coat. He's wearing jeans and a big Fair Isle jumper like a farmer. He has on brown sandals in the middle of winter and he hasn't shaved for a couple of weeks at least. Without asking he leans over and pulls Mona up.

'It has the same effect on everyone,' he says, 'it's like being eaten alive.'

He points to a pair of red leatherette armchairs and they sit down.

'Sorry, sorry,' he says immediately, 'should have said. I'm Bob. Bob Wright. William's my patient and I'm a senior psychiatrist here.'

He shakes her hand. 'You're Desdemona, William's wife. And I apologize for being late. Well,' he says and claps his hands. 'Here we are. We haven't come very far with William yet. What we do know we've had to get out of him bit by bit. We knew nothing about you.'

'Didn't he tell you he was married?'

'William has hardly spoken since he was admitted.'

Mona puts her tea on the floor and takes an envelope out of her bag.

'It's all in there,' she says. 'William's birth certificate, my birth certificate and our marriage certificate.'

She holds the envelope right up to the doctor's face because she knows she looks young for her age and that lots of people don't bother with marriage these days but she and William did and she has the proof.

The doctor puts his hand on the envelope and gently pushes it away.

'That's okay, we don't need any identification. We're glad you're here and that William has someone who cares about him. At the moment he doesn't care very much about himself.'

The doctor starts to smoke, tapping the ash into the palm of his hand.

'Let me start at the beginning,' he says. 'It may be difficult for you but it's best that we're clear about William's mental health.'

'He's mental?'

'He's sick. Very sick.'

Without warning Mona feels a rage towards the doctor and his scruffy clothes, who can't even be bothered to get up and use the ashtray or the bin, who can't be bothered to look at three pieces of paper and doesn't own a shirt and winter boots.

'Why hasn't he contacted me?' she says.

'He's on some rather powerful medication, I'm afraid, and as I say, he hasn't told any of us about you.'

'Can I see him? I mean, he can come home, can't he? He hasn't done anything. He hasn't broken any laws.'

The doctor takes two drags of his cigarette before he speaks.

'Forgive me, but no, he cannot simply come home. I've spent some hours with William since he was admitted. He has had, in simple terms, a breakdown, an emotional psychosis. He's tried to harm himself and others. Quite seriously, I'm afraid. William presents a risk both to himself and to the public.'

Mona says nothing and the doctor smokes his cigarette.

'Does he have a history of mental illness?' he asks.

'He does not,' she says. She can hardly hear her own voice. Her throat is tight and the words have to struggle out.

'According to the police report, he was found drunk in a shop doorway having cut his wrists.'

Mona gasps.

'It was a serious attempt, Mona, although not very expertly executed. He lost a great deal of blood before he was discovered. In hospital he became very violent, attacked two nurses and a police officer with a screwdriver, then turned on himself. Stabbed himself in the arm, here. William is what we call "detained", that is to say he was admitted to this psychiatric hospital under a compulsory order for his own safety. He's given us precious little in the way of personal details, name and address and so forth, so we had no way of contacting any of his relatives. Had you not been in touch with us I doubt whether we would be any closer to knowing anything about William.'

The doctor looks down at the stub of his cigarette which is now dead.

'Since your phone call yesterday we have spoken to William. He's not tremendously forthcoming but it appears that you and William recently lost a baby.'

Mona nods.

'I'm sorry.'

Mona gets up quickly, picks the wastepaper basket up and stands over the doctor.

'Here,' she says. 'Put it in here.'

The doctor takes the bin from her, tips the ash and the butt in and puts it back on the floor. Then he lights another cigarette.

'Do you?' he says, offering Mona the packet.

'No.'

'Sensible. What we're not clear about is the bomb.'

'No, he had nothing to do with that, he wasn't even there if that's what you're saying.'

'No, you misunderstand me,' says the doctor. 'What I mean is that William has a number of injuries and we wondered whether he was a victim, whether he was in the pub when it was blown up.'

'He was attacked for being Irish. On the night of the bomb, he was attacked. His friend and himself, and Tom is blind in one eye. Englishmen attacked him and I want to see him.'

'I see, yes.'

'And then when he went home I wasn't there and he came straight to the hospital because he was worried about me and that's when he found out that our baby had died.'

'Yes, I'm very sorry for your loss.'

'She didn't breathe at all. I knew earlier on in the day, in my heart I knew, but William had no idea. She looked perfect, like she should be alive, but she just wasn't. I did nothing wrong. It wasn't because of anything I did, if that's what you're thinking or if that's what he's thinking. She died inside me but there was nothing I could do. William couldn't have done anything either. It could not have been prevented.'

'No.'

'He wouldn't hold her. I held her up but he couldn't. He looked at her, I think. I don't remember. He never took her in his arms. He had blood all over his face and dirt and dust in his hair and his clothes were filthy but I only realized after he'd gone that something must have happened to him as well. Something happened to me and the baby and to William all on the same night. None of us knew where he was. Not his aunts. Not me. Not anyone.'

She is crying but she doesn't care.

'If he's tried to kill himself it's because of the shock and when it wears off he'll get better. I've had to deal with it. And I've managed. He just needs time and to be among his own people. I'm taking him back to Ireland. Have you any idea what it's like to be Irish in Birmingham? Have you?'

She points down the corridor. 'It's me that should be in here, not just him.'

'I think that myself sometimes,' he says quietly. The doctor isn't really that old. He has a bit of grey hair but his face isn't lined. His eyes look ancient and his shoulders sag in his massive jumper. His skin is the same colour as the grey walls in his office.

'Look,' he continues, 'this is impossibly difficult for you. And the same goes for William. To say he's fragile is an understatement. He is unwilling to come to any of the group sessions which we're pretty keen on and which really do help. What we know about his feelings comes to us in fragments in his own time, in his own way. It's very early days. What we want to avoid is William becoming dependent. We have many patients that come in for short periods and then go home. They come back for a bit longer. They go home and this is repeated. We don't know for sure yet if William is acutely ill or if this is a one-off episode. There are people who are referred to us by the courts for assessment, people who need to be here and one or two people who don't. We do our best.'

He stands up, smokes the rest of his cigarette and grinds it out on the side of the bin. 'Would you like to see him now?'

Mona nods.

'I'll say this again. William is fragile. He is quite serious when he says he doesn't want to be here, that is to say, he doesn't want to be alive. He is in pain, mental pain, the same pain you feel when you break your arm or cut yourself except that it's here,' he taps his forehead, 'where no one can see and where, unfortunately, we have the most difficulty in helping people recover. But they do recover, you know. Many of our patients we never see again.'

The doctor opens the door.

'The hardest question for William to answer is "why". Why he's tried to take his own life and why he feels the way he does. So don't ask him. Don't talk about the future, it can be overwhelming. If you talk about the past, make it short, positive and as neutral as possible. A holiday you took together or a pleasant shared memory. Something like that. He's going to find your visit difficult because you will remind him of the events leading up to his admission. Go lightly, Mona.'

He buzzes her through a door and shakes her hand.

'We'll talk again.'

The secretary leads her back down the corridor to another locked door marked 'Day Room'. There are bars on the windows and the lights are too bright. The room is thick with heat and clanging laughter from the television. Low chairs cluster around plastic tables and through a wall of wired glass Mona can see two nurses at their desks and a big golden sign that says 'Merry Christmas'.

Mona scans the room. There he is, in a chair facing a window. She walks slowly and stands in front of him.

She didn't know what she expected but not this. Not half of him. And not that half looking past her, his mouth forming words that never come. His tongue lolls out of his mouth. He's wearing the dreadful clothes of an old man, baggy and out of shape.

She draws a chair up close and puts her handbag on her lap. He might run away if she touches him so she doesn't.

'Hello, William,' she says. He licks his lips. 'How are you?' She leans forward. She wants to see the whole of his face. It's sallow, puffed out as though someone's blown him up from the inside, but it's not good living nor good food that's done it. He has the yellow remnants of bruises and a scabby gash on his cheek. He juts his chin towards the glass as though telling her to look outside, at the winter garden and the wooden troughs of purple winter pansies. Mona wonders if they are planted by the inmates as some sort of compulsory work. She wonders if the troughs themselves have been made by men like William who are shut away from their families and people that love them.

'Lovely,' she says, 'lovely flowers.' She sounds stupid as though she's talking to a baby. But what can she say? Where have you been? What have you been doing? Why did you try to kill yourself?

'William, I'm really glad I've found you.'

He starts running his tongue over his teeth, down the space between his lips and gums, gurning, letting his jaw go slack.

'And your aunts will be pleased. Teresa and Margaret. They send their love.'

A thin thread of spit spins down from William's bottom lip on to his chest.

'No,' he says.

'No what?'

There are people all around them. A middle-aged couple sit close together, holding hands. A young man, a boy almost, sits in front of them, rocking from side to side, almost jumping out of his seat. He's smiling and talking, his fingers flickering in the air as though he's conducting a symphony. But his parents aren't laughing. They watch him with watery eyes and slumped shoulders. At a small coffee table on the other side of the room, two people work side by side on a jigsaw. They have the same head, the same face, like brother and sister. They sit in silence, quietly working away, passing pieces to one another, trying and rejecting a fit, sorting methodically through the pile. A black man stands in a corner, writhing and turning his head over and over, his eyes closed, his fists clenched against his chest. There are other patients with no visitors. Visitors with no patients. There is William and Mona. She puts her hand on his knee.

'You don't belong here, William.'

'No,' he says, letting his tongue loll on his wet lips. His eyes are dull, his lids are heavy. His long black hair is thick with grease and hangs in uneven hanks around his face.

'You'll get better if you come home,' she says. 'I'll help you. As soon as you're out of here you'll be well. You don't belong in here, William. Come home. We'll get you some tablets. I'll help you.'

He jerks forward and grabs her handbag, shoves it into her stomach and she yelps. He pushes her backwards and she topples out of her chair. She scrabbles to her feet as William begins a gentle rock like he's trying to balance on the bow of a ship. He stares past her out of the window, his eyes fixed on something outside.

'William! It's Mona.'

She tugs her coat straight. Two nurses stare out of the wired glass window but don't move. People are watching. The parents of the boy, the jigsaw woman.

'William, I'm here. Look. William. What are you looking at out there?'

Mona walks out, down the corridor, and turns immediately right and across the front garden, skirting the building, looking for the wooden troughs. All the gates are locked, all the fences too high to climb. She finds a route through some trees but it only brings her to a brick wall topped with barbed wire and a sign that says 'Private Property'.

William is in there somewhere. She retraces her steps and tries to go round the other way but there is no way into the grounds. If William is only going to look out of the windows then that's where she will be. He can't ignore her for ever. But the other way is just the same. 'No Entry. Keep Out.'

33

The next day she finds him in the same chair. She's brought clean, warm clothes in a carrier bag, some soap and a shaver, a comb for his hair. She has to give everything to the nurse in the office before he can have them, for his own good, they say, as they look through the bag. Mona has brought sandwiches and a pork pie, a bottle of lemonade and some biscuits. She can't take the bottle, they say, but she can pour him a glass if she wants.

She sits next to William, draws her chair up close and smells the sweat on him, the stench of the other man who owns the clothes, the boiler-suit man maybe who sits with his jigsaw and his sister or the man with the twisting neck.

'Hello, William,' she says and pats his hand. She notices the bandages on his wrist and the bruises on his knuckles. 'Are you well?'

Nothing.

'I brought you some food, they said you can have it later. Your favourites, William.'

The tongue droops out of his lips.

'You have to eat if you want to get better. Teresa would say that, wouldn't she? They both send their love. Teresa and Margaret. They've both been worried sick. We all have.'

The television is louder than ever. Horse racing, the commentary running like a single word at fever pitch and no one watching. She's too scared to turn it off.

'There are some jigsaws over there. Will we do one together, William? You like puzzles.'

William leans forward and puts his head on his knees.

'Are you not feeling well? Are you faint? Will I call a nurse?'

His arms hang loose, fingers on the carpet. In the corridor

Mona can hear an argument and scuffling. There are mad people everywhere, no one knows what they might do. This isn't a place for her husband, who's grieving and in shock.

'Shall I take you home, William?'

He shoots up on to his feet. He kicks furniture out of his way as he strides out of the room and then he is gone. Mona looks at the nurses through the wired glass but they are drinking tea and laughing, sticking little green holly shapes on the window and ignoring her. The lady with the jigsaw smiles but Mona won't be coming here when she's thirty to visit anyone, she wouldn't let anyone put William in a boiler suit and lock him up for ever. She'll never abandon him.

She strides down the hallway to Dr Wright's office. His door is open. He turns when he sees Mona.

'Come in, come in.' He's shuffling papers on his desk, picking up whole piles and putting them down again. 'It's here somewhere,' he says, 'a letter about the treehouse I'm building for my little girl. Planning permission. Not granted. So I'm going to appeal. Almost half an acre of garden and they say it's inappropriate or something. What was it now? Not inappropriate. Can't remember. Something like that. In other words, I can't build a little house for my daughter. So I'm going to appeal. I'll show them.'

He rifles through piles of letters and reports, files and prescriptions, moves two coffee cups and a dirty glass and then stands at a filing cupboard and starts to do the same.

Mona watches his slow uselessness, wanting to tell him to be methodical, tidy the surface off or at least start from one corner and work his way across to the other. She wants to tell him to shut up and pay attention to the terrible things they are doing to William. She wants to hit him for keeping her from him, for not healing him and making him well with all his learning and tablets and long words. He's just making William fat and doe-eyed, slobbering in a cheap, baggy jumper which is not his own that makes him look like an imbecile. Can't they wash him? Comb his hair? Let him go?

'Oh, for God's sake,' the doctor mutters with his back to her. 'I'll have to get them to send me another copy. How is he?'

'He looks terrible. He's not getting better.'

He looks at her and then behind her. He quickly walks to the desk and slips a piece of paper from a pile.

'Aha!' he says. 'Look, if William is looked after and has rest and therapy he may well be fine. Eventually. We do have to give it a little while yet.'

Mona sets her face. 'I don't like what you're doing to him. I don't agree with it. He's not himself. I know him,' she says. 'You don't.'

'I agree,' says the doctor, folding the paper in half and putting it in his pocket. 'But I do know mental illness and I do run a compassionate and caring hospital. At least my part of it.'

'I think he should come home. I don't think the medicine is agreeing with him.'

He stands by the door and gestures to her. 'You can visit William whenever you like and you can talk to him. But he is under my care and I'm afraid he is subject to Part IV of the Mental Health Act 1959. It is a legal requirement that he stays here at least until he is assessed and I'm afraid that assessment is not yet complete. We will keep you up to date on his progress. What he needs is quiet, stability and time. He also needs medication regularly and perhaps permanently. We shall see.'

As she leaves he calls her back. 'Tell me, are you seeing your own doctor?'

Mona shakes her head.

'You should. After what you have been through, you should be talking to someone.'

Mona looks at the long corridor that leads to the Day Room. She hears the industrial cleaner on some other long corridor, buffing the lino to a dull shine. She turns right and buzzes the door to be let out.

Pestilence and Famine are in the kitchen.

'When are we going home, Margaret?'

'When we bring him with us, Teresa.'

Mona pushes the door open and Pestilence clears her throat.

'Mona, love. We'll make the tea. You sit down.'

'He's the same,' says Mona. 'No, he's worse.'

'Should we come ourselves?' says Famine. 'Should we speak to the doctor?'

'There are four horsemen, aren't there?' Mona says.

'Horsemen, love?' says Famine.

'Of the Apocalypse. What are they?'

Pestilence tuts. 'What's that got to do with anything? It's not run by the nuns I hope. They're not filling his head with all that mumbo jumbo, are they, Mona? We don't want him coming home a religious nut.'

'War and Death,' says Mona. 'That's what's missing.'

Famine gives Mona a squeeze. 'Now, now, the two of you should come home with us for a holiday. He promised when you got married you would come over for a couple of weeks but then you were pregnant and . . . think of the nice long rest you could have. The beach around Renvyle is world famous, Mona. You've not a scrap of fat on you. Come to us. Get yourself well.'

Pestilence folds her arms. 'None of this hatred. He'd be better in no time away from England. You both belong with us now, Mona.'

The women sit and make their plans. Pestilence and Famine will return home to look after William's father. They will support Mona's request to the hospital to discharge William into their care. They'll give an undertaking to make sure he takes his medication, to keep him safe, anything, but they have to let him go. He's a citizen of the Irish Republic after all and they wish to take him home. Mona and William will then take the next aeroplane to Galway, never mind the cost. They'll recuperate together. Their next child will be born among its own people.

The aunts go off to their boarding house to pack and Mona sits on the sofa. She holds a mug of tea against her chest. The warmth seeps through her dressing gown and spreads down into her belly. It will be Christmas soon. They made no plans other than to be together, hunkered down by the fire, the three of them. Their dreams hadn't gone beyond Christmas and here she is on the third of December in a place she could never have imagined.

She feels the tears on her face and wonders when, like the milk in her breasts, they will finally dry up. She looks down at the cradled mug. Her robe has fallen over the rim and she feels only the heat. She moves the mug into the crook of her arm and arranges the pink candlewick until it covers the cup completely. She rucks the material up, more and more, until it makes a little bundle with the warm mug in the centre. She lays her head against the back of the sofa and her eyes close.

The short sleep she has is the first that gives her peace. When her eyes open again, the scrumble of cloth has not shifted. She peels it back and sees that the mug of tea is cold but intact. She puts her hands to her cheek. She has not cried.

She will talk to the doctor and bring him home. They will be looked after by Famine and Pestilence and sit by the fire, listening to the sea. They will lie together again in cool cotton sheets in an attic bedroom with the beams creaking in the wind, the weight of his arm on her waist, his breath on her neck. Long walks, yes, and new family to meet, and maybe William will sing again and the life will be back behind his eyes.

The following day, at the coach station, there is an almighty queue. Famine has stuffed jams and chocolate and liqueurs into her suitcase and can hardly carry it. Pestilence is determined to be first on to the coach so insists they stand right up close to the vehicle door in the ice-cold draught that blows in off the main road. Mona can't feel her hands nor her feet nor her heart. She stands between the two women, listening to the unspoken worry in their ceaseless arguments.

Eventually, the coach driver waddles over from the canteen and climbs into his cab. He fiddles with some buttons and then gets out again and begins checking tickets. He pulls open a wide door in the side of the coach and people begin piling their luggage inside. Famine stows the suitcases, kisses Mona and huffs on board while Pestilence checks their tickets.

'It's a long journey and it's one I'm not looking forward to,' she says, 'but I have no choice. I have himself at home and I have William here.'

Pestilence puts her head to one side and looks at Mona like she's sizing her for a suit.

'You've got a good bit of William in you, child. Stubborn to the bone. And I thank God for it. I have no fear for him while he has you.' Her voice is soft and even. 'You'd never leave him.'

Famine begins knocking on the window like a child, gesturing her sister on board, and Mona puts her arm round Pestilence.

'I'll bring him home,' she says.

Pestilence puts her handbag on her shoulder and sniffs. 'If I believed those fairy stories I would pray for you. Pray for you both. For the three of you, I would. But I have more faith in you than I ever had in the Church.'

She quickly kisses Mona and grips her shoulder.

'I'll come back alone. After Christmas, I'll be back. If anything changes, send a telegram. You're not alone.'

Then she gets on board and Mona watches her haranguing her sister until the coach pulls out and they are gone.

She sleeps all the following day. Across the city, William is locked in some terrible room, dribbling on to his pillow, missing her and missing their baby and still reeling from the shock of it all, like she is. She rehearses little speeches she will make to the doctor, framing and reframing her request – no, her demand. She will take his passport. She will, if necessary, go to the Irish Embassy and get a letter. She will get a solicitor. An Irish doctor. But first she will start with a polite request. She thinks of Bridie O'Connor and what she would say and what she would wear and how she would put her handbag square on her lap and cross her feet at her ankles and say firmly and sweetly that William is to come home. Set him free.

Dr Wright is waiting for her and gestures her into his office.

'Please,' he says, showing her a chair, and before Mona can speak he squeezes her hand. 'I'm afraid I have some bad news.'

Mona nods because somehow she knew that William was dead. She knew that in the night or in the day when she wasn't there, when she was sleeping or washing or sobbing on her bed, he had stopped breathing like their baby. That he'd gone and left her all alone.

'He's dead,' she says.

Dr Wright shakes his head. 'No, no. No, he's not dead but he had a bloody good go at it.'

He lights a cigarette. 'We can't watch everyone all the time although in fact we were keeping a very close eye on your husband. He made one or two attempts at escape yesterday and was quite violent. And then in the middle of the night he – well, he tried to hang himself. Used a sheet. The staff here are very vigilant and he was discovered before . . . and he's in the hospital wing now. Heavy sedation, I'm afraid.'

Dr Wright seemed to recede then like he was being pulled back at terrific speed, pulled away from her down a long corridor, and she could only just hear what he was saying. Something muffled about William's determination to die, something else about danger and things being unfortunate.

'Unfortunate?' says Mona but he doesn't answer. He just stands up and says, 'I'll take you there myself.' They walk down fetid corridors, hung with Christmas streamers, tinsel and cut-out angels that look like hordes of grotesque white bats, things that might come alive at any moment. Her shoes squeak on the polished floors. Dr Wright stops outside the door to a single room. 'He's a very ill man. This may take some time but we are committed to whole-person care here. We can work with him but he has to want it, Mona. Talk to him. Make him want it.' He squeezes her hand again and she goes inside.

34

Mona will always remember the last time she saw William in the hospital. He's lying on the metal bed with the blanket up to his chest, the skin around his neck burnt red and sore where the sheet had caught him when he dropped and hung. He's heavier than he's ever been, swollen from the drugs, full of water and sorrow, and so sour a smell Mona wants to hold her nose. Or wash him. Wash him properly from head to toe with their own soap and dry him with their own towel until he is hers again. There is a plastic cup of water on a little cabinet and a clipboard fastened to the bedstead with William's name on it. Someone has put a Bible on the windowsill.

And she will always remember the way the low winter sunlight screams against the window and a single shaft lights up his head like some kind of halo, mocking them both.

She sits next to the bed. She has no idea if he is asleep or in a coma or wailing crouched in a corner of his mind like a small boy in a big room. Wherever he is, it's far away. His hands are cold.

'Hello, William.'

But he is saying nothing so maybe he doesn't hear. Mona takes a handkerchief from her bag and wipes the corners of his mouth where spittle has dried and turned white.

'That's better,' she says.

He's wearing a blue striped pyjama top that someone has buttoned wrongly. She folds the blanket back and re-fastens it, talking to him all the while as Dr Wright has asked.

'So, the journey here is a terrible thing, William. And it's cold outside, freezing actually. I wasn't sure if I should wear a hat because they're so old-fashioned but in the end I didn't care. I thought I might get frostbite on my ears.'

She tucks him up and pats his chest, rising and falling slow as the tide.

'Are you coming back to me, William?' she whispers.

She wonders who put cream on the sheet burns under his chin and whether they were kind to him, whether it was one of the young good-looking female nurses or the big blokes that look like bouncers. She wonders whether William has lucid moments when he might share a laugh and a joke with whoever is washing his private parts and his armpits and whether he's alive behind his eyes, just waiting for her to leave so he can wake up and get out of bed.

'Is that what you're doing?' she says. 'Trying to get rid of me?'

There is nothing kind in her voice. She doesn't care.

'What do you think it's like for me? I'm bleeding still, William, and our baby is dead. Our baby is dead. Our baby is dead.'

She grips his fingers and squeezes them hard.

'I'm here all on my own. And it's Christmas, William. Where have you gone? Are you coming back to me, William? I can't bear it any more.'

She lifts his arm and lets it drop back, lifts it again and lets it drop. She peels the blanket back and looks at him from head to toe. If the nurses come in they'll think she's mad and maybe lock her up as well but so what? She could do with a rest. William's ankles are fat and his skin is yellow; no one has cut his toenails. Could she move him over and sneak in beside him? Does she even want to any more?

Suddenly he turns his face from left to right.

'William? William? I'm here. It's me. Mona.'

He breathes in like he's about to speak and then lets out a little belch, rancid and medicine-stenched.

Mona bites down on her lip and tastes her blood. She'll cover him up and make sure he looks decent. She'll ask about the welts on his neck and what they are using. She'll ask if someone can brush his teeth or if she is expected to do it as she is his wife and maybe she should do all the intimate care after all. And also she'll bring in some pyjamas that have not been worn by other people, by another madman who's tried to hang himself or maybe a man who succeeded. She is so tired. She'll come back in a few days, after Christmas, with nail clippers and a little vase of flowers if they are allowed and she'll ask for the Bible to be removed. Neither of them has any faith left. She will do all this next time. She kisses him goodbye.

She turns the key in the door and sits at her kitchen table. The idea of Christmas alone is mortifying. William will be days and days getting better and Mona cannot bear to be alone. She has no present for him, nor him for her, and their flat is full of their baby's unworn and beautiful things, things that she would have hand-washed in perfumed soap and ironed with rosewater, precious things that would smell of milk and innocence. Mona picks up the telephone and realizes there is only one person left to call.

On Christmas Day, Mona sits at Bridie O'Connor's cold and elegant dining table, pushing meat from one corner of the plate to another. She spent the first day avoiding Bridie's questions, determined to tell her nothing. After each fruitless enquiry, Bridie would veer off only to return again to the source of Mona's troubles like a magnet returning north. Of course, Mona regretted getting in touch as soon as she heard her voice on the phone.

'Mona! It's been more than a year and I was beginning to worry. The last I heard you were still working in the factory and someone said you were married.'

Mona said she would be coming alone.

'I see. Well, naturally, you'll come here, naturally. Where else would you go?'

There had been all sorts of fuss since the moment she stepped through the door. No tea-making for Mona this time. She had to sit by the fire under a crocheted blanket and take sherry on the hour or brandy in strong coffee. There had been great long pauses between them with Mona's lips clamped shut on the whole sorry tale and Bridie waiting for the curtains to open on whatever tragedy had brought her back to Kilmore Quay.

Mona refused to go to mass and now she's here, sitting across from Bridie O'Connor as still and poised as a stone Madonna.

'You're not hungry, lovey?' says Bridie.

'No.'

'Wait while I make you a bit of Christmas pudding. Will you eat that?'

'No. No thank you.'

Bridie puts down her knife and fork and sits back in her chair.

'Come on, we'll go and sit by the fire. This room is a bit chilly after all.'

Bridie pours them both a little tumbler of something sweet and Mona realizes that the two of them have been drinking steadily for the past two days. She has slept well and that's the reason why. She throws the whole tumbler of sticky wine to the back of her throat and holds the glass for more. Bridie fills it without comment. It's almost dark outside.

'When are you leaving?' Bridie says quietly. Mona shoots her a look but Bridie's staring into the fire. 'You can stay, of course, but you'll want to go back, won't you? Go back to England away from here. You never could wait to be away.'

'Yes, I am going. Yes,' says Mona.

'Ah, well,' she replies and the sorrow in Bridie's voice cuts Mona to the quick.

'I live there now,' Mona added, gentler now. 'I've got a flat and a job. And I have a husband.'

Bridie nods and sips from her drink. 'A husband? Good. Good. I loved your father from the very day I met him.'

Mona can hardly move.

'I fell in love just once and it was with your father. Married I was, with a young baby, and happy enough. We had this house and everything was fine and dandy and then your mother, God rest her soul, brought Robbie round to meet us and it just happened.'

Mona glances up and back at the fire. Bridie's voice sounds dreamy, far away.

'I don't know if he knew. Not a word ever passed between us.

Not a word. Not a touch. Not a look. While I was married and while he was married I would never have said anything or done anything. I respected my husband and I was a good wife, a good mother. Robbie and Kathleen were as happy as anyone could be. You know that, don't you?'

Mona nods but cannot speak. Bridie tops up her glass from the decanter at her elbow.

'When your mother died and I was already a widow I thought things might change. I said nothing while he was grieving and he had the sole care of a little daughter, of you. I wanted him to recover and come back to himself. I watched him hand in hand with you stalking the sand up at Forlorn Point and I wanted to comfort him. Oh, I wanted him. Yes, I did.'

Bridie's eyes are wide and glassy, staring at the flames, her head leaning on one side.

'I said nothing. Then time went on and you began to resent me. You saw how I felt. I knew that while you were still here Robbie and I would never have a chance so I waited and you left. He was upset for a few weeks, more than upset. He missed you terribly and worried about you but he wanted you to have your own way, wanted you to have a chance.'

Mona goes to speak but Bridie raises her finger.

'Don't,' she says. 'I know. You missed him too and you intended to come back and then he died. You've already told me.'

Her voice is hard now. 'You see, in those few weeks before the accident he had begun calling for me in the car on little pretences, a book he wanted from Carey's, a first look at the Camross Ballroom, a run out to Fethard. Anything. He was coming round. Without a word, after all those years and all that waiting, he was coming round.'

She sniffs. 'Then he died, Mona, and all my waiting had been for nothing. My restraint and my decency had all come to nothing. I lost him.'

Mona is hot. The drink and the wild flames and Bridie's confessions boil her blood. 'You never had him.'

'Ha!' says Bridie and throws her head back, laughing. 'I had the chance of him, my darling. I had the chance of him. And let me tell you this. The chance of something is a good meal when you're starving.'

Mona bites into her cheek. The woman is drunk. 'I don't know why you're telling me this now.'

'Neither do I. Unless it's as a warning. Unless I just wanted to tell someone, to confess, to hear my heart speak.' She drains her wine. 'I've made a will and you're to inherit this house and everything in it. You'll have the top field and the old farm where the Goreys live but I wouldn't want you to throw them out. You won't throw them out, will you?'

Mona shakes her head.

'I have a bit of jewellery too. You already have the rent from the cottage so when I'm gone you'll be well off. It's what Robbie would have wanted. We would have made such a plan had things been different.'

She gets up then, slowly and deliberately. She smooths down her skirt and slides her glass on to the little side table next to her chair.

'Goodnight, Mona. Tomorrow we will talk about something else entirely.'

Hours after, when the fire is dead and the old house begins to moan against the wind, when Mona is beginning to feel the cold, she gets up and goes to her bedroom. The curtains are still open and just faintly she can see the moonlit tips of breaking waves, the little islands far off the coast and the bay where she used to walk with her father. She wonders for the first time if, after she left, he walked there alone and what he felt standing out there with his hands in his pockets, what he was thinking. She remembers watching him lean over the arm of his chair to look at something Bridie was showing him, how he laughed at her observations and always added a quiet word when she'd finished. Had he loved her? Had Mona stood in his way?

She lies down in her clothes and because she doesn't sleep she sees the sunrise and the night change from pewter to lilac and then the pale blue of morning. She's up before Bridie and downstairs with a blanket over her shoulders, busy in the kitchen. She takes two good strong mugs from the cupboard and fills them both from the pot. She knocks on Bridie's bedroom door and finds her sitting up, puffy-eyed and pale.

'I overslept,' she says as she gathers her nightdress round her chest. 'I'll be up in a minute.'

Mona puts both mugs of tea on the bedside cabinet and sits carefully on the bed. 'I lost my baby, Bridie,' she says and begins to cry.

35

There is nothing good to be said of November. Mona buttons her coat and tucks the ends of her scarf inside so the wind can't whip them away. She's never suited a hat but she wishes she had one anyway no matter what she looks like. She has her overnight things in a small suitcase with wheels, she has a handbag, gloves and – as always at this time of the year – a sense of dread.

She's told him once but she will tell him again. So she bumps the trolley over the cobbles and makes her way to the station via the carpenter's workshop. He's using the electric saw and doesn't hear her enter. She watches him work. She could walk over unseen and pull the plug on the machine. She could smack him a good one on his back and make him spin round in surprise. She could grab the front of his shirt and shake him until her fingers bleed. She could just call out and he would turn round, so that's what she does.

He takes his goggles off and stares at her.

'I'm going now. I'm getting the 8.38.'

'Yes,' he says.

'I'm early,' she says and she looks at her watch.

'Yes, yes you are. Are you walking?'

'I am. Do you want to come?'

'I've this to finish.' He gestures to a long plank, to his circular saw, and he shrugs.

'I'll go then,' she says. 'Just thought I'd tell you.'

He turns away. 'Goodbye,' he shouts over his shoulder and then the noise of the saw and his back hunched over it.

At the station, she buys coffee and a sweet pastry while she waits. On the train, she works her way through a packet of sweets, one after another until her tongue is sore. She keeps her eyes on the barren fields, on the naked trees, and she keeps her memories in check because there is time enough for that sort of thing. She changes trains in London and then settles herself down for the journey to Birmingham, just over an hour, two stops, quick as you like. The train is full and busy and she's glad of the noise and distractions.

There's no need for Val to meet her off the train but of course she's there, waving and smiling. Her embrace nearly squeezes the tears out.

'It's been too long, Mona. And look at your hair!'

'Oh, I know, I know.'

'Are you all right?'

'Grand, fine.'

'Come on then.'

Val hooks her arm through Mona's and they walk together through the town centre.

'Everywhere's different,' says Mona. 'And the station's unrecognizable.'

Val shakes her head. 'I don't drive into town any more. I've no idea where these new roads go. I got a ticket for driving in a bus lane a few months ago and I said to myself, "That's it." So I get the bus now.'

'Every year it gets more and more like somewhere I don't know.'

'Me too and I live here.'

Mona puts her case in Val's guest room. Lovely Val, who's put a single white flower, a daisy, in a little vase next to the bed, who's never missed a year. This will be the worst visit and Mona knows it but doesn't know why. She must say nothing to Val, who's good enough to put her up and stand by her side.

They sit in Val's little dining room overlooking the dual carriageway.

'They've come and replaced the double glazing at last. Can you tell?'

'I can,' says Mona, 'lovely and quiet. What about your mother now?'

Val shakes her head. 'Bloody social services. They've put her in a home in Pype Hayes. That's forty minutes on a good day and I don't know how much petrol. You have to pay to park there if you're a visitor. They put her there without any consultation and you still have to pay. I mean, she's safe enough I suppose. Sometimes she doesn't know where she is, doesn't realize she's moved house. She recognizes me, more's the pity, and can still find the right words to complain all the time. Always wants food bringing in so I take her a packet of biscuits or some cheese and crackers. I used to make her a proper dinner, you know, cottage pie or something, but the care staff told me that as soon as I'd gone she put it straight in the bin.'

'She's getting worse then.'

'Downhill all the way.'

'Is that what we have in store, you and me?' Mona asks.

Val whistles softly. 'Bloody hope not. Not for a good few years yet. We're still young, Mona, for God's sake.'

'Are we?'

'Sixty's the new forty they say, even if it feels like fifty-nine.'

They sit together with the muffled thrum of the cars and lorries outside, in the sour afternoon light, and say nothing. Val gets up suddenly.

'Nearly forgot!'

She runs upstairs and comes down with a little box wrapped in turquoise paper, a silver bow on top.

'Here you are.'

'Oh, Val, you shouldn't have. Your card was enough but this is lovely, thank you. Honestly, there's no need.'

'Don't be daft. Go on, open it. It's only two months late.'

It's a paperweight. A little silver bird trapped in a heavy bubble of glass.

'It's lovely, Val.'

'Do you like it? I thought that you could use it in the shop, you know, to keep the papers from blowing around when the door opens.'

Mona holds it up to the light and turns it slowly. She mustn't cry so she laughs.

'And it's good for throwing if I have a robber!'

Val smiles. 'Yes.'

Then there's nothing for it but to get going. Val drives and when they reach the cemetery she links her arm through Mona's and they walk up the long lane towards the high brick wall.

'Twenty-eight years, Val,' says Mona.

Val's answer is a squeeze of the elbow.

'Wish I'd done things differently.'

'You say that every year, Mona. You didn't know where she was, no one did.'

'Yes, you're right. But still.'

'Some people never find their babies. At least you've got somewhere to come.'

'She doesn't know though, does she? She doesn't know that I come.'

Val says nothing.

'And he doesn't know.'

They skirt the chapel in the centre of the graveyard and carry on up the path that becomes narrow and covered in moss. A sprawling yew throws low branches over the grey headstones and part of the back wall has crumbled and perished in the damp of the dark shade. The two women pick their way through the narrow paths and come to a haggard patch of green with a slab of black marble set to one side.

'Here we are,' says Val. She stands still. Only Mona moves forward. She takes off her gloves and taps the headstone lightly with her fingers.

'Hello,' she says. 'Arthur Samuel Fielding. I pay my respects to you and thank you again for taking care of my daughter.'

Mona opens her handbag and takes out the tiny linen doll with black curly hair and a thick blue winter coat. She holds on to Val's hand and lowers herself to her knees. The ground is damp and cold as she knew it would be. She will get wet and maybe the edges of her coat will get dirty and stained. She props the doll against the headstone.

'Hello, my little angel. Well, Beatrice, there's a new toy for you,' she says. 'It will be gone in a few days, I know. But it's there anyway. I made it for you.'

Mona sinks down on to the weeping grass.

'I have something to say to you, Beatrice. I hope you'll understand. You see, I don't know how much longer I can come, sweetheart. I really don't. I'm sixty now and you've gone. And you went a long, long time ago and wherever you are, it's not here.'

There is, as always, the sense of stilling time, of the air and the noise of the day being hushed, the same sense of monumental grief. There were times in the past when she would stay for an hour or two. When Val would walk back to the car and wait there with the engine running to keep warm. When Mona would talk about William and what he was like and what plans they had made. There was the time when she sat and finished the doll by hand with a few stitches before she laid it down in a little leather pouch. And the very first time when she had so much more to say, when she had to say sorry for taking twelve years to find her and they had years to catch up on. But these days, Mona is realistic and knows she talks to tiny bones, if those tiny bones still exist. She leans close to the earth.

'I love you,' she whispers. 'I miss you. Still sleeping, Beatrice.'

She pats the grass twice. Wipes her face with the back of her hand and Val helps her stand and passes her a tissue.

'Thank you, Val, love,' she says. 'All done.'

They are slow to make the journey back to the car. The wind cuts across the open space and stings Mona's cheeks. Her hands are freezing and her legs feel light, full of air.

'Did you mean it?' says Val. 'About not coming any more?'

'I don't know,' Mona says after a while. 'I've just been thinking about things.'

'I've been worried about you, you know.'

'Oh, I've been worried myself. I think it's just my birthday, you know, it makes you think. I mean, how much time have I got left? I have to have a life, Val.'

'You're preaching to the converted, Mona. What have I always said? And you said you'd met someone. Been out on a date, you said. Come on, details, please!'

'Oh, you needn't get excited,' says Mona and makes her walk on. 'I've probably gone and ruined it. Gave him his marching orders a couple of weeks ago.'

'Why did you do that? Who is he? Where did you meet him? Does he know about –'

'No, no. I've told him nothing really. He's a bit older than me and he's very different but he's a gentleman. Got a sort of elegance about him, speaks different languages and everything. Very knowledgeable about things, you know, wine and food. He's travelled all over and he's refined. Yes, refined is what you'd call him.'

'Oh, very lah-di-dah,' says Val.

'Oh, not refined then, that's not really the right word, and anyway, I've ruined it. I gave him the brush-off when he tried to kiss me.'

'Is he not fanciable then, this gentleman?'

'It's not that.'

'No,' says Val. 'I didn't think so.'

Val's booked them a table at Purnell's. Mona wears a black dress with a brooch that she found in a second-hand shop. The stones were loose but she eased them back in. Everything goes to the dolls, it's time she kept something for herself.

'I'm not coming out with you again if you're going to outdo me all the time,' says Val. 'You look great, Mona.'

They sit at a window overlooking the street. You wouldn't need telling it's near Christmas, there's a sparkliness to everything, a festive feeling, like the whole place is waiting for the party to start. The menus arrive.

'We're having champagne,' Mona says and holds her hand up when Val goes to speak. 'No. Say nothing. My treat. This is for my birthday, remember, and anyway it's been too bloody long since I had champagne and I want it in one of them champagne saucers as well. A coupe is the right word.'

'He's rubbing off on you then, this posh bloke with fifteen languages.'

They order extravagantly, bread and olives which neither of them eat, red wine with their starters and steak, side dishes of buttered greens and sweet potato fries. By the time their puddings arrive, Mona has sunk a little in her chair, her cheeks are red.

'Can I force this in?' says Val, holding a spoonful of chocolate mousse in the air. 'I haven't got any space left.'

Mona shakes her head and digs her spoon into a bowl of ice cream. 'There's no harm in a mousse. It will slide down and settle in the gaps.'

Val closes her eyes. 'Hope you're right,' she says. 'I'm going to have to undo a button in a minute.'

But neither can finish and they end up shoving their dishes away and pouring out the last few inches from the bottle.

'Do you remember the 24-Hour Girdle, Val?' says Mona.

Val splurts her wine and dabs her giggles with a napkin. 'It wasn't twenty-four bloody hours. It was the 18-Hour Girdle by Playtex.'

'Was it?'

'Yes, it was. Who wears a girdle for twenty-four hours?'

'Could double up as a chastity belt,' says Mona. 'As I remember, there was a girdle and a panty girdle. What was the difference?'

Val holds two fingers up. 'One had built-in knickers, I think. The other had them white plastic hooks for the stockings. My mum had them, both varieties. I tried them on once. When you sat down they rolled up and cut in like cheese wire.'

'The 18-Hour Cheese Girdle,' says Mona.

'The 24-Hour Chastity Cheese Girdle.'

'With built-in crotch support.'

They're still laughing when the waiter brings their coffee. Mona leans across the table. 'That reminds me,' she says, 'there's this couple on their honeymoon.'

'Please,' says Val. 'I'm in agony here.'

'No, listen. A man and a woman on their honeymoon. It's their first time, you know, doing it. She's kept herself pure for their wedding night.'

'Idiot,' says Val and they laugh again.

'So anyway, she's under the covers waiting for him. He comes in and stands by the bed to get undressed. He takes off his socks and she looks at his toes and they're all gnarled and hairy with the nails all set in at a terrible angle. "Oh," she says. "What's wrong with your toes?" He ums and ahs and says, "Well, I had toe-cilitis." "Toe-cilitis?" she says. "I've never heard of that." "Yeah, yeah," he says, "it was terrible but I'm over it now." She thinks to herself, "Well, all right, I can live with toe-cilitis." Then the husband takes off his trousers and she sees his legs. He has these knees all crooked and bony with terrible pitted scars and when he sees her looking he says, "Ah, yes, I had a touch of kneasles." "Kneasles?" she says. "Yes, it was a bad case of kneasles but I'm all cured now." "I see," she says and watches carefully as he takes down his underpants. She has a good long look and folds her arms. "Don't tell me," she says. "Smallcocks."'

36

Val takes her all the way to the station and kisses her goodbye at the ticket barrier. 'It's my retirement do on the nineteenth. You coming? Just the nurses and staff from Dudley Road, a few from the old days at Selly Oak.'

'Yes, yes. I'll put it in the diary.'

'Remember what you said, now, Mona. You have to have a life. Your words, not mine.'

It rains on the way home. Rain on the cusp of ice, slanting against the window. Mona can see nothing through the thick fog of condensation that she won't wipe away. She chose a quiet carriage so it's nearly empty, she has a little table to herself and no one in the other three seats around it. She bought a newspaper at the station but sometimes train reading makes her feel sick. So she leaves it where it is, rolled up in her bag, and she feeds her hands up the sleeves of her coat like a geisha. She closes her eyes.

She'd never usually sleep in a public place but the noise of the engine and gentle rolling motion of the train is as soothing as a lullaby, and anyway, there's no one around to steal her bag and no one nearby to stare, and if she nods off, the train's final stop is London and that's where she gets off. The guard would wake her surely and she might feel better for a snooze. She's seen other people napping on long journeys, with their heads jerking forward every few minutes, their mouths hanging slack and loose. No one seems to mind.

Sometimes on Sunday afternoons, Mona sits between her parents on the old sofa while they listen to the radio. Well, it's on in the background, with the door open if it's fine and the fire on if it isn't. Sometimes they all play cards or read books. Mona's mother sews or knits and her father fills in the crossword or reads the paper. Once in a while, they all walk out to the cinema or to visit Bridie O'Connor or one of the other families in the village. There is a dance once a year and the agricultural show at the end of August with stalls and competitions. The years seem to blend into one another, one long golden road flanked with flowers, Mona walking between her parents holding a hand each all the way along the strand to Ballyteige for the fair or to St Catherine's to the park or right out to Ardamine beach for a picnic. Mona wanders off and returns to find always, always her father and mother in a quiet embrace, her head on his chest, or the two of them lying on the grass side by side watching the cotton-wool clouds shift across the sky.

Once the three of them get caught in a storm. It comes in off the sea as quick and angry as a wild bull and they have to run the length of the beach to shelter in the dip of a sand dune. Mona's father takes his shirt off and cloaks it around Mona's shoulders, his broad, naked chest heaving from exertion.

'Are you all right, Kathleen?' he says, wiping the water from his wife's face.

Mona catches the look that passes between them, a secret look. He with his hand on her shoulder and her with a summer dress stuck to her chest and between her legs.

'I'm soaked, Robbie. It's obscene.'

But she's laughing and so is he.

'That's your opinion,' he says and with a kiss.

Mona's mother becomes ill later that year. She begins to lose weight and energy and has to rely on Maureen O'Shea to help her every week to cook and clean and get through the household chores. Mona's father moves out of their bedroom and makes a little cot downstairs by the fire. The doctor tells them that Mona's mother needs absolute peace and even Mona can smell the sickness on the sheets, the sweet miasma of decay that more and more bleeds down, through the rafters and into the fabric of the house.

Shortly before her mother dies, Mona finds her parents hand in hand sobbing together on the bed. Mona hears them talking and creeps upstairs, watches them through a gap in the door.

'I can't bear it, Kathleen,' her father says through his sobs.

'Robbie, pet, don't.'

She kisses him. Not the sort of kiss that Mona gets. Not the sort of kiss that says 'Goodnight' or 'Clever girl'. It's the slow kiss she saves for him alone, that she gave him on the beach, that made him miss her even before she died.

London is dry but bitter cold. It's already high Christmas season even in November and the shops are lit up with flashing snow-flakes and neon fir trees. In the window of a little stationer's there's a nativity scene made of brown paper origami figures, with baby Jesus on a bed of shredded straw. Mona stops and notices Mary's carefully painted face, a look of wonder and joy with a few strokes of a brush. She could get the carpenter to make a couple of Marys and Josephs this year and maybe a manger or two. A little late now to go adding orders and new designs but next year perhaps. Next year.

Mona takes the bus to Farringdon for the train to the coast. She's already bought the few presents she needs so won't stop at any of the big department stores. She has her little trolley and a handbag and that's bad enough to manoeuvre through the crowds. She stands on the platform and waits.

Next year she'll make the same journey and make the same decision to hurry home, put her case in the cupboard and hang up her coat. Next year she'll climb the stairs to the carpenter's work-shop and be greeted by his back bent to the lathe, collect another few dolls and paint them alone in her workroom, talking to her-self about colour combinations for their clothes and the hairstyles they might wear. And next year she will be sixty-one and then the year after sixty-two and the panic catches in her throat like a sharp stone.

The train rattles in. As Mona gets on, the wheel of her trolley catches on the door. She yanks it but it only twists, doesn't come free. The carriage is full of shoppers and noise and aftershave and young men with headphones and young girls in thin jackets and a couple in their prime with their two prime children and a toddler asleep in a pushchair. Nobody moves. In a moment, the door will close and Mona's trolley will be ruined or an enormous alarm will sound somewhere and everybody will look. Mona puts both hands on the handle and pulls and pulls, and then, right in front of her, a man bends down and frees the wobbly wheel from the lip of the carriage door. He picks the trolley up and twists the neck of the wheel and something clicks into place. He settles it back down by Mona's feet. He's not young either, grey hair with a side parting, a woollen overcoat with a tartan scarf at his neck, and he's sixty himself, maybe, with a neat little beard and moustache.

'Thank you, thank you,' Mona says as she sits down and smiles up at him.

'The mechanism's worn on that rogue wheel,' he says as he sits down opposite Mona, 'but that should fix it for a while.'

Mona opens her mouth to speak about unreliable luggage and cold hands and an awful journey in weekend traffic and thank you again but before she can say anything, the man reaches for the woman next to him. The woman is Mona's age, better dressed, with leather gloves and a sheepskin coat. She's wearing a glamorous fur hat like someone from *Doctor Zhivago*. She hardly turns her head when the man rests his hand on her lap but she clasps his glove, a move that Mona knows she's made a thousand times before. He leans a little so their shoulders touch and the woman, his wife surely, still looking straight ahead, blinks slowly as if to say *Lovely*.

Mona puts her handbag on her lap and holds it tight. The man and the woman don't speak, they have no need, and Mona sees that they have lots of carrier bags from high-quality shops, presents for their friends and relations, for children and grandchildren, neighbours; not food yet probably, except for a bottle of port maybe or some jellied fruits. They will shop for one another in secret, things neither of them needs because after all it's the Christmas card that counts, the inscription inside, the handwritten dedication.

Just before their station, the man says something to his wife but his words are lost in the screech of the wheels and they both stand. Mona tries not to be nosy but she must watch as they get off. He takes all the bags and lets his wife off first. He guides her, with perfect manners, his hand in the small of her back, and just before the doors close, they link arms and disappear.

It's early evening when the train at last brings Mona home. She walks first to the off-licence opposite the station and parks her trolley by the counter.

'Now,' she says to the shopkeeper. 'I had a good bottle of wine the other day but I couldn't tell you what it was.'

'Red or white?' he says, folding his arms.

'Red.'

'Peppery? Bold? Heavy? Rich? Strong? Give me a few clues.'

'It tasted a bit like wood or resin. With vanilla. It was very strong.'

'Spanish? Chilean? French?'

Mona shakes her head. 'Begins with "M".'

The man narrows his eyes. 'Did you get a look at the label?'

Mona makes a square with her two hands. 'White, I think, with big black letters.'

'I've got a Chilean Merlot with a cat on the front?'

'What's it like?'

'It's like twelve ninety-nine.'

'Oh. That's a pedigree cat then. I better have a look.'

Mona lets him show her the bottle but she knows she'll take it anyway because the choice in the shop is overwhelming and he's the best judge. She doesn't want to end up with a bottle of vinegar. She lets him persuade her into a long, silver gift bag and then walks towards home.

37

Mona gets the bus to Dublin and flies home. She takes the number forty-five bus from the airport into town and then the number fifty home. She pushes her little suitcase inside the door and gets the bus straight to the hospital. Half of her wants to make herself some toast and tomato soup. She imagines dragging the blankets to the fire and watching the television, putting some money in the meter and running a hot bath with bubbles, soaking her bones until they are warm through. The bleeding has stopped.

She's brought William a Christmas present, a silver flask that she found in Bridie's house. They polished it together with baking soda and wrapped it in a silk handkerchief before she left. The wrapping paper is covered in cartoon holly. It's a long walk from the hospital entrance to the ward and Mona is surprised to find that she's gone to the wrong place after all because William's bed is empty. It takes her a long, long time, maybe five or seven minutes, to find the duty nurse and explain that she would like to see her husband because she went to Ireland to recover and she's been away for too long and maybe she never should have gone but she's better now and she's come back.

It takes the duty nurse one minute twenty seconds to find a private room and tell Mona what has happened and another five minutes to make Mona the cup of tea she never drinks. Mona straightens the watch on her wrist and does what the nurse tells her, which takes another one hour and twenty-seven minutes, going to different rooms and talking to people that tell her different things and ask her if she's all right. Then Mona finds her way back to the hospital entrance but keeps getting lost and because she's carrying William's personal effects in a white cardboard box she feels exhausted like she could fall over or fall asleep and the box feels like it weighs three stone and not three pounds. There is virtually nothing inside, just his clothes and shoes but no wedding ring because he is wearing that still, at least. It will still be on him. There may be lost minutes or even hours when she listens to a different doctor or a nurse or an administrator or someone that makes her sign papers while they give their apologies and explanations and tell her what to do next and who she should contact but Mona never can account for that time even years and years afterwards.

She remembers getting home somehow, maybe she walks, but by the time she opens her front door it's pitch black and her fingers are frozen into claws where she's gripped the box in the freezing wind. She throws it down on the kitchen table and drops into a chair.

When she comes to, still wearing her coat, she finds her purse and feeds coins into the phone.

This time, Bridie asks no questions. She opens the door and Mona walks past her, straight upstairs, and sleeps for ever. The house is so quiet she might be the last person in the whole world. There's just the sound of the sea, constant and familiar as her own heartbeat. Bridie comes into Mona's room every morning and opens the curtains but Mona squeezes her eyes shut. She comes back with tea in a cup and saucer and sometimes but not always a bit of toast or fruit cake. Bridie closes the curtains at night and when Mona is in the bathroom she fluffs the pillows and eiderdown, leaves a cut-glass dish full of lavender or dried rose petals. Days go on. Mona says nothing.

Then, one morning, Mona hears Bridie laughing in the kitchen. It starts as a little giggle and soon she's hawing and roaring like a trawlerman. Mona goes to the landing and leans over the bannister. She can hear voices in the kitchen. She tiptoes down the stairs. It sounds like a party in there and then quite suddenly the door is flung open by a young woman with curly red hair tied up in a headscarf. She's holding a bunch of yellow dusters in one hand, a chocolate biscuit in the other. She's bursting out of her dress at the top with her ripe and ruddy cleavage. Mona stares at her and the woman raises her eyebrows.

'Heard you were back,' she says. 'Pamela.' She stuffs the biscuit sideways into her mouth and shakes Mona's hand. 'Right,' Pamela calls behind her. 'I'll start in the parlour, missus. And don't forget my tea.'

Bridie is filling the kettle when Mona walks in. 'Ah, you're up. I'm late with the tea because of that one.' She gestures to Pamela singing and scraping furniture on the wooden floor in the front room. 'Don't you recognize her? Pamela O'Shea. Her mother used to clean for us, the whole village. Maureen O'Shea, don't you remember? She's passed the business on to her daughters now, Pamela and Diane. You'd never think they were twins.'

Mona sits at the table. Bridie puts butter and jam in front of her.

'She just told me about Pat Holmes. Did you hear he's wearing a wig? In black? I'm completely in the wrong listening to tittle-tattle but by rights that girl should be on the stage. She has him down to a T.' Then Bridie does an impression of an old man with a walking stick that isn't funny. Not one bit. When she sees Mona's face, she stops and makes the tea. She pours three cups, takes one to Pamela, and when she comes back she sits down opposite Mona.

'We shall get along, you and I, Mona. We have each other now, just the two of us. We have a good house here and your own is bringing in some rent. We are as different as night and day or at least night and dawn, shall we say, but we like one another and fate has brought us together. If I was you, in your situation, I would take a job in Wexford where you can meet people at least. There's a couple of shops that need good people like yourself and the town is looking up these days. It's fairly busy and there are opportunities. When you came here, you needed peace and you needed rest. You've had both. Quite enough of both, Mona. We can settle all your affairs in Birmingham from arm's length. You're young and fit. Work is the best thing for you.'

The spring comes and Mona is manoeuvred back to life. Bridie leaves Mona's clean, pressed clothes on a hanger behind the bedroom door. She drives her into Wexford and introduces her as a 'niece come home' though half the town already know Mona's story. Mona finds work in Dooley's selling bras and girdles, nightdresses and knickers, and the other women are lovely to her, motherly and understanding.

One midsummer's eve, there's to be a dance at the Camross Ballroom. Bridie folds the paper in half and shows Mona the announcement.

'Your dresses need replacing, Mona.'

Mona has found the soft places in Bridie's character, can hear, like a tuning fork, the notes of reprimand and the notes of love.

'I will if you will,' she says.

'I have good clothes already, Mona, and at sixty-three none of them are quite right for a young person's ceilidh at the Camross. No, you will go with Pamela and her sister. It's arranged.'

It wasn't quite a ceilidh, more like a country discotheque with half the night taken up by a live band and the other half a DJ with nearly current records and the love of his own Dublin patter.

'You's wouldn't want to go home without a girl, would you, lads? Ask her for a slow dance to "Lovin' You" by Minnie Riperton. Lots of beautiful ones here tonight and no mistake. Waiting on you, lads.'

Pamela and Mona stand on the balcony and watch the rotating couples below. Pamela has a name for everyone. 'See there, Dracula's Cousin dancing with the Koala Bear. I wouldn't want those incisors near my neck. And, Mona, will you look there, at two o'clock, Stumpy with the Wandering Hands. He's the right height for a knee in the gonads. It wouldn't topple you over, if you know what I mean.'

At the end of the night, there's a bus to Kilmore and a cup of tea in the kitchen. Bridie has waited up. Mona tells her about the evening and that she's volunteered to serve at the bar the following week. Bridie smiles and presses her cheek to Mona's face.

'You'll be better in the by-and-by, Mona. You're home now.'

And Mona finds herself returning every evening to Bridie and a hot meal at the dinner table, conversation, sherry or whiskey at the weekend, walks arm in arm around the beach and the repetition of weeks and days and months and years like balm on a sting.

38

Mona tries to work it out as she walks up the hill. She lives on the third floor so Karl must live on the second. His flat must be in the right-hand corner of the building as she looks at it from her window, so that means on the left if she's standing outside. And there must be four flats on each floor, so he would be number nine or number twelve. Whatever happens, she'll know which it is when she gets there.

The bottle of good wine swings from her wrist, and she has her handbag on her shoulder. Her little overnight trolley bumps along behind her, smooth as you like, still full of her overnight things, toothbrush, toothpaste, spare knickers. The air is as fresh and sharp as a new knife, with a bit of prickle in it too, the hint of something sparkly because it's getting near Christmas, or maybe there's a party nearby and she's caught the atmosphere on the wind. She puts her fingers to her mouth and remembers the mash of Karl's lips against her teeth. She won't tell him to stop this time.

There's already someone standing at the front door as she nears the foot of Karl's building. He's a boy from KKK, dressed in his white uniform with a green baseball cap and the logo on the side. He has a paper bag with the same logo, a bottle of Coca-Cola sticking out of the top. He buzzes a buzzer, the door pings open and he walks in. Mona quickly follows him in and across the lobby. He holds the door for her at the entrance to the staircase.

'Lift's bust,' he says as though he knows she doesn't live there.

'Thank you, love,' she answers and smiles. 'You're working late, are you?'

He nods. 'Yeah, five more hours. Don't get off till two in the morning and it gets busy later. Like, everyone comes in from the Drum and Monkey or the Butler's and then the Alexa closes.

There's supposed to be me and Adam but it's, like, just me. It can get really busy. Like, really, really busy.'

He's a slow talker with big cow eyes. He hums as he plods up the stairs and Mona struggles behind him. At the first floor she's nearly out of breath trying to keep pace with the youth. He turns and sees her panting.

'Want some help?'

He doesn't stop for the answer, just bends down, grabs her trolley and heaves it on to his shoulder.

'What floor?' he asks.

'Next one. Second, I think,' she says. 'It's a surprise visit.'

He waits for her at the top, holds the door open to the grey-lit landing and gives her the handle of her suitcase.

'You're a kind young man,' she says. 'Should be more like you in the world.'

But she feels the hammer of her heart both from the exertion and the brave and bold thing she is about to do. She wants the boy to walk off so she can gather her thoughts. A sign on the wall says 'Flats 9–12'. She follows the arrow and finds she is following the boy all over again.

At the second door, the boy stops and knocks.

'Come!' she hears. 'It's open.' Karl's voice.

The boy opens the door and walks in. Mona stands outside for a moment and as the door swings to close she sticks her foot out. The boy doesn't notice, he's gone inside, and Mona listens.

'Ah, Gary. Good. Good.'

'All right, Mr Ritter. Large meal deal. Keith's Kebab special with fries and onions. One-litre bottle of Coke. Twenty per cent voucher here for next time. Night.'

Mona doesn't have time to move before the boy comes back. He smiles and holds the door wide open.

'Got a visitor, Mr Ritter,' he shouts behind him and walks off down the hall.

Mona takes a step inside but keeps the door open. Karl appears in the hallway. He stands a few feet away in a pair of check boxer shorts, in a white vest, no socks, no shoes. He is wearing a hairnet. His pause is less than a heartbeat.

'Mona,' he says simply and makes a slight flourish with his hand towards his outfit. 'You find me *en déshabillé*.'

His gesture turns into an invitation to the living room and she has no choice but to let the door go and walk in.

The living room is unbearably hot. An old gas fire hisses blue and orange flames against a blackened wire mesh. The pine mantelpiece is cluttered, a packet of biscuits, newspapers, brown envelopes propped up behind a brass carriage clock. The carpet is covered in three different overlapping rugs, lumpy and uneven under her feet. Faded green velvet curtains are drawn over the window where she sees him standing at night with his coffee.

Old beer, stale food, the laundry he has not done and, as faint as an old scar, the scent of the same herb he brought to her house and used on the chicken. Now, over it all, like perfume on sweat, is the smell of the oily kebab that sits still in its carrier bag on a coffee table in front of a sagging Dralon sofa. She sees it all in a second.

'Sit, please,' he says and points to the only other chair in the room, a kitchen seat of white plastic that stands alone near the television. Too loud. Three contestants are fighting their way out of a cage filled with balloons. 'Who's going to win!' screams the compère.

'Excuse me,' says Karl as he squeezes a button on the remote control. But for the puttering of the gas fire, the room is silent.

Karl shakes his head. 'It's not everyone that can eat and watch *Celebrity Gladiator* at the same time. But this meal goes particularly well with the show.'

He grabs the coffee table, laid for one, and drags it between his naked legs. He holds the paper bag in the air and swings it from side to side. 'Supper,' he says.

She notices an open bottle of wine at his feet and a dark purple stain in a small tumbler. She notices the black hairs that cover his toes. She knows she should speak but has nothing to say.

He's careful opening the box. He lifts out the steaming kebab with both hands and lays it on his plate like it's a precious thing, a vase of new clay. He takes a paper bag of chips and spreads them around the plate and lastly a plastic container of fried onions, greasy and brown, that plop audibly over the lip of the cup. He picks up a knife and gestures to the meal.

'Keith is no chef,' he says, 'and yet . . . what do you think? Would you like some?'

Mona shakes her head. As Karl cuts the kebab in two, he slips two chips into his mouth and chews. He nods as if to say 'yes', and then quickly looks at her.

'I didn't expect to see you again,' he says. 'As you see, you've caught me off guard.'

'Excuse me,' says Mona but there is a cut in her voice and he hears it.

Karl sits back suddenly, the knife still in his hand, and puts his head to one side. 'You seem upset.'

She can see through his vest, the pelt of grey hair on his sagging chest and the dull silver down on the top of his legs. And though she tries very hard not to raise her eyes, she is drawn to the hairnet, to the silvery sheen of the close plastic weft, to the symmetrical waves that lie snug against his head, caught entirely, heavily, at the back of his neck. He is vain. And he is an old, old man.

'I'm very sorry to have disturbed you, Karl.'

'Really?'

'I was just passing.'

'Just passing. I see. You brought wine though?' He nods to the bottle in the bag.

'Yes, yes I did. To say thank you for the other night. I forgot to say thank you.'

'I recall that you did say thank you, Mona. I distinctly remember you saying thank you before you shut the door.'

'Well, anyway.'

'Come, come,' he says. He slides the knife on to the plate and sits on the edge of the sofa. 'Let us speak frank, you and I. And let us drink your thank-you present together.'

'No, it's all right. I don't want a drink.' Of course she should

240

never have come. 'I didn't mean to embarrass you,' she says and clutches the handle of her trolley. 'I'll leave it here for you. You can have it later.'

'On my own?'

'Yes, if you like.'

'But I do not like, Mona. I would rather drink it with you.'

Mona stands up and puts the bottle on the table. 'Actually, I think I should be going, Karl.'

'I would rather you didn't,' he says simply. 'I would rather you stayed and took a glass of wine with me if it's all the same with you. I would prefer it if you would do that before you go. I think it would be polite.'

There isn't a hint of give in his request. Mona sits back down and watches him struggle off the sofa, walk past her into the kitchen and return with another tumbler. On the way back, he slips her wine from the bag and peers at the label.

'Very good. Rather expensive, I think, but I have some already open.'

He picks up his bottle and pours for them both. He hands Mona her glass. He is right in front of her but she cannot look up at him.

'Cheers,' he says but makes no movement.

'Yes, cheers, Karl.' She puts her lips to the glass and wets them with the wine. It's peppery and strong. She will drink no more. She makes a little cough and puts her handbag on the floor next to her suitcase.

'Have you lived here long?' she asks.

'I have lived here since Andreas died. You see, he had rather a long illness and the family wanted him to die at home. So they took him back. Reclaimed him, you might say.'

'So you moved here.'

Karl gives a snort and sits down. He shoves the table away, shoves it almost into the fire. He lounges back on the sofa and swallows all of his wine in a few gulps.

'This,' he gestures to the room, 'is another thank-you present. I seem to be collecting them. This apartment is a thank you from Andreas's family. You are no longer needed, Karl. You've been loyal, Karl, et cetera et cetera. Here you are, Karl. Here in England, several hundred miles from Andreas, here is your home, number twelve in one of the several blocks we own. Oh, and while you are there you might attend to a little caretaking on our behalf. Yes, it seems I am a sometimes janitor now.'

On the fireplace is a framed photograph of Karl with another man.

'Is that him,' says Mona, 'Andreas, your friend?'

'Andreas, yes. Count Georg Leberecht Andreas Graf von Everstein-Ohsen.'

'I see.'

'Do you see, Mona?' Karl leans forward and pours himself another glass of wine. 'What do you see?'

'I can see that you're upset at the death of your friend.'

'Ha! Now you want to talk about my friend. Now! Well yes, yes, let's talk about him. He was in fact my employer if you want to be strict about it. Yes, I was paid, not very much, naturally, but something. I stayed in the most beautiful houses, the most beautiful palaces, on yachts and winter retreats in all of the world. Name a country!'

'Lovely,' says Mona.

Karl takes a long swig of wine. 'Lovely? Do you think so? My father was a gardener on the estate, we grew up together, Andreas and I.' In another few gulps the glass is empty. 'And now he is dead.'

'I'm sorry.'

'Andreas had epilepsy. It was rather an embarrassment for the family. You can imagine, can't you? Poor Andreas rolling on the floor at a banquet. Frothing from the mouth at the party. He was one of life's innocents, Andreas. He could manage nothing on his own. Not his love affairs, not his bank account, nothing. Epilepsy. Stroke. Cancer. Death. These things he managed very well. That is the way of things.'

As Karl pours another glass, Mona picks up her handbag and moves her trolley by her side.

'Do you know the saying, *Manchmal muss man mit den Wölfen heulen*?'

'No.'

'Sometimes we must howl with the wolves, Mona. Make the best of things. I have a home and that home is here. And yet I intended to sell it so I could move back to Hamburg but when I consulted a solicitor, more than one, in fact, it seems that I have this apartment only in trust, only until I die. It is not mine after all. So this evening,' he thrusts his glass in the air, slops of wine splashing his vest, 'I am howling with the wolves,' and with that Karl bellows until he coughs, then swigs back the last of his wine.

Mona looks away. 'I think I've been here long enough, Karl. I'll be saying goodbye,' she says, but Karl continues.

'I am given a trunkful of a dead man's clothes. I am given a few thousand pounds and a pillow for my bed. *Machen wir das Beste draus.*'

Mona closes her eyes and shakes her head. 'I'm sorry for your loss, Karl. But I must be going now.'

She stands up and Karl springs from the sofa. 'Why?'

Mona takes a step towards the living-room door. 'I think I might have caught you at a bad time.'

'Bad time? Sitting in my own home having a take-away. What is bad? Talking about my troubles to a friend? We are friends, aren't we? Or perhaps this is a bad time for you, no?'

She shrugs. Karl's vest has faint yellow half-crescents under the arms, it's old and out of shape. She would wash her windows with it and put it in the bin. She dare not look at his shorts. The thin string of elastic around the hairnet cuts deep into his skin. There will be a tell-tale crease on his forehead when he takes it off. How many hours does it take for the crease to disappear? She imagines him counting the hours on his fingers, working backwards from the time he arranges to meet her, then slipping the hairnet off and tucking it away somewhere, so she would never suspect.

'You came for something?' he says. 'What was it exactly?' He nods towards the suitcase.

The heat from the fire is vicious. Her mouth twitches and she looks away, finds herself focussing on a mountain scene in a gilt frame that hangs crookedly over the fire. 'Just for a quick visit,' she says. 'To see where you lived.'

'And now?'

'I think I'm going now,' she says. He gestures for her to stay and when he begins to speak he is almost laughing.

'Mona, Mona, Mona. You are disappointed, no? What did you expect? Did you think I would be wearing a velvet jacket and leather slippers? Did you expect drapes and marble, crystal goblets on a silver tray carried in by a waiter, a valet?'

'I don't know what I expected.'

'I am that valet, Mona.'

She takes another step towards the door.

'You do not pass my house, Mona, and you do not buy wine because you do not drink, well hardly. You came here to spend the evening with me, I think, regretting perhaps your rather inelegant behaviour a few weeks ago. True?'

'Inelegant?'

'Inelegant.'

'My behaviour? I beg your pardon. I had no idea you were coming. I didn't invite you.'

'Quite.' He raises his eyebrows. Silver prickles of hair cover his chin and neck. He has not shaved. He scratches himself, stretches his neck and rakes his fingers against the stubble. Mona shakes her head.

'Look, I'm sorry and I'm going.'

He leans in, close to her face. 'Where?'

'Home.'

'Home? Or to see the carpenter? Isn't that where you go when you leave me?'

'You're drunk, Karl.'

'Maybe you will take your little overnight case to the carpenter?'

Mona draws herself up and faces him square.

'I beg your pardon?'

'The carpenter, the carpenter. Every day, the carpenter. How many dolls he makes. How he works. How cold he will be. And you declined my offer of champagne for a quick visit with him. You prefer him, do you not?'

She goes to speak but he holds his finger up.

'Let me tell you something, Mona. You are in love with the carpenter. Or at the very least, you have strong feelings for him. You are, for whatever reason, dishonest about those feelings. I don't know why. But we begin our friendship, more than friendship, I think, and I take your promptings at face value and respond, then you slam the door. Such dishonesty is unattractive in a woman.'

Her face burns and the collar of her coat itches against her sweating neck.

'At least I don't pretend to be the Count of Monte bloody Cristo.' She is almost breathless. 'You live in a slum if you don't mind me saying. You go on and on about cooking fancy meals while you're buying yourself monster orders of chicken kebab or whatever it is. Talking about antiques and grand living all the time. How you go about things is none of my business but don't make out I'm the one who's living a lie.'

'The Count of Monte Cristo. Very good. I like it.'

He folds his arms over his chest. 'The Count in fact was the master of disguise. He was a nobleman who became a prisoner and then returned to his rightful place. He did some rather wicked things as I recall, all in the name of love. We make mistakes, do we not, usually involving those whom we love. Let us take the carpenter, for example.'

He walks round her and warms his legs by the fire.

'The carpenter, whom I have seen incidentally –' he holds his hands up as though to make brackets around a whisper – 'I took a walk along the beach to see for myself – looks unwell – no, sick, actually. He's very thin, isn't he?'

Mona bites her teeth together.

'Clearly, he has turned you down in the past or perhaps you have not declared your love for him. Not visited him with your suitcase and your bottle of expensive wine? If it was me, and I

245

speak as a friend, I would make him a good meal. Chicken livers are full of iron, sautéed with apricots and raisins, delicious. Serve it on thick bread, rye, lightly toasted.'

'For God's sake.' Mona puts her hand on her suitcase. He is still talking.

'Yes, the carpenter has featured in almost all of our conversations these past several weeks. I feel the carpenter and I have almost become friends.'

Mona turns quickly. With one pace she could reach him, slap him, make him stop. 'Just shut up, Karl! The carpenter! It's you that keeps talking about the carpenter all the time! I don't! He's nobody. Nothing.'

Karl smiles. 'So loudly he is nothing?'

'You have no idea,' she hisses. 'No bloody idea what he's been through. What I've been through. What do you know? You've lost a friend. Lost your job as a bloody manservant. All right, I'm sorry for you. But you've had a good life, haven't you? That's what you keep saying, all the things you've done and seen. Some of us have had a very different time. We haven't all spent the last fifty years as a playboy's companion.'

He closes his eyes and peels off his hairnet. He picks up the wine bag and puts it in her hand. He walks past her and opens the living-room door wide enough for her to pass. He ushers her along the hallway and turns the lock on the front door.

'Life is not easy, Mona. We live as we must.' He sounds weary, far away. 'I am a plain man. You are a complicated woman. And unhappy, if I may say. Maybe the carpenter is the same. Goodnight.'

She feels his hand in the small of her back but this time pushing her over the threshold and out into the dingy hallway.

'Wait,' he says and leans forward, kissing her on both cheeks. 'I wish you happiness, my dear. *Viel Glück*.'

Bridie is small now, shrunk over the years somehow, white-haired and delicate as a feather. She lies in the middle of her bed, neater than ever and dignified even now. She talks from time to time, mostly to herself, sometimes to Mona and once or twice to someone else.

'I love you, Robbie,' she says and her thin fingers strum the blanket.

It's one o'clock in the afternoon when she opens her eyes and smiles at Mona.

'It's all yours, you know that.'

'I know,' says Mona. 'You told me. Ssshh now.'

'I have been quiet too long. And I've been selfish.'

Mona straightens the straight blanket and smooths down the smooth edges of the pillow.

'You should have gone years ago,' says Bridie. 'This is no place for you. Forgive me, I wanted you all to myself. Needed you.'

Mona can hear the whistle in the old woman's throat as though her breath comes up from an empty place.

'I've had you these twelve years,' she says, 'but you have to leave now as I do. And find him again,' she says. 'Don't wait too long. I waited and it got me nothing.' She's crying and Mona is too.

'I know you've tried, lovey, but it's no good, is it? Even Duggie Hannah, God bless him, was no good for you. You broke his heart, I think. And the others.'

'Ssshh,' says Mona because she agrees, and anyway, this is an old conversation, an old spiral she rides again and again and comes to earth with a bump. But Bridie won't quieten. She grips Mona fiercely with a strength she shouldn't have.

'Find him and love him again, Mona. There's people you

can pay to help you find him. I have the money. Whatever it takes. Have another life. Have another baby. You're young yet. Promise me.'

Mona nods and wipes her sleeve across her face. 'I promise.'

'Remember me as someone who loved you. And loved your father. We were happy, weren't we? Me, you and Robbie?'

There was no sun the whole day. There were only three grey hours when Mona stood at the window watching the rain stream against the glass and pool on the drive. When Bridie died, Mona let herself return to William and to Beatrice and imagine where they might be and where she might look and what she might find because without knowing and without thinking and without planning she'd been waiting and waiting and now she had to go. She rang for the doctor and watched him cover Bridie with a sheet and make the sign of the cross.

'You'll be all right alone here, will you, Mona? You're welcome to come back with me.'

'No, I'm fine,' she says. 'I'll bury her and then I'm going back to England.'

40

A rogue wheel, that's what the man called it, as though the thing had a personality and had decided to cause trouble. It bounces off down the stairs all the way to the ground floor and comes off entirely on the last step. Mona scrapes and wobbles the suitcase all the way across the lobby and out again into the street. A surge of roiling blood courses thick in her veins and she could, in a moment of intense pleasure, rip the other wheel off and fling it like a missile a hundred miles away.

She stamps down the hill, with the trolley grinding against the tarmac, screeching on the pavement. She hardly feels it, hardly hears it. The gift bag of wine bounces against her hip, the damp, freezing wind cuts welts across her cheek, but she raises her head, lets fingers of ice squeeze her throat and chivvy the tears off her cheek.

She stops suddenly at the crossroads and looks down towards the beach. The windows are closed but light leaches out between the wooden boards of the workshop. She turns towards it.

The door is unlocked because there is nothing to steal. She barges the trolley in, sets it at the bottom of the steps and marches up. It's dark but she has, of course, like a fool, been up and down the ugly metal contraption so many times in her life that she could waltz up backwards with her eyes closed and never falter.

She reaches the top, pushes open the door and sees him, standing by the stove with a bowl of soup in his hand. He has a spoon almost in his mouth but he stops dead when he sees her. His lips go slack for a moment and she sees him gather his emotions up like the pieces of a broken plate and tuck them away wherever it is that he has hidden them all these years.

'That's your dinner, is it?' she says. 'Not a kebab, then.'

He only stares at her. This too is a place of jarring smells. Oh yes, there's linseed and pine and the sniffle of old dust but also there's the smell of the man himself, his bleach and his detergent, the rough laundering of his rough sheets and the soap he rubs into rough skin. The skin she has had to keep her hands from touching and holding and stroking all of the years of womanhood.

And it's freezing in the workshop. Of course it is. It's not the draught and it's not the weather. No, lifelessness has seeped into the bricks and the rafters and floorboards and the off-cuts and the long wooden bench and, over the years, into her.

She begins to pace around. On the workbench, a long piece of squared-off walnut lies dull and unvarnished, a folded piece of sandpaper on top like a dropped handkerchief or a secret letter. She traces a line in the dust, silky between her fingers, fine and soft as talcum powder. She blows it off into the air and sees her foggy breath in the half-light. And he stands, gargoyle-still, crouched almost, watching her. And because she knows him so well, she knows he wonders what she wants, knows that he's worried.

'Oh, don't worry,' she says. 'I'm not staying. No, no, you needn't worry on that score.' She rubs her hands together but can bring no warmth. 'It's not as if you've ever given me an invitation to stay, have you? Took me, what? Twenty months? Yes, nearly two years to find you. Tracked you down like a bloodhound. Remember when I first came up them steps? I was so happy. I thought you'd jump at the chance. I asked you to come back with me. What did you say? Remember? "Go away, Mona." That's what you said. "Go away." '

Mona shakes her head.

'So I went away like a good girl. Did as I was told but I crept back and I crept back and I brought you little bits of food like a bloody great bird with a chick. And I kept coming, didn't I? Week after week, never more than you could bear, never disturbing you more than I had to. Oh no, William isn't to be disturbed.'

He says nothing. His mouth is open, wide as his eyes.

'I've wasted my life keeping you alive. What have I got out of it? What have you done for me? Nothing.'

She can hear his answers though he says nothing.

'And don't say the dolls neither. It's the one doll you won't make that matters. How many times have I asked you for that bloody doll? All this time and nothing.'

He puts the bowl of soup down and puts his hands over his ears.

'Don't you dare!' she hisses. 'Don't you bloody dare!'

She almost runs across the room. Her handbag drops from her shoulder. She catches his narrow wrists and yanks them back.

'You will hear this, by God you will. Shall I tell you where I was yesterday? Shall I? I was visiting our baby, William. That's right, our baby girl has a grave, a grave I found many years ago after a long search. A search I couldn't ask you to join because it would have tipped you over the edge and not tipping you over the edge is very important. William can't be upset. William can't manage. William might kill himself. Well, you're good and strong when you want to be, aren't you?'

She is shouting, she can feel the muscles of her throat straining. 'Not upsetting you has been my life's work. What about me? What about my upset? Did you ever think of that?'

He tries to pull his hands out of hers but she grips him hard and sucks the air in through her teeth.

'No, you don't. You will hear this. Let's talk about wood. You like to talk about wood. Do you know what coffin our baby has?'

Mona pulls him, drags him towards the bench and the slab of walnut.

'This?' she says. 'Do you think our beautiful baby girl has a walnut coffin? Or mahogany maybe? Or teak? Well, I don't know, William, but I doubt it. She's buried in with an old man who died in the hospital on the same day as our little girl. That's what they did in those days. They took her tiny little body and they put her in a coffin with a man who nobody claimed, who had no family. They threw her in and nailed it shut. Her cold body in the freezing earth at the feet of a tramp.'

He hunches suddenly, wrests his hands from her and curls his back over, bending double as though she's hit him.

'Yes, go on, William. Think on that, why don't you? All these years I've kept quiet. Now you can bear what I have to bear. And good luck to you.'

She watches him drop to his knees.

'Wait, wait, wait, William.'

He looks up at her and she sees the boy still and if she wasn't so cold and wasn't so tired and if there was no such thing as a rogue wheel and inelegant behaviour and she wasn't sixty but twenty-one, she might have crouched there with him.

'I've something else for you,' she says. She places on the dead metal of the pot-bellied stove her wedding ring. She picks up her handbag and turns to look at him for the last time.

'Life's not easy, is it, William? We all live as we must.'

She has to hold on tight as she goes down the steps. She rattles the trolley back along the streets and before she knows it she is at the edge of the black sea. She listens to it shush and shudder, fall towards her and fall away. She wonders if the water that soaks her shoes will one day end up at Kilmore, wetting the shells and the sand that was once her home.

She holds the bottle of wine and tosses it gently into the waves. Maybe it will wash up in the harbour and one of the old soaks from the town will think it's a miracle.

'Cheers,' she says.

She brushes past her trolley as she walks past. She will have quiet for the long walk home. She strides uphill, feels the muscles strain in her calves and the heave of her chest. She feels the pain in her arm first and then in her neck and then the thump of her heart, stronger and stronger until she can't breathe.

41

So this is how it ends. On a white cotton sheet, on a narrow trolley behind a hospital curtain five miles from the sea at the very edge of England.

The little cubicle is over-bright, clean as you like and hot as a sauna. There are notices everywhere alerting the patients to all variety of dangers, posters on the wall about using your mobile phone, using hand wash, having patience at busy times and, in a big red circle, a warning about aggression towards the staff. Mona wonders if someone somewhere has made a connection between impatience, filthy fingernails and the temptation to rough up the duty doctor.

Mona wears the gown they gave her, polyester brown check untied at the front. No bra. She holds it closed across her chest while the nurse takes her blood pressure, squeezing a tight elastic band round Mona's upper arm and inflating it until Mona's finger-tips tingle.

The nurse is as neat as a button, her skin as dark and lovely as polished teak, her black hair oiled and scraped back in a velvet ribbon, her beautiful slim fingers perfectly fit for the piano or harp. She looks up and sees Mona watching her.

'Do you have anyone with you?' she asks and Mona, to her immense embarrassment, begins to cry. Cries, right there in front of a stranger.

The nurse takes Mona's hand and squeezes it. 'No?' she asks. 'Would you like to ring someone? Make a phone call?' But the tears have started now and she cannot answer. She bites her lips together and feels her heart thumping again.

'No,' she says.

The nurse gets up quickly and leaves the cubicle. She's probably gone to find someone with more medical expertise. Maybe she thinks Mona is having a heart attack.

And bring a priest! Mona thinks. But it's not funny. She might come back with a crowd of trainees with the two big paddles they place over your breasts to zap your heart back into obedience. They will all see her limp bosom, that sunless private skin, and what will they think? They'll have seen worse, no doubt. And better.

It's a terrible sight, the two empty chairs next to the bed. Some people come in with a worried husband and grown-up children or a whole troop of cousins and aunts. Sometimes there will be standing room only, people fighting for space when two chairs aren't nearly enough.

But the nurse is gone for ages so Mona has time to gather herself together. She sits up straight, smooths her hair down at the back, runs a finger over her eyebrows, things that will make no difference. She has no pain at all and that's the truth of it. Hasn't really had it since she walked into A&E although she told a little lie to the nurse on reception. 'I think I might be having a heart attack,' she said and noticed a couple of people turn in their chairs to look her up and down.

No wonder everything is taking for ever. There'll be real emergencies somewhere in this hospital tonight. Ambulances full of disasters from multiple car pile-ups and brawls in boozers, falls from ladders and industrial accidents. People with life-threatening wounds and injuries. Bombs. Mona's a fraud. The lovely nurse will be out there somewhere in an operating theatre tugging the doctor's arm and saying, 'Excuse me, sir, I can see you're stitching up that open throat, but there's a barmy old Irish woman in cubicle five with indigestion. Will I give her a couple of tablets and send her home?'

There's someone in the next cubicle. The sobbing is awful to hear, great long gulps and swallows as though the woman's heart is breaking. She's probably got her mother or a friend in there on one of them two seats, helping her through it, whatever it is. Still, it's hard to sit and listen.

★

The doctor is a big, smiley man squeezed into a pale-blue cash-mere jumper, pills of wear at the wrists. He taps the side of his head with a biro while he reads Mona's chart then carefully opens the front of her gown. He presses a stethoscope to her chest and says, 'Big breath.' And then again, 'Big breath,' and that goes on for a while, front and back. He gives nothing away but apologizes for the cold metal on her warm skin, looks over her chart again and taps his teeth with the end of the pen. Finally, he shows her his smile again. One of his easier jobs, he says, is quite simply reassur-ance. It's always nice after a busy night, he whispers, to be able to tell someone that there is positively, absolutely nothing wrong. Mona nods. He asks her about stress and her job and where she lives and whether or not she has troubles or concerns that keep her awake and he asks her about what she eats and drinks and if she takes any medication – just checking, he says – and then asks again, does she have anyone at home. No, she answers, no. No to everything.

She takes a taxi home. She takes the lift instead of the stairs. She opens the door to her empty flat and slips off her shoes. She brushes her teeth, washes her hands. She dabs cream on her face and rubs it in, notices again the blue of her eyes paling with time, the slight give of the skin on her cheeks. That first time, William said she was beautiful and she believed him. She has been a fool.

When she lies down, she presses her hand to her chest along the same route the doctor took and feels the slow and steady beat beneath.

It does not end this way.

42

Buttons, zips, thread, needles, antique thimbles, scraps and remnants of suede and silk and leather and fur and good old linen and calico. Old earrings, necklaces that are half unstrung, pearls and beads and fasteners of every description, vintage lace and edging, velvet cushion covers that Mona has eaten into over the years, tapestry, jacquard, a bit of a faded wall hanging that was used for a portmanteau, Fair Isle jumpers and Norwegian cardigans, Aran hats and scarves. The accumulation of a lifetime's quiet and careful industry and all to be packed up. A school might want it or an evening class.

Mona stands in her dressing gown at the window in her workroom. It's strange that she so seldom looks east. The view of the sea is interrupted by the new marine centre, blue glass and beige concrete. She has a mug of tea and half a piece of wholemeal toast. She won't be able to pack it all in a day, maybe not even in a week, but there's no rush.

It will be good to see her father's cottage. It must be thirty years since she sold it, it will be changed no doubt, improved. And she will need to give notice to the tenants in Bridie O'Connor's old house and put her flat up for sale. There will be furniture to keep and some to sell and shipments to be arranged and bills to settle up but nothing she can't do and nothing she's afraid of. She's only been home three times since she left and two of those were for funerals. If she had kept up some sort of correspondence with her school friends and neighbours then maybe . . . but anyway, it doesn't matter. She's of the land and soil and the sand on the beach and her father is buried in St Mary's Field. Where else would she go?

By the end of the afternoon, she has seven black plastic bags neatly labelled and tied. She has four plastic tubs of accessories, the sewing machine is unplugged and covered and there is a box of scraps for the binman. The shop will be rented out and any stock there can be sold half price. There's only the wooden box to think about. She drags it from under the bench and places it on the empty table.

Of course, there's no name engraved on the top and the rocking horse is covered in dust. For all she knows moths have got in and eaten into her baby's shawl and the cardigans she knitted but how could they? The box has been unopened for nearly forty years. She turns it quickly from side to side just in case mice have burrowed in but the sides are sound, white-painted smooth and barely touched in all that time.

It takes a deep, deep breath and a slow hand to open the lid. Oh. She hardly remembers covering everything over with crepe paper and tucking lavender down the sides. She lifts it off and sees how careful she was and organized. All the tops, jackets and bibs on one side and all the bottoms, dresses and leggings on the other. A good pile, something to be proud of. The shawl she embroidered is double-wrapped in white tissue and the edges folded in. She can't actually see it but she touches the raised stitching through the paper and remembers the design, whorls of buttercups and ivy that simply took for ever. She can smile now at the memory.

She closes the lid and goes to the window again. The soot-black sky has no moon and no stars and it will be lonely at first in Kilmore Quay. Bridie O'Connor's house will need painting and airing, it always was a fusty building, but that can be remedied too. Things must have changed at home. Some people will have moved on, of course, but it's not a tourist town and there are generations of people who will have had the sense to stay where they were. She will be remembered. There's a little catch in her throat but she doesn't cry.

Five o'clock and more than a day's work done. Enough to let her sleep. A long hot bath and a good night's sleep and back at it tomorrow. She's washing her hands at the sink when she hears the doorbell. There's no need to answer it if she doesn't want to. If it's Karl she will tell him plain that there's no animosity between them, at least not from her, and neither is there romance. She picks up a tea towel and rubs her hands as she walks down the hall. She's tempted to wear it as a bandana and to call him the Count of Monte Cristo again. Ask to join his brigade. She can't help smiling as she opens the door.

'William.'

He nods for an answer and then nods again. 'Hello, Mona.'

'How did you know where I lived?'

'You told me once,' he says. 'You thought I wasn't listening.'

'Oh.'

She cannot say more. She can feel her feet on the carpet and her hand on the doorknob. She can feel the cold air that slips in from the hallway and she can feel William's heart beating from where she stands. He takes a half-step towards her and she moves aside. He walks in, his soft tread and lolloping gait.

He has a bundle with him, like a sack of laundry. He has no coat and she catches herself fearing for his health. She shakes the thought away. He stands like a surveyor in her living room, looking up at the ceiling and down again to the carpet.

'Like I imagined,' he says and Mona can't find a reply. He looks about some more, a few moments, less than a minute, and then turns to her. 'Just like I imagined.'

Then he puts the bundle in her arms.

'I was losing you, Mona.'

In her workroom, she unfurls the sheet and sees what he has made, what he has carved and chiselled and polished and polished again, all from a few minutes of memory. She holds it once in her arms and remembers Beatrice. She feels the weight she felt before and, by luck, she has no need to stoop underneath and drag the wooden box forward. She opens the lid and peels the tissue paper from the embroidered shawl. A puff of sweet lavender. She wraps Beatrice so he can see her face and when she comes back to the lounge she sees he has found her seat, angled to the tall windows and the sea beyond. She brings their baby to him and he holds out his arms.

'Close your eyes, William. Feel the weight.'

She leads him home from the maternity room to their little flat on Alcester Road and to the crib he made.

'Remember?' she asks.

'Yes.'

She then leads him to their bed and the feel of Beatrice between them, to the smell of their baby's skin and the silken down of her hair. They can hardly sleep for looking at her. Remember Pestilence and her unexpected tears and Famine and how many cakes she made?

'How many?'

Two per day for the visitors and friends. And the presents they all brought, booties and rattles, teddies and trinkets in silver and porcelain. Bridie O'Connor sent a silver picture frame, bless her. Good old Tom upstairs took his wages and stood the whole pub a round to wet the baby's head. And home then for Christmas with Beatrice only four weeks old on the ferry to see the rest of the gang in Clarinbridge, William's father and his first grandchild. Oh, he was happy and not drunk and more unexpected tears. And the first hold he had, proud as punch and careful as you like.

And every Christmas for five years they crossed the water but then what did they do? Back to Ireland, of course, because of the good schools and the way of life and the sweep of the bay and the sand and the sea and Beatrice's little legs dancing in the waves. She squeals and William runs after her but she's fast. 'Come back, you little devil,' he shouts and Mona watches, shielding her eyes from the blinding sun.

Beatrice has William's artistry. If she's not colouring in, she's drawing a horse in a field or a flower, just like Mona used to sitting at the kitchen table. They're living out in Clifden now, where the river meets the sea that disappears into the sky, where there is nothing left of the land. Little white boats bob on the blue-green water and the three of them take a picnic up to the hill and look out towards America.

'Next stop New York,' says Beatrice every time.

William has his own workshop in the village. He makes tables and chairs, and people come from far and wide to see him working with his daughter apprentice. Why not? It's what Beatrice wants and there's no reason to say no, they're a modern family and she's a modern girl as stubborn and headstrong as Pestilence with all the kindness of Famine, the grace and looks of her mother and the deft and clever hands of her father. She wears her hair short. Of course she does.

'I didn't want her to go to university, Mona. I was glad when she stayed with us.'

'I was too, William.'

'Dublin is no place for a single girl and she's so beautiful.'

'I know, I know. What else?'

There are wet, silver tracks on William's cheeks but no cry in his voice. He's as simple and open as a country boy. He talks and talks and Mona chimes in because she has her own memories of the things they did and the places they went together, the three of them. Did he remember the day before Beatrice's wedding when they took her to the shore and they held hands and William said in his plain way that her place would always be between them and that if ever she needed to come home . . .

'You wouldn't wish that for her,' says Mona but William says nevertheless it was important that she knew.

'If anything went wrong between Beatrice and her young fella,' he says, 'there would be no judgement, she should just turn up, bags or not, money or not, no questions asked.' The three of them would return to how they were.

'She knew we meant it as well,' says Mona. 'As I recall.'

Then she sits by William and they cradle Beatrice together. Mona adjusts the shawl and William moves one arm and places it round her shoulder.

'Can we go home now?' he asks.

'We can.'

43

The boarding house is crawling with men from the building site, four beds in a room with another weary body on the floor. There is nowhere for Mona to stay. They tramp around the town for ages but find themselves with lots of others, sheltering at midnight under the dangerous cliffs with only their coats to keep them warm.

'It's not too bad,' William says, shuffling up to her. 'We'll be grand here for one night, won't we, Mona?'

'We will,' she says and kisses him.

'I can't believe you came all this way. I love you for it, I do.'

A few yards away there's a couple already dozing in an enormous sleeping bag. They came prepared.

'Are you warm enough?' he asks.

'I am. With you I am.'

He draws her into his arms and rubs her back up and down, pulls her coat collar round her neck. 'Look at the stars,' he whispers.

Mona looks up, the indigo sky pierced with little diamonds spread out past the curl of the waves and beyond, the horizon.

'Oh, it's beautiful.'

'It's been like that for ever and ever. Can you imagine that? And it will be like that way past you and me.'

'We'll be old one day, William.'

'Aye.'

'And I'll be grey.'

'I'll be bald, God help me. Bald and bent over like my father.'

Mona giggles. 'You'll have to carve yourself a walking stick. And make one for me while you're at it.'

He says nothing.

'I might get fat,' she says. 'And wear Crimplene.'

He doesn't answer.

'Then you'd have something to say, wouldn't you? A fat wife with rollers in her hair and a face full of wrinkles.'

'When's this?' he asks.

'Oh, I should imagine I'll be sixty. You'll be even older obviously.'

'Will you love me then?'

'Will I love you?' she asks.

'Yes,' he says, 'I'll be old and you'll be old and we won't be like we are now.'

Mona sits up. She can just see the light in his eyes and the worry in them. She can't imagine him scared of that, can't imagine his doubt.

'All that is true,' she says, 'but it's a long way away, William MacNaughton. We have a whole lifetime in front of us. And anyway, we'll be back home by then, Kilmore maybe or Kerry where the palm trees grow. Somewhere in a little cottage with a proper fire. I dream of a proper fire.'

She puts her hand to his cheek. 'And one day, we can come back here and remember the day when Mona crossed the country to find you and then got no sleep on the beach, back when we were young, and when Mona got a sharp stone in her knickers, when William had most of the coat and definitely most of the beer.'

She puts her hand out. 'Deal?'

'Deal,' he says and kisses her.

They lie down.

'To be fair, Mona,' he whispers after a short while, 'you did eat most of the chips.'

She laughs. 'I can't wait for the future.'

Acknowledgements

My thanks and gratitude to the many people who have helped me, supported me, made me laugh, held my hand, mowed the lawn, mended my back and my heart, looked after my children, showed up, washed up, talked to me – sense and nonsense – spurred me on and cheered me over the finishing line.

I would particularly like to thank the knowledgeable, helpful and compassionate duo of Anna Nella and Beverly Archer who helped me with details of Mona's stay in hospital and general midwifery research. Thank you to Dan Burden, the carpenter, for expertise, advice and suggestions, and to Marcus Gaertner for his help with German names and customs.

My profound respect to the mothers who told me their stories.

My thanks also to Marie-Therese Cox-Keegan and Karen Whitlock for their keen eyes, to Benedicta Norell for her invaluable input and for streamlining my life, to Julia de Waal, Sophie Morgan, Justin David, Annie Murray, Nina Black, Sue Underwood, Lezanne Clannachan, WRB, Anna Lawrence, Beth Charis, Steph Vidal-Hall, The Dark Elf, Tom Downham, Fool, Leather Lane Writers and Oxford Narrative Group for general loveliness.

To my agent, Jo Unwin, I acknowledge a huge debt of gratitude for her wisdom, friendship and unfailing support. To my editor, Venetia Butterfield, I send my thanks as always for every bit of editorial advice and for helping me to tack into the wind and steer this book home. To everyone else at Viking, cheers.

To Conkers, Dog, Kimbob, Trenz and Karn, love, always.

Again, this book is dedicated to my beautiful children, Bethany and Luke, who I am lucky enough to know and love.